T0368413

THE TWISTED HAND THAT BUCKY PLAYED

PEACHES DUDLEY

authorHOUSE®

AuthorHouse™
1663 Liberty Drive
Bloomington, IN 47403
www.authorhouse.com
Phone: 833-262-8899

This is a work of fiction. All of the characters, names, incidents, organizations, and dialogue in this novel are either the products of the author's imagination or are used fictitiously.

Published by AuthorHouse 09/27/2024

ISBN: 979-8-8230-3495-1 (sc)
ISBN: 979-8-8230-3496-8 (e)

Print information available on the last page.

Acknowledgements

To my son Kobe mommy loves you

Wanda V. Addison thank you for always being there for me throughout the years

John Welcome Richerdeen Chisolm "Big Mama" Naomi Dickerson thank you for always listening to my stories

Chyna "Jane Doh" your creativity inspires me to achieve

Heather L. Nared your unselfish love and friendship means the world to me

Lashera Upson aunty loves you, keep on reading

Christine Dudley Julius Dudley Michelle Clarke A.J. Hattie Williams Dawn Dudley

Matthew Dudley Veronica & Jessica Julia Dudley, your constant love motivates me to reach goals

Terri White Lynn Easter Mamie Tate Lakeesha Murray thank you for all your support

Kevin Miles you always know how to keep a smile on my face a definition of a loyal friend

Pastor David Wright Lady Geneatha Wright Jai Wright your friendship equips me to win

Edye Boyd Chyna Vilanueva Dr Lynn Saxton Jake Langley thanks for your support

Contents

AUTHOR'S PREFACE

Growing up in a traditionally loving household that reinforced the importance and significance of enjoying family gatherings in the hot southern coastal city of Mobile, Alabama the young man Tyrone is compelled to make hasty decisions while facing sudden family tragedy. From dominating the basketball courts in his home state as a youth to mastering the hot kitchens inside the restaurants located in Mobile, Alabama the young man Tyrone is suddenly faced with navigating his cousin's BMW through the detoured storm hit streets filled with hustlers and heated gang violence. Can the family aid Tyrone in this crisis as they gather and will the family's strong religious morals positively impact any of his decisions. Will the family's professional musical abilities and music careers be able to handle Tyrone's long steamy love affair and the criminals lurking around the hot streets of Mobile, Alabama. This emotional story is filled with high tensity family drama and mysterious actions. This eye-catching entertainment out of the deep hot south reads like a thriller.

Peaches Dudley resides in Harlem, New York. She's an author, poet, song writer and respected singer. Her unique voice and true style exhibit her activeness in the community. Being well-traveled, there is no place in the United States her feet haven't touched. She is known as a great storyteller.

CHAPTER 1

RETURNING ON A STORMING AFTERNOON

It was a clear and beautiful night. The rain that pounded hard upon the green leaves which hang on the Alabama trees had finally moved on. The treacherous storm which lit up the Alabama sky earlier with its thick black clouds that roared violently while swiftly moving loudly all afternoon through the widespread Alabama fields now relocated to another destination. I was glad not so much that the heavy rain had stopped but that this time in my area there were no tornado warning sirens loudly ringing and no reports coming from the local newsrooms of severe wind damage of down trees from the fierce strong winds that blew roughly rocking things throughout the Alabama fields all afternoon. Or any of my neighbors knocking on my front door with an emergency report of injuries from the rock size hail that I could hear dropping down from the sky earlier this afternoon onto the gravel in my driveway.

Everything now seemed to be quiet. Another hot and humid Tuesday in Alabama. As the sound of crickets chirping together outside my window loudly continued, I began scrubbing and rubbing together my two favorite pair of boxers against my washboard that had been soaking in the detergent filled basin inside my bathroom tub. I could smell the strong scent of cinnamon cornbread which had finished baking that was now covered up inside the large pan on my stove. The cabbage mixed with thin slices of bacon that had been steamed is in the pot next to the cornbread. My tender marinated meat was all chopped up and fully cooked. I was now waiting for my popular BBQ sauce to thicken up in the pot which is why I lowered the flame on top of the stove from medium to low. Exactly like Pop-Pop, used to do when Nana would invite us over for Sunday dinner at their house.

I learned from who I called the best. I modeled a lot of things like my grandfather. Growing up under his watchful eye I took plenty of notes. As a tall young boy fastened under my father's wings, I always positioned myself in a ready posture being eager to learn from the elder men in my family. My grandfather had my full attention when it came down to operating the grill. Many say I looked and acted just like him. But in my opinion, all of us Vendridge, boys, looked like one another. We all look like our daddies and our daddies look like their dad. Pop-Pop is the name we all called our grandfather. He was handsome with extremely strong genes. Nana kept us all together every chance and opportunity she could, taking pride in her large family. She enjoyed watching her family happily grow together. Though we resembled each other in looks our personalities and interests were very much different. My cousin Blaire enjoyed karate. He always made us play ninja along with him as kids while my cousin Derrick loved fashion and he was always seen playing dress up with my cousin Brenda modeling our Nana's wardrobe on family day. Derrick also had fun playing with my sister Debbie's Barbie dolls. My cousins Jill, Jimena, Jaquie, Joshua and Joe loved to sing and always harmonized the latest songs on the radio together as a group in Nana's living room. Vocalizing their gifts and riffs in song. My cousin William was always quiet and kept to himself. My cousin Bobby and Bam always had a football in their hands while my cousins Tiny, Tanya, Tommy and myself always had a basketball in our hands. Shooting hoops and talking stuff to one another was our thing. On Sunday nights our grandparents' house was filled with delicious hot food, good chop BBQ and laughing children that were identical in features but who would display themselves differently in their characteristics and hobbies.

Now my uncle Bucky, Blaire and Brenda's dad loved to play the saxophone. He was a member of a jazz band called the Brown Bucky Blues Band, while his new wife Rebecca, their stepmom worked in a small bakery that her father had owned. For their real mom our beloved aunt Betty died in a factory fire she worked at some years ago. They were the only ones who brought us dessert and cinnamon cornbread to Nana's house on Sunday nights. Aunt Rebecca would always have extra Sweet Potato pie and Rum cake for everybody. Uncle Bucky would serve us entertainment with live music blowing his heart away on that Saxophone. My five cousins would eventually harmonize themselves in a song vocally along with whatever tune Uncle Bucky was blowing. We always were and still are a tight-knit family. Groomed and raised to enjoy one another's company.

Turning off the hot water as I rinsed my boxer shorts out for the very last time, I could hear what sounded like car wheels rolling over the wet gravel that laid across my driveway. Hanging up my shorts over the bathtub to air dry I quickly made myself over to the hallway window to see who was rolling up in my driveway at this time of the evening. Pulling back the purple curtains that hang down covering my hallway window, I saw that a white Chevrolet Silverado 1500 with black tinted windows came to a complete stop in my driveway. As I heard the driver turn off the engine, I slowly walked up my hallway towards the front door.

The strong scent of freshly chopped garlic, chipotle peppers mixed with onions, ketchup, molasses, brown sugar and vinegar were now giving off a heavy but sweet aroma from the sauce simmering on top of the stove throughout the entire house. As the smell of Pop-Pop's, BBQ sauce, our renown famous family recipe that I inherited, mastered and presently cooked was now filling my nostrils, I couldn't help but wonder who would come to my crib unannounced. My mind started pondering, looking for clues from the unfamiliar vehicle with just the slightest hint of a remembrance. I was unsure who would be coming to my house without giving me a call. As I slowly reached for the doorknob, inhaling the aroma of the BBQ sauce, my mind then began racing on who would come to my house on a surprise visit this time of evening driving a white pickup truck that I have never seen before. Could it be someone who has the wrong address? Could it be someone who has lost their way and maybe in need of some direction on the rough Alabama roads? Maybe there was some severe storm damage to the Alabama roads which required detours. Perhaps a new neighbor that may recently have moved into this Alabama neighborhood and wants to get acquainted. As the smell of sweet BBQ sauce began to get stronger meaning it was just about ready to be spread all over the chopped meat in the pan, I paused anxiously awaiting to see who this mystery person was now in my driveway. I heard the truck door open that was parked in my driveway. I turned the doorknob slowly, cracking open my front door slightly to see who it was that came unannounced to my house.

"*Wait, it couldn't be! No, it isn't*" I said to myself. Slowly moving my body further out through the cracked door.

"What? Is it really her" I quietly moaned to myself in a whisper. My body movement paused as I steadily positioned myself in between the cracked door.

"Wow! It just couldn't be" I then shouted to myself. While leaning my body out the door so only my head could be visibly seen on the porch, my eyes staring directly at the white pickup truck which driver side door was now fully opened. I inhaled heavily and as I exhaled quickly, I verbally shouted out loud.

"Can I help you?"

Stepping out the Chevrolet truck in heel stilettos, wearing a pink mini skirt that fitted tight around her thighs, onto the wet gravel in my driveway. Was a black woman sparkling in hot designer pink. I then pushed the front door all the way out so my whole body could be clearly and visibly seen by the sparkling hot woman. As she leaned forward to pull down the bottom of her miniskirt towards her knees as if the tightly fitted pink material could even reach past her thick shaped thighs. I quickly seized the opportunity while she was bent forward by looking around her to see if someone else had been traveling with her or perhaps somebody else was seated in the passenger seat. But there was nobody else. As she reached for the truck door using it as a form of support while slowly lifting her curvy body, she opened her mouth and with a high-pitched voice loudly spoke *"well, hello my love."*

I remained completely still on my porch and calmly kept completely silent.

"Are you just going to stand there like a bump on a log

or are you going to give me some sugar babe?" She then bellowed out.

"Are you asking to borrow some of my brown sugar out of my brown cabinets mam?" I replied while stepping out onto the porch as I folded my arms.

> *"I know the little bit of sunlight we had today is now long gone and the bright stars are beginning to light up the evening sky. But it's not that late Mam. There are plenty of stores that are still open at this time of the evening, and I am pretty sure you passed one or more on your way out here that supplies sugar in whatever flavor you want"* I said in an unexpressive direct tone.

> *"Babe!"* she shouted, slamming the truck door with confidence as if she had a personal invitation to come to my crib.

> "Babe!" She shouted again wiggling her hips from side to side while popping her chewing gum in her mouth taking her beautiful black hands and long pink colored designed fingernails gently passing them against her wiggling hips. She then started rolling her hands gently around the edges of the miniskirt making sure there were no wrinkles in her outfit.

7

"*My love, I know your mama raised you better than that*" she said looking down at her pink heels while tossing her long black hair off her shoulder.

"*Mr. Vendridge, I know you are not going to stand there and ignore me? That's not you, my love. You know how to treat a woman. Your mama raised you much better than that*" she repeated herself while making her way to the bottom step on my front porch.

"*Well, it seems that you know a lot of things Mam*" I sarcastically responded as I unfolded my arms while widening my stance into a military attention position as if I was about to salute the general and come into the presence of superior authority.

"*That knowledge you display, may be a good thing. However, mam, you do know that trespassing is illegal and can be offensive here in Alabama. Now that is definantly not a good thing*" I said dropping my arms to my side.

"*Driving up on someone's property this time of day unannounced and not invited may not be good for someone as pretty as you*" I continued to say a mellow tone.

"*Someone like who, Babe*" she loudly replied.

"*Are you telling me I'm unwanted? Cause I clearly don't see a shotgun in your hand my love. Neither do I see a guard dog growling at your side to scare me or to back me off causing me to retreat from you. So clearly there's no offense. Now where are your manners*" she said while slowly wiggling her hourglass frame of body up the porch steps.

"*I know your fine butt is just as happy to see me as I am to see you, my love*" she continued to say while stepping up from the last step onto the porch.

"Whose truck is that belong to in my driveway Georgia Mae?" I asked slightly tilting my head to the right looking around her as if the white Chevrolet pickup truck looked even sexier than the beautiful attractive black hourglass figure shaped woman who is now boldly standing in front of me on my porch.

"Why are you so concerned my love?" Georgia Mae replied popping her chewing gum as she tossed her long black hair off her shoulder once again.

"So, you going to answer my question gal?" I asked sliding my hand into my pants pocket.

"I'm still waiting for my sugar babe" Georgia Mae softly replied.

"So, pretty lady you telling me that you have driven to my house and interrupted my evening for a bag of sugar? And in whose truck did you roll up on my driveway in to only to get this bag of sugar Georgia Mae?" I asked firmly.

"My sweet Lord! What is that delicious smell my nose has captured? Dear God, I can smell the chop BBQ from out here! It smells yummy! Like, an invitation for my belly to indulge in and from what I am smelling you still got it Tye" she shouted, moving closer to me while reaching her arms out as if we were going to embrace each other in a long a waited hug.

"The truck belongs to me Tye" she softly confessed, finally answering my question, while slowly moving her long pink painted fingernails across my chest.

"So, what punk you stole that new truck from Georgia Mae?" I asked, shifting my eyes down towards her face as she moved her hands around my rib cage towards my

back. Then clasping her brown hands together around my mid-section and gently laying her soft gorgeous head onto my chest muscle, Georgia Mae softly whispered,

"I missed you very much Tye. I have driven my new white truck through the dangerous tornado weather just to come and see you, Tye."

Georgia Mae like me was from Alabama. As children we didn't know each other and as teenagers we attended rivalry high schools. Our bond was so strong that when we had met it was as if we had known each other all our lives. Her cousin and I were crib babies as they call it in the South. Georgia Mae and I are simply kindred spirits. The intense chemistry we even shared as a couple was so genuine, so real and believe it or not so pure that if a person was to evaluate our relationship, they would conclude that Georgia Mae and I have been an item since childhood. We had a lot of similar interests. She enjoyed eating good cooking and I was developing myself into a master chef. Georgia Mae liked to go out dancing into the night and I loved to DJ the latest music released from the hottest new artist on my bedroom stereo. She loved to dress in the latest fashion, and I loved to stare at her sexy body watching her walk. Her body is mesmerizing. Georgia Mae was popular with the fellas around the neighborhood, and I was a popular all-star high school jock. I always had the latest vehicle and Georgia Mae was forever happily sporting my ride around the different neighborhoods. Driving herself places and burning out my gas. We were urban hood compatible. We were a power teenage couple. If there was ever such a term for young strong lovers. I respectfully enjoyed our sexual chemistry while we were together. And I boasted about that fact! Her beautiful juicy glossy lips serving me plenty of pleasure was my message to my peers. I had a Baddy who was a real delight, a truly bad girl. I always felt like the whole state of Alabama knew that statement was a fact. Stylish pocketbooks, neatly curled hair and fashion wardrobe doesn't make a beautiful black woman a hot commodity. Their involvement in street life activity can code their identity as a baddy. Her aunts and mother were well known and respected as street hustlers. I overheard some years ago one night as I played in a poker game one of the players referred to her aunt as the Godmother. Her five brothers were very loyal to their cousins, and nobody messed with them. I remember Georgia Mae mentioning to me that when any of her family members walked through the neighborhoods that nobody dared to even make eye contact or look at them.

One night her older sister and uncle rolled up at a basketball tournament that we had just won and in the middle of the victory celebration they pulled out a 9mm pistol and pistol-whipped one of our teammates. No one even intervened in the beating as I stood there shocked in silence. No one stopped them from publicly hurting the athlete or calling the local police. Coach never mentioned the incident or talked about that teammate ever again. The very next day in practice we had a brand-new teammate playing in that position. Her family street influence and respect were incredible.

Georgia Mae's family street influence and respect was visibly noticed. Even though she was one of the baby children of her family, she was just as tough as the rest of the older well-known family members. I always assumed being the baby girl amid those older male siblings toughened her skin. I once saw her beat up a boy from our high school in the skating rink parking lot. That was a hot Saturday night at the rink. Rumors in our neighborhood about her boxing matches were constantly rehearsed on how she beat up one of her math teachers and sliced up a school safety agent for messing with one of her younger brothers. I know she beat up my ex-girlfriend in the gas station, while we were dating. Putting the girl in the hospital after she called the house catching a case of amnesia forgetting that Ms. Georgia Mae and I were now together by getting loud with me on some nonsense about how I still owed her money. Yes, there are hearsay and street tales. I didn't need a story to respect her street credibility. The way Georgia Mae handled my body in the bedroom I in return adored the ground she walked on in public. I made sure personally within all my athletic muscular power that nobody dared mess with my girlfriend. I respected wherever Georgia Mae wanted me to go. I represented the fact that we were a power couple daily and I enjoyed giving her my respect.

"Babe, you know that you really want to kiss me" Georgia Mae said to me keeping the sarcastic greeting

dialogue going on as she began to squeeze her arms that were now fully wrapped around my muscular body tighter while we were standing together on my hot humid Alabama porch.

"Georgia Mae, have you been driving for a long length of time?" I asked, trying not to give into her seductive greeting.

"I am glad the storm that just passed didn't do a lot of damage Georgia Mae. For a good 40 minutes I was a little nervous because of the sound of the roars coming from the strong winds. I kept looking out the window hoping I would not see a funnel cloud that might have come viciously pounding through this neighborhood being destructive to our neatly kept property" I honestly said. Admitting how my true feelings had been throughout that afternoon.

"Yes, Tye, that was a heavy downpour and a real dark gloomy sky. But you as a nervous black man on the other hand is a surprise. I couldn't possibly imagine you being a nervous black man" Georgia Mae softly replied.

Black man was a term I took seriously. She chooses her words wisely in my presence. Only someone close to me or in my sphere of influence would be familiar with how that term powerfully and positively affects me. A term I took a lot of pride in growing up as an African American male in the South. Training as an athlete brought a competitive edge to my personality. I honestly admit I was and still am a very competitive person. I didn't just play street ball with my friends and the local neighborhood boys at all the local park basketball courts. I competed in school tournaments throughout the state. Daily practices and everyday gym workout routines helped to develop my skills towards possibly becoming a professional ball player. It wasn't just black faces I was playing up against. There were plenty of white boys on the opposite teams. Some of the battles were on the basketball courts or at the school gymnasiums. Few of them were neighborhood rivalries and some were plain racial wars with white boys from other neighborhoods. At the end I always won. School basketball games, at the local park, shooting hoops or a neighborhood fist fight. I was an all-star athletic champ. Being a muscular 7ft tall dark skin black boy had its advantages especially in intimidation. One time I stepped out of my best friend's car and the guys took off running. We laughed about that occasion for months after. Plus, I enjoyed fighting so putting my fist through some smart mouth punk was at times a joy. On and off any court I was a winner.

It was off the court I won Georgia Mae's, heart. It was off the court Georgia Mae, had my fully undivided attention. It was off the court I freely gave her my heart. After graduation I landed a job at a local waffle house and being an active student in a culinary program on the other side of town, I quickly became the main chef. So, I had a descent income coming in which I used to get my own crib while eagerly trying to become a master chef. My schedule was growing hectic, and it needed some type of balance. My dad was upset with me because I didn't join the military. My Uncle was upset with me because I didn't go on to play college ball or go pro by going on to the NBA. But how can you play professionally if you're not drafted. How can you play college ball if you're fighting in the Army. I don't know about dribbling a ball with an AK-47 wrapped around your shoulder. Plus, I never saw a tank roll up and soldiers pop out to shoot hoops in any of our basketball games. Now I have seen plenty of exotic cars exhibited from time to time and plenty of high fashion worn all around the school, specifically showing themselves off at our basketball game tournaments. There were a lot of high rollers in, Alabama. Plenty of entertainers as well as local spectators who loved to attend the tournaments and watch the after-school basketball games. Plus, I was in love with Georgia Mae, and our relationship elevated my popularity in the area with a baddy on my shoulder. My heart was steadily beating for her. So, I wasn't giving up our solid relationship to travel anywhere in the world to sleep around a bunch of guys dressed in any type of military uniform.

With some of the money I won from the local hoop matches or the betting I did as a side hustle I fixed my house up nicely. I furnished my crib with style. Not only am I a card shark but I was always taking another suckers money at the hoops. I didn't save up my money to buy that Bentley's I"m driving, I had I won it off a professional local producer and businessman that summer I vacationed in Miami for 2 weeks. Can you imagine only being in town for 2 weeks for a short, planned vacation and became the owner of a new Bentley's. I came into town on a crowded domestic flight, but I left out of Miami driving another suckers Bentley's. You already know Georgia Mae put more miles on my ride than the previous owner or myself. Like I said, I always had the latest vehicle, and I was known for rocking a foreign. I did notice how many of her family members started speaking to me publicly after I had got the new ride from Miami. I personally knew it was because of how I obtained my new whip rather than the fact that I had a new foreign parked in front of my stylish crib. I am sure she told her brothers the detailed version while driving them around in my car.

Even though I then had a heavier schedule than what I was used to having I still tried my hardest to continue keeping up with the rigor exercise and gym routines. My gym buddies were different than my high school friends or my teammates. They were actual athletes themselves. I did occasionally hang out with my teammates as well as worked out with them periodically in our school gym however they were not my official work out partners. At the time when I was attending high school my dad and coach thought that was a better solution for me. Together they felt it would help me to be more focused on my gym goals and get better physical results by being less social during my exercise times. I must admit hanging with my guys from school we did tend to get silly. Being around each other all day even as teammates there was always something to gossip about and someone to crack jokes on. So, we would focus on entertaining each other with wise cracks and horse play than setting body building goals. Now my gym buddies that I eventually ended up working out with at that time and still to this day are very serious about exercising. They're even flexible around my work schedule. Two of them had additional little ones now to add to their own schedules, so with that extra mouth to feed they had extra responsibilities themselves. Being out of high school we helped each other out in any possible way that we could plus we were known as a wolf pack. And together we thrived on that public image. When we walked into the gym it was the instant Olympians takeover.

"So, you missed me huh? I am glad to hear you say that to me. Honestly Georgia Mae I wasn't too sure if I would ever see you again. I was trying to remain single in hopes your sexy curves would one day be in my grasp" I said to her looking down into her beautiful brown face.

"Wait! Remain single? What are you mumbling to me Tye? I know you're not trying to imply that there is some chic in these Alabama hills on my wood" Georgia Mae said while slightly raising the tone of her voice.

I cracked a smile and started laughing because Georgia Mae always had a way of getting me to loosen up around her. Yeah, I was a tough guy, a high school jock who thrived on an image as a giant slayer. A fantasized Olympian, but this beautiful vivacious sexy woman always had that sweet smooth personality that warmed my heart.

"Your wood" I calmly replied. Slightly tilting my

head altering the expression on my face to a sudden look of admiration.

"*Tye now I know there's not some desperate tramp eating up my man's sauce*" she sarcastically said.

"*Looks like you came back in time for my sauce Georgia Mae*" I gently replied.

As we embraced each other intimately, our arms squeezing tightly around one another's body, we began to slowly kiss our lips gently but firmly touching while our tongues met twirling around one another locking together. We stood on the porch squeezing one another and sucking each other's lips.

"*You bring out the passion in me Tye I can't lie. I know I'll feel even better when we finally go inside*" she said while licking her lips and looking up right into my bedroom eyes.

"*That's where you want me to make you feel better when I get inside? Sounds more like you just want to taste my meat,*" I said.

"*You know I'm going to enjoy that meat of yours, lick up all that good sauce Tye that's a promise*" she quickly replied. As we entered the house Georgia Mae made her way up the hallway to my bathroom while I held down my kitchen finally turning off the low flame and pouring the sauce all over my meat. The cell phone began to ring when I answered it, it was my cousin Tanya. She works in an automotive shop on the East side of the downtown area.

"*Hey cousin, how are you?*" Tanya said over the phone.

"I'm not going to even lie cousin" I said with a big smile on my face.

"I'm feeling right at this moment cousin" I said in an even louder tone over the phone.

"Is that so big head" Tanya loudly replied.

"Cuz I'm feeling like myself right now and you know it's been a minute since I've been my real authentic self" I told my cousin Tanya over the phone.

"Well, I'm not going to block your shot champ you got this" Tanya said. *"I was on my last break, and that grimy guy Larry was being nice to me by giving me a lot of unnecessary conversation. I in return stood with a stone face looking back at him until he mentioned your name Tye. But cousin I'll let you go and do your thing on the court scrub"* Tanya said.

"Well Tanya, I just finished cooking dinner, so you know it's going down in my crib tonight. The sauce is ready whenever you get off work chump" I said to her over the phone.

"Thanks for the heads-up cousin sounds delicious and as I lick my lips right now to the wonderful sound of your invite, tell Georgia Mae I said I'll catch you'll later" Cousin Tanya said to me over the phone before I heard the clicking sound. As I hung up the phone, I heard the bathroom door open, and the sound of stiletto heels walk across my wooden floors.

"Yummy", *it sure smells sweet up in here this evening. You have the whole house super lit babe!! Can't stop licking my lips my love. You are the master chef Tye. I'm sure you know that babe. A sexy black man who knows his way around the kitchen. An attractive black man who enjoys leaving his underwear all over the bathroom."* Georgia Mae said while

19

easing her way over to my dining room table. As I continued to pour the well-loved steamy sauce all over my meat.

"It's my crib you freely roaming around in beautiful, and I can let hang what I please" I quickly replied.

"Yeah, Tye, you are right about that but I'm a girl that is not into sniffing negroes' underwear. I'm not into smelling dirty drawers" she replied while putting her purse on my dining room table. Pulling back one of the chairs from the table so she can ease her voluptuous hourglass shape body down to sit.

"Babe you are a master chef who can sure enough cook! I pulled up just in time! Hot damn! It smells good in your kitchen Tye" Georgia Mae shouted out!

"So, Georgia Mae you seen your boo Larry lately?" I asked lifting my eyes slowly from the pans in front of me while I continued to prepare the meal.

"What are you talking about now Tye? How did we go from a very intimate moment to including someone who has no interest in anybody in this room right now" she innocently replied.

"Girl don't fool with me. Have you been in the company of your boo Larry lately?" I asked slamming a lid on top of the pot of cabbage.

"Yeah, I heard he got out and is supposedly now back out here in the hot south" Georgia Mae said while scooting her chair up closer to my dining room table reaching her long finger nailed hands towards the inside of her pink purse which she placed on top of the table.

"Yeah, that bum came home from jail and is probably

doing something right now at this present time to get himself locked back up!" I loudly replied.

"But my concern right now in my comfortable drama free home is why is that something letting him take her to jail? Your feelings for that bum are that strong that you'll want to get locked up together? Oh, wow how cute is that picture an incarcerated couple! Two cute, caged jail birds! He's your boo so that means whatever nasty scam he will attempt to pull you surprisingly are now going to do along with him" I continued to say in an angry tone while slamming down the large spoon next to the pot of cabbage on top of the counter.

Georgia Mae pulled out a large fingernail file from out of her pink purse. Tossing her hair from off her shoulders once again as her eyes slowly maneuvered up towards my direction

"Tye why are you switching the mood with an inappropriate attitude? Stop getting yourself worked up over nothing that has to do with me or you. Whatever you think you know or feel you may know babe let me say to you it is not so. Negro, I aint, nobody's hoe! Whatever rubbish someone has told you is not true. He is not my boo. I am not dealing with him in any way shape or form. So, my handsome jealous strong black man can at this moment in his drama free home relax himself and breathe easier. Tye, I drove all the way out here because I wanted to see you. My lips don't lie. I miss all of you Tye. My body is craving for some Tye. My heart is beating for you. My steps demand me to be here with you. My lips speak truth. But they're watering right now cause of all this delicious food you skillfully and wonderfully have prepared. That is a right

21

on time surprise for a hungry lady. Let's just sit down together and enjoy your sauce" she replied.

I was never into playing any games. I never carried myself like a punk, I never dressed like a punk, I never behaved like a punk, I never surrounded myself with punks and I'm not going to let anyone come into my house and punk me. It's not going to happen. I heard what her juicy lips were saying but her actions were giving me another uncomfortable vibe. I'm not embracing any sucka street scams! No punks sneaky move! That punk Larry's track record speaks of trouble and Georgia Mae's affiliation with the punk is what swiftly changes my whole entire mood. She can surprisingly sit at my table across from me and enjoy my cooking with a soft beautiful smile on her face if she so desires to. She can sit at my table across from me and play with my feet with her feet under the table making my penis erect knowing I'm aroused if she so desires to. Georgia Mae can sit at my table and lick the BBQ sauce off the bone with her luscious juicy filled lips if she ever so wants to. However, that punk Larry's new move is still a serious issue that is out on this table, and I will continue to discuss this subject in my house with an attitude until I am informed of his current agenda with Ms. Georgia Mae.

CHAPTER 2

THE COUSIN'S CONCERN

Boom! Boom! Boom! The loud hard sounds of knocks coming from someone banging on the front door of my house. Ding-dong, the doorbell on the front of my house door repeatedly rang. Boom! Boom! Boom! The loud hard sounds of someone knocking at my front door continued. Behind this noise was the sound of early morning birds harmonizing in the trees around the windows with their loud symphonic chirping boldly letting everyone know it's the start of a brand-new day. Along with the rooster who was perched in the yard area on the right side of my house backing them up with a loud crowing sound. Boom! Boom! Boom! The sounds of hard knocks on the door continued followed by the constant ringing of the doorbell on my front door.

Then a sudden yell came from off my porch.

"Yo, cousin! You here? Ah, yo, cousin, can you hear? Cuz, I know you can hear me" Tanya screamed as she continued to knock even harder on my front door.

"Now I know you can hear me" she sarcastically said followed by an outburst of laughter.

Pulling back the silk sheet from off our warm bodies barely able to open my eyes I slightly rolled my body over from one side on the king size mattress slowly moving Georgia Mae's sexy sleeping body from off me. Rubbing my eyes with my index finger trying to open them up wide enough so I would be able to see the current time displayed on the panel of the clock on top of my dresser, my cell phone began to ring.

"Get your butt up and open the door Tye", Georgia Mae softly whispered while wrapping up herself with that end of the silk sheet that I had pulled back from off me.

Picking up the cell phone from off the dresser I slowly answered it.

"Wash your butt you, funky smelly chump and come open up this door scrub" Blaire boldly said in a loud tone without any hesitation over the cell phone.

"Well, hello to you also punk" I softly replied, still rubbing my index fingers around my eyes trying to get a clearer vision of the things all around my bedroom.

"Did I hurt your funky feelings chump? Get your nasty smelly butt up and come open this door so I can run this garden hose that I see outside here laying across this front yard of yours straight into your dingy jacked up bathroom to wash your dirty butt down with cold water and bleach! You smelly chump"

my cousin Blaire loudly screamed on the cell phone followed by an outburst of laughing.

"Tell Cousin Tanya," "I said stop banging on my damn door! She is going to need to save that hand for her little girlfriends" I replied while slowly getting up off the king size mattress in my bedroom walking over to a loveseat that is positioned in the center of my master bedroom which had a pair of my boxers and a pair of pants thrown over it.

"Ahh Tee!" Blaire yelled over towards his cousin Tanya.

"Tye asked why all the hard door banging this early in the morning? He asked why you didn't just use the window and climb through like you do at night with your little snow bunnies who are comfortably still living in their mama's crib" Blaire shouted over the cell phone followed by another outburst of laughter.

"Tell Tye, to watch his mouth scrub! I didn't want to climb through his house window and embarrass him by climbing into his busted bed to finish the job that he never can seem to handle. Serve that box up a real orgasm it came all the way back down here to Alabama for." My cousin Tanya loudly replied while laughing loud as she stood next to Blaire outside on the front porch.

"Oh lewd! Here we go! Cousin Tye, Tee is out here on this porch now speaking in tongues" Blaire loudly said followed by another outburst of laughter.

As I opened the front door my cousin Tiny was standing in the doorway on my porch with a huge smile, an unopened pack of large paper plates in one hand and a box of aluminum foil in the other hand.

"Come over here to get me some leftovers and try to get me some early morning breakfast from my all-star cousin. Now what's popping in your kitchen this morning for me" Tiny said while dropping the plates and aluminum foil into my arms as he began pushing his way through my front door. My cousin Jimena was right behind him bulldozing herself through my front door with her new 5-month-old baby girl snuggled tight in her chubby thick arms. Delores Blaire's pregnant wife came rushing inside my house marching right behind Jimena along with their 6-year-old son pulling him by his t-shirt from behind her through my front door with her right hand. Cousin Blaire who was still standing outside my porch laughing along with Tanya had the baby stroller in his left hand of course always trying to give the persona or image of being a perfect gentleman while loudly laughing hitting Tanya in her left shoulder with the cell phone in his right hand.

"I see you'll are a bunch of silly comedians this morning" I said while attempting to close the door leaving the two of them laughing foolishly outside on my porch.

"Come on scrub, don't be wimpy like that I'm just here taking you up on your invitation. Isn't that right Blaire? We just here because of the thoughtful genuine invite our champion all-star cousin extended to us." Tanya replied while extending out her right hand like she was going to give me a high five.

Turning away from the door, letting it close, I just walked back inside the house ignoring them both.

"Big hip sexy! Where are you at? Big hip sexy come out of hiding because my cousin Tee got real action for that cat" Tiny said while sitting on the sofa in my living room, throwing his feet up on top of the wooden coffee table as if he was sitting comfortably being king of the castle in his own home. Blaire's pregnant wife Delores slowly sat herself down on the sofa next to him. Her son sat Indian style on my waxed wooden floor in the middle of my Livingroom.

"You need help with the breakfast Tye?" Jimena politely asked while pulling out one of the chairs from under the table in my dining room so she can sit and rest her chubby legs.

"No thank you cousin" I sharply replied in a heavy tone.

"I been meaning to ask you Tye, how is Jason? Is he still working down there at the docks lifting freight off those big ships?" Jimena softly inquired.

"I thought they got rid of that wimpy guy?" Blaire said in a loud tone now standing over the kitchen sink washing his hands with the little bit of dish detergent soap he had seen in the bottle that was placed on top of the kitchen counter by the faucet.

"No, Blaire it wasn't Jason those racist supervisors canned over there at the docks. They need that good looking dude down there. You know how they operate and make illegal but legal moves. It was that tall negro Jamie who got the axe" Tanya loudly said while taking the baby stuff from out

of the baby's bag that she also had carried into the house placing it on top of the kitchen table next to Jimena.

"No, no, no Jamie still works down their girl. I was with him, Eric and Larry at the bar last week for Candice's big 30th birthday party. I specifically heard them talking about the loads they've been maneuvering over the past couple of days at the docks. And my ears overheard Jamie who came right out his face and said I'm going to have to call a meeting with them suits for an increase in salary if they keep working me like this" my cousin Jimena said while adjusting the pacifier in her newborn baby girl's mouth.

"So, you were hanging with Larry last week?" I asked aggressively walking over to the kitchen table.

"Is that what she said Cousin Tye? Because I clearly had heard her say that she was getting her party on at that bar last week and while she was making her baby fat bounce all over that bar for big mouth Candice's cake, Jamie and Larry were talking about their present problems down there at them docks. Now that's what I thought I had heard! Scrub you may need to take your mean self to church. It might be that time. You know Gods ways are not our ways and Gods time is not our time. God has a way of making his will be known. It may just be your time to mosey on over to church and let our blessed Bishop cousin Joe lay his hands on your ears. Ever since I have been here today, your hearing has been in question. Can't hear the knock on the door, you can't hear the doorbell ringing, you can't answer the phone properly and you can't even hear anything someone says to you even if they're a foot away from you in your own damn kitchen. It may just be your time for a blessing" my cousin Tiny said while pushing the buttons

on the remote for the television in the living room as he sat laid back comfortably on the sofa.

"Well, hello their family aren't we all a lively bunch to see this morning in my handsome babe Tye's house" Georgia Mae said, as she came quickly wiggling into the kitchen wearing one of my sports jerseys' over her, hourglass shaped body fitted looking like a lovely dress. Making her way toward my cousin Jimena who was seated at the table in the dining room to see her newborn baby girl.

"About time you come out of hiding and hit the stage for us sexy gal. I know you heard me summoning you when I came through the door quietly into the house. I know you heard me constantly calling for you to come into our presence and to show my cousin Tee your stuff! There may be a problem with your hearing too Georgia Mae. However, you came into our midst just in time for a real treat. That is whether you can hear good or not. A heavenly miracle. You're going to witness a sudden turnaround in Mobile, Alabama. That's why I love God. God can turn it all around just like that. Watch the turn around happen in this house. Cousin Tye is about to go to church and receive a blessing" Tiny loudly shouted as he reclined himself on the sofa with his feet on top of the coffee table.

"How are you doing this morning Tiny?" Georgia Mae implied while standing over Jimena gently pulling and tugging at the newborn baby girl clothes with a soft smile on her face.

*"Did you hear what I said gal? **I am Blessed**! Maybe you need to go to church too. Alongside your hard of hearing boo Tye. Get double for your trouble"* Tiny loudly replied.

"So, you went to Candice's party girl? How was it?" Georgia Mae asked Jimena while still standing over her and the newborn baby at the table. Purposely ignoring Tiny's suggestions.

"Girl it was super lit! Lot of faces I haven't seen in a while" Jimena replied.

"Lot of lying faces too. It seems as if fake fellas are fearing telling the truth these days about how bad they are really doing with their broke pockets. They would rather parade around a party profiling and telling lies" Blaire said while opening the refrigerator in my kitchen and pulling out the opened gallon of milk for himself to drink.

"I am telling you'll Jamie does not work at that dock anymore. And if any of you'll ever listen to me when I share my work stories then each of you can remember that I'm his mechanic and I have been working on Jamie's truck for years. That tall negro got the axe. You cut off! Goodbye! Is what those dock supervisors said unto him" my cousin Tanya jokingly shouted while standing next to me with her hands in her pants pockets.

"How was the music at Candice's party girl? Who was the DJ for the party that night?" Georgia Mae inquired wiggling her way over to the refrigerator to pull out the pots and pans of food I had previously cooked the night before.

"That skinny tall dark skin Jamaican fella. DJ GAN. He had his crew there too" Jimena loudly replied.

"You are talking about hearing some good music. Bishop now has a new band giving that choir a brand-new sound. That church over there is where it is at. Heaven is calling for *you Cousin Tye. I know you can't hear the invites because of waxed filled ears, but I'm sure you will be able to see God clearly over there at the church"* Tiny said as he sat up on the sofa removing his feet from off my wooden coffee table.

"My God is blessing every, every, every day and God has a big blessing on the way oh God is going to show up for you today" Tiny sang while stomping his feet on my floor as if he was a professional gospel quartet singer.

"Oh, Gods is going to show up for you every, every day, watch God bless you every, every day" my cousin Jimena started to sing harmonizing joining in with Tiny lifting her 5-month-old newborn baby girl slightly in the air so we could all sing directly into her future.

"So how long was you conversing with that bum Larry at that Wack party?" I aggressively asked.

"Him and Eric were rocking together at the bar all night from what I did see Cousin Tye. As a matter of fact, they had on the same colors that night. But you know Eric stays hot on my tail. Honestly, he's been pushing up on me since my first baby daddy and I separated. He just knows now he can't get rid of Quincy, so he doesn't try as much as he used too" Jimena said with a huge smile on her face.

"Ooh so you saying he had something to do with the disappearance of Matts father. You let that smelly breath negro run your baby daddy away" Tanya said, while leaning her body into me.

"Yes, Matts my little man! Dats my heart right there! He can play some ball now. Got shots for days! That explains why he plays better than Quincy" Tiny loudly interrupted.

31

"*That's it. My first born a baller just like his daddy*" Jimena replied with a big smile on her face.

"*What? Are you crazy! That loser couldn't play no Ball! Tye, Tiny and I always had to bail that negro out on the court. He and Quincy both had too much mouth. Matt gets his ball skills on the court from me! I schooled my little cousin on the game for real! I taught him all of that*" Tanya shouted as she moved her way into the living room towards her cousin Tiny.

"*I'm with Tanya on this one Jimena, why you let Eric thirsty musky smelling self-run your baby daddy away?*" Delores sarcastically said while rubbing her pregnant belly with her hands.

"*Would you like something cold to drink DeeDee?*" I asked Delores in a loud tone.

"*I'm pouring her a tall glass of freshly squeezed lemonade right now babe*" Georgia Mae loudly said while standing in the kitchen over the sink with the giant size pitcher of lemonade.

"*Thank you, cousin, Tye I always love your hospitality*" Delores said to me as she continued rubbing her pregnant belly with a smile now on her face.

"*You want something cold to drink also little cuz?*" Tanya asked and said to their 6-year-old son who was sitting on the living room floor Indian style with his hands on his knees.

"*You become a black belt yet boy?*" I intervened loudly to ask him, turning my body towards the living room area but still standing directly over my cousin Jimena with my arms folded.

32

"*Not yet sir*" he softly replied to me.

"*That's little GI Bruce Leroy meditating over there in that living room. You'll better watch yourselves with Master Lee in there*" Jimena loudly said followed with an outburst of laughter.

"*Mighty ninja Joe young who will go ape shit on you. Jungle style like his father standing there in that kitchen*" Tiny jokingly said.

"*Forget, both of you chumps. You'll just be mad because my son can kick butt like his father always has. And believe it or not he is not even one of my class leaders. Now don't get me wrong he's a great martial arts student who has wonderful potential and a disciplined son if I can say so myself. My boy is tough like me! A strong muscle. You'll know when I had that karate school built, I had my boy in mind because I wanted him to have all the opportunities and advancements afforded to him that I didn't have*" Blaire said walking over to the dining room table standing directly next to me.

"*He's a good kid Blaire and you're lucky punk. That's a good turnout you have received from the students who seem ready to learn from you. Ever since you opened the doors of that martial arts school out here in Mobile, Alabama*" I replied turning around walking towards the stove to fire up some breakfast for my hungry annoying family.

"*Master Lee massage my knee come on baby soothe me*" Jimena jokingly said to Blaire looking up towards him while kicking out her chubby leg followed by an outburst of laughter.

"*You heard what DeeDee said about that thirsty punk Eric. Trying to bully them bums away from you Jimena. You*

33

may need to hire her son to guard your hot butt from now on. His young self will Kick some sense into a punk quick with no hesitation" I said while turning on the flame of the stove to heat up a frying pan.

"I'm surprised your waxed ears heard anything anyone said Cousin Tye, with your tall mean self. I know I just overheard why Quincy can't ball like his son Matt. Tee done showed him the family moves" Tiny responded while shifting his body up off the sofa, reaching out his right hand to give Tanya a pound as she reached her right hand down towards him.

As Georgia Mae wiggled her way into the living room to serve them the glasses of lemonade she had poured. Blaire pulled out the chair from under the dining room table to sit across from Jimena.

"Big hip Sexy. You squeezed the juice out them lemons yourself this morning?" Tiny loudly asked Georgia Mae as he laid his body back onto the sofa.

"No Tiny I did not squeeze any lemons this morning. Your very handsome muscle bodied cousin Tye made this sweet refresher to go along with the delicious dinner he cooked last night" Georgia Mae replied wiggling her way back into the kitchen wearing my basketball Jersey.

"That's what I came here for! To get that tasty chop!" Tanya shouted out.

"That was a bad storm we had yesterday. The winds took out the power on our side of town" Blaire said as he sat at the dining room table roaming through Jemena's baby bag.

"Were there any damages to the property at your school?"

Jemena asked, as she rocked her baby back and forth cuddled in her chubby thick arms.

"*Yeah, I meant to ask you that man? Your Karate school good after that madness yesterday?*" Tanya asked as she walked slowly over to the dining room table.

"*That was a heavy down pour on yesterday I had to navigate and drive through!*" Georgia Mae shouted as she put the jar of lemonade back into the refrigerator.

"*No damages to my martial arts schools building. I really must thank God that everything remained intact throughout that severe windy mess*" Blaire replied.

"*Just our home lost power and we thank God that was the only serious problem we faced. Because our entire neighborhood obtained a lot of damages*" Delores said while opening her pocketbook to look for her cell phone that kept chirping alerting her of new text messages.

"*I heard there was a bad accident on some freeway too. I'm just not sure which one. My neighbors were talking about last night*" Tiny said in a loud tone.

"*Yes, Quincy didn't come home until around 4 in the morning. However, he did call me last night to inform us that it was a deadly pile up on I 20. The emergency room was chaotic all late afternoon way into the night. That's probably the accident you're speaking about Cousin Tiny*" Jemena said softly while giving her newborn baby kisses all over her face.

"*So, when did you buy that monster truck Georgia?*" Blaire asked pushing his chair back away from the dining room table.

"*Yes indeed,*

that bright white stallion is something to see.

Having the keys and papers to that ride puts you in the lead.

Now that ride is a real beauty.

Looking real litty and sitting real pretty,

outside on your driveway.

Seriously stunting in the morning sun. Ms. Big hip Sexy is on the scene.

The horse race has already begun" Tiny rhythmically said.

"You'll butt kissers admire my style and I see your loving my taste" Georgia Mae softly replied.

"You can save that kiss and love for your bedroom drama with our cousin. We just want to know when you bought that white monster truck?" Blaire asked looking out the hallway window catching another glimpse of the White pickup truck on the driveway.

"Are you'll ready to eat?" I asked.

"That's what I came over here for this morning. That delicious Barbeque cousin! What's the deal with the meal" Tanya rhythmically said, making her way back into the kitchen towards me.

That's when my cell phone rang. Usually, I don't answer calls when I'm maneuvering around the kitchen. However, considering the hour of morning, this is the time when stores would contact me about deliveries running late or possibly being cancelled. Answering it I can hear crying in the background.

"Hello, hello!" I continued to loudly say not really

recognizing the phone number displayed on the caller ID.

"Hey, Uncle Tye it's me Libbie your niece" a soft voice whispered over the phone.

"Morning lil-bit, what's the matter? Sounds like crying I'm hearing. What's going on? What happened" I loudly asked.

"Um, Uncle Tye, um oh God help! Lord why?" She screamed out while crying over the phone.

"Lil-bit! What happened? Talk to me! You know your uncle is always there for you. Tell me why you're crying baby girl" I nervously asked standing over the stove.

"What happened Tye?" Georgia Mae asked in concern, stopping what she was doing making her way over towards me.

"Cuz is everything O.K.?" Tanya asked with concern.

"The police are here Cousin Tye" Blaire said standing in the hallway by the front door still looking out the window.

"What? Wait, what is going on?" Jemena loudly asked and said jumping up off the kitchen chair with her newborn baby wrapped tightly in her arms quickly making her way to the window towards her first cousin Blaire.

"Two police cars just pulled up in Cousin Tye's driveway!" Blaire shouted.

Tiny's cell phone began to ring amid all the sudden commotion of concern now on everyone's faces in the house. He quickly reached his right hand in his jeans pocket to answer it.

"Yeah Rev. what's going on in Alabama this morning?" Tiny loudly asked responding to the incoming phone call. *"Yes Rev. I have. I'm in Cousin Tye house right now sir"* Tiny said quickly standing up on his feet moving into the kitchen towards Tye.

Ignoring my cousin Tiny's phone conversation, and Georgia Mae's sudden questions of concern in my ear as she now stood next to me.

"Lil-bit whatever it is you can tell me. You know you can trust your Uncle Tye. Stop crying baby girl your uncle is here for you" I said in a stern voice standing in the kitchen looking into Georgia Mae's eyes.

"No, the police are now here for you! Three cops are stepping up onto your porch steps cousin Tye" Blaire said making his way towards the front door.

"Oh My God! Oh No! NO! Say it's not so! Oh God not Cousin Debbie!" Delores loudly shouted as she started stomping her feet on the wooden floor. She began crying, continuing to scream while holding her cell phone up in the air. Her son jumped up from off the wooden floor, snatched the cell phone and quickly ran to the front door towards his dad Blaire giving him the phone so he can read the text messages that was sent to his wife Delores phone.

"Lil-bit where's my sister? Is she there with you? Stop crying for a second and hand Debbie the phone baby girl. Let your uncle Tye speak to his sister. I'm here for you but give my sister Debbie the phone so I can speak with her Lil-bit" I frantically said. As my heartbeat began racing faster and the sounds of the room got quieter to me.

"She's dead Tye" Blaire said holding up the cell phone in the air that his son had just handed to him.

"No! Say it's not so! Oh God not Cousin Debbie!" Delores screamed out while crying and stomping her feet on the wooden floor in the living room.

"Yeah, Cousin Tye, Debbie is not here with us anymore. I am deeply sorry for your loss on this morning man. Bishop is on the phone right now. He's over at your parents' house with Aunt Rebecca and Cousin Brenda" Tiny said holding his cell phone to his ear while putting his hand on Tye's shoulder.

Ding Dong the doorbell rang.

"Yeah, who is it?" Blaire yelled standing at the door.

"Good morning, sir, it's the police if you could open the door, we would like to have a word with you."

"lil bit what's happening in my house right now? Talk to me baby girl! Where's my sister?" I frantically asked and loudly said as my heartbeat started pounding even faster. Uncontrollably tears started to fall down my cheeks as I ignored all of my cousins.

"Open the door Blaire" Georgia Mae said.

"Yeah Cousin, let the police come in" Tanya softly said while grabbing the crotch of her work pants.

"Oh God No! Dear God, why so?! Not my beautiful Cousin Debbie!" Delores continued screaming out her mouth while holding her pregnant belly as she began to lie across the sofa in the living room crying and still stomping her feet on the wooden floor.

"Go in their comfort and sit with your mother boy"

Jenema loudly said to Blaire's son while reading the text messages from his sister Brenda on Delores cell phone.

"Uncle Tye my mommy is dead" the soft voice whimpered out as Lil-bit finally answered her uncle's desperate plea.

"It hurts me so bad! Uncle Tye. They killed my mommy Uncle Tye! Why did they want to hurt me? They took my mommy away from me!" Libbie yelled out over the phone.

As Blaire reached for the door. Jemena quickly ran into the kitchen towards the stove, turning the knobs on the eye of the stove to the off position. Then turning around pushing Georgia Mae out of the way with her newborn baby still wrapped tightly in her thick arms she quickly embraced her cousin Tye in a bear hug.

CHAPTER 3

THE DEPUTIES HOME VISIT

"Good morning, sir I do apologize for the sudden intrusion on this early Alabama morning. I'm chief Reginald, this is sheriff Wesley and deputy Davis are you, Tye?" The Stocky policeman said as he and the officers stood in my hallway.

"No man you referring to my cousin that's him standing over there in the kitchen talking on the cell phone. As you can see officers, he's being comforted right now by our big cousin" Blaire loudly said looking at the Chief of police directly into his eyes.

"Well, I'm very impressed seeing that news does travel fast around Alabama. I guess you'll beat us here, not that it's a race of any kind excuse the expression of speech. I don't want to be offensive. Heavy news does bear weight, so I am glad that someone who is familiar and comfortable with the family is here to help bear this kind of bad news. It makes the assignment

smoother. I am also not surprised that you all are here before us given the time of the event when everything actually did occur" the chief sharply said while looking directly into Blaire's eyes.

"No chief! Unfortunately, we just found out ourselves. The Pastor, who is also our cousin, is the one who informed us this morning and he is on the cell phone right now as well as Tye's niece" Tiny loudly stated, while standing in the kitchen next to Tye and Jimena still holding the cell phone to his ear.

"Yes sir, we were all just gathered here at Cousin Tye's house for morning breakfast" Tanya said while holding her crotch in her pants.

Still ignoring everyone talking around me in my own kitchen as the fast-paced heartbeats pressed against my chest making it even harder for me to hear anyone. While my cousin Jimena still held me tight in hug along with her new bundle of joy now pressed up against my chest.

"Why are the police here in my house lil-bit? Who messed with my sister? Where's Debbie?" I loudly asked my niece.

"Uncle Tye, it hurts me! Uncle Tye my mommy" Libbie sadly said as she continued to cry on the cell phone.

"Where is my sister? What is happening baby girl?" I screamed out as tears kept falling from my eyes uncontrollably right down my cheeks.

"Give me the cell phone cousin" Tanya calmly said, reaching her hand out towards me.

"Please cousin, let Tanya speak to her. She's not going to hang up on her I promise you all-star. You have my complete word. I won't let her hang up the phone until my sweet little cousin Libbie answers all your questions champ." Tiny calmly said.

"*Come on Cousin Tye let the phone go. Just give it to her*" Jemena said while still hugging me in a tight bear hug swaying my tall athletic body back and forth with her thick arms.

"*Oh God! No, not Debbie! No God not my beautiful cousin! Say it's not so!*" Delores sadly yelled out as she continued to cry while still rubbing her pregnant belly and stomping her feet on the wooden floor. Her body was now slain across the Livingroom sofa while her 6-year-old son hugged her tight trying to console his mom from the text messages Delores received on her cell phone from her sister-in-law.

"*You must excuse my wife this morning chief. This is just a shocker and a heavy blow to our entire family*" Blaire said, turning his head to the other two officers.

"*I'm sure it is and there is no reason for apologies*" The Chief clearly lifted his voice and spoke.

"*We completely understand sir and like the Chief just said you don't have to apologize for anything*" Sheriff Wesley calmly said.

"*And sir if you don't mind may we enter the kitchen and speak to Tye ourselves? Once again Like the Sheriff said, we are very sorry to intrude on your family breakfast this morning, but it is an urgent matter that brings us out here to speak with Tye*" Officer Davis clearly said.

"*We don't mean any harm and I'm truly thankful that you guys are here for your cousin. But your uncle and aunt told* us that their son is the one we need to speak with this morning" the Sheriff loudly said.

As Blaire made his way into the kitchen with police officers Georgia Mae quickly pulled out one of the dining room chairs from under the table and sat down crossing her legs.

"Hey Tye, man give Tanya the cell phone right now so she can comfort your niece! Listen here these police officers want to speak with you. They were sent here by your mom and pops" Blaire loudly commanded as he walked over and stood by the refrigerator.

Jemena finally let me go of her tight hug. Turning her chubby self around in my kitchen and making her way back to her original seat at the dining room table while Tanya quickly took the phone out of my hand.

"What is going on in my house man?" I loudly asked and said to my first cousin Tiny who stood next to me with the cell phone in his ear.

"God is with you cousin. God got your back all-star" Tiny clearly replied while holding his cell phone to his ear with their cousin ------ who is now a Bishop and the pastor of a church in Alabama where his sister and parents attend.

"We all got your back Cousin Tye!" Jemena yelled out while taking a bottle out of her bag for her newborn baby that was on the dining room table.

"Good morning, sir my name is chief Reginald, I am here with two of my officer's Sheriff deputy highway state trooper Wesley and officer Davis who is our certified chaplain. We were sent here by your parents. I am sad to announce to you

Tye that on yesterday afternoon during that monster storm we had here in our town in the State of Alabama your sister Debbie was killed in tragic car accident on Interstate 20. Her body was discovered late last night in the wooded area off the Interstate. The car had already been towed when the body was discovered. We assessed that because of the impact she had been ejected and due to the high winds of the storm her body had been thrown into the woods and covered by debris." The chief loudly said.

"Oh My God! Dear Jesus no!" Jemena cried out, dropping her head into her chest as tears fell from her eyes while rocking her newborn baby in her thick arms.

"We ran the information from the plates to find out who the owner of the vehicle and who the possible driver of the vehicle might have been. According to the Drivers Motor Vehicles, the car was registered to your sister Debbie" Sheriff Wesley calmly said.

"Like I stated her body was finally discovered last night and it was brought to my attention she was pronounced dead by the EMT on site. Her body has been transported to the morgue located in ------- hospital, downtown Mobile, Alabama. Now to confirm all the information we have so far, we are still going to need a positive identification on the body that was discovered at the wreckage site.

Going by the records we have on file that matched the information we received from the Drivers Motor Vehicle, is what led sheriff Wesley and myself to your parent's house." The chief calmly said.

"Once again, we express our deepest condolences to you Tye and to your family. We know this heavy news as the

chief clearly stated, is so unfortunate and strikingly painful. Our hearts are saddened with your family for this horrific loss of precious life, and you all are truly in our prayers. We only come in such an efficient manner because it is our job. The information regarding details of what occurred yesterday is still pending. The shared reports from victims and eyewitnesses are still sketchy and nothing is concrete at this present time. Now what will help these law enforcement agencies and what will bring a little bit of comfort to your family is if we can get a positive identification on the body that was discovered at the crash site that is now in the morgue at the hospital. After speaking with your parents earlier this morning, Tye, they led us to believe that you would be the best person to do that in assisting all of us in doing our daily job." Chaplain Davis calmly said.

"Oh no Lord not so! Why my beautiful cousin? No not so! Not my Debbie, she didn't deserve it!" Delores continued to scream out as she laid across the sofa cuddled in her son's arms as she continued to stomp her feet hard on the living room wooden floor.

"We believe that her wallet and personal items if she was carrying them with her yesterday that they still maybe located inside the car. The car itself is of course totaled and severely damaged. So, any obtainable items found in the vehicle as well as her personal identifications you can claim them Tye with the police officers on duty at the precent parking area where the vehicle has been towed and is now located" The Sheriff loudly said.

"Oh, Debbie my beautiful cousin you have gone too soon. May her sweet, sweet spirit now find heavenly eternal

rest" Jimena said while the tears fell from her eyes as she continued to rock her newborn baby tightly in her arms.

Tiny handed Tye his cell phone.

"Cousin Tye, your pops want to speak to you" Tiny softly said.

"Baby girl we love you. I heard what the officers just told your uncle. We are coming to get you! Okay? We are not going to let anything else bad happen to you this morning. Your grandmother is already on the case. Your grandfather is releasing his entire family on them people right now you hear me? Baby girl we love you. Go ahead and cry, it's okay. I know it hurts. We are coming to get you" Tanya said to Libbie, as she paced back and forth in the living room holding the cell phone to her face.

CHAPTER 4

THE UNWANTED GUEST

"Global warming has affected and changed our way of living drastically. These storms have grown worse enormous in size and uncontrollably disastrous" Bishop Joe said as he sat next to his crying aunt Tye's mother while holding her cold shaking hands on the back yard porch. Seated directly next to him on the backyard patio furniture was his cousin Joshua who was holding the pastor Bishop Joe's cell phone while he scrolls through the emails.

Joshua is very loyal to his cousin Bishop Joe. He respects him as man of the cloth, and he serves him efficiently. They were always close as teenagers. Even though Joshua was more outgoing in personality, when Joe was ordained, a Bishop there was no question in anyone's mind who would be his assistant. He lets everyone know that Joe is his pastor and should be respected as a man of God.

"Nephew, my daughter Libbie, is going to need you more in her life now than ever! You hear me son?" Tye's father shouted across the backyard as he stood at the foot of his porch holding a tennis ball in his hands preparing himself to throw the ball further into their backyard for the families pet dog a Golden Retriever to chase and eventually bring the tennis ball back to him.

"Yes sir!" Joshua replied to his uncle.

"I texted Libbie a few minutes ago to see if she needed anything. She replied to me that Cousin Tanya and your son are with the police now and they are on their way to pick her up to go and view Cousin Debbie's body" Joshua continued as he replied to his uncle.

"No! No honey! That baby doesn't need to see her mother in that condition! No, it is too soon!" Tye's mom shouted out loud as the tears fell down her chubby soft cheeks.

"Wait, what's going on out here? Who's seeing who? What are you all talking about now? Who, don't need to go and see what?" Aunt Rebecca yelled as she quickly came outside onto the patio busting through the back door of the house while holding a small paper plate with a slice of bread pudding in her hand.

"Here sis, taste this! It just came out of your oven" Rebecca said as she shoved the plate with the slice of hot baked bread pudding into her sister-in-law's nervously shaking hands. Pastor Bishop Joe quickly grabbed the plate helping his aunt to hold the plate as she continued to cry about the loss of her only daughter due to the tornado that touched down on yesterday.

"Where is my piece mama?" Brenda loudly said finally

lifting her head from texting and chatting on her cell phone. While rocking back and forth on the wooden rocking chair that's placed by the steps to the backyard of the patio.

"You need to get your lazy butt up out that chair and go into the kitchen yourself and get your own slice" Rebecca sternly replied to her daughter.

"Auntie you delegated the responsibility of your daughter and the assistance with the authorities to Cousin Tye. Let your son handle it. You gave them your permission and released it on to Tye for a reason. So, allow your only son Tye to make the decisions that will help this family get through a tragic situation" Joshua said as he continued scrolling through the emails on Bishop Joe's cell phone.

"Hey Joshua, call my son and tell him don't take my daughter to see her mother badly bruised maybe deformed body laid out on a cold mat in a cold morgue!" Tye's father shouted out loud while trying to pull the tennis ball out of his pet dog Golden retriever's mouth.

"Now everyone let us all calm down. Let's all take a deep breath and settle our nerves for a minute. I feel we all need to try and eat a little something, maybe drink a cup of ice-cold lemonade to cool and refresh us. Gather our emotions and finally exhale" Rebecca sternly said.

"Who was that I heard at my door 10 minutes ago?" Tye's mom weepily said.

"Your niece Jill and her husband. They are in front of the house with your brother. They had been arguing since they entered the house. I told them to take that noise outside, this is not the time for all that unnecessary bickering" Rebecca said.

"That's so unfortunate my uncle had to come over here this morning and be a part of their toxicity. He can't even calmly comfort his own brother in a time of family tragedy" Bishop Joe loudly said.

"That's your parish pastor. Isn't my beautiful niece a leader at your church. How is she going to be running things with all that anger and verbiage spuing out of her mouth every time there's a public event? You may need to intensify your bible school lessons or start imputing marriage counseling into your sermons on Sunday" Tye's father loudly said as he threw the tennis ball again out into the yard for the dog to chase.

"Uncle I've sat with them in my office personally many times. I've even met with them at their house dozens of times. But with Cousin Jill it seems to be a weekly battle with her husband" Bishop Joe replied while holding the plate of bread pudding for Tye's mom as she wiped the tears from off her face.

"More like a daily battle Uncle" Joshua sarcastically said lifting his head up from Bishop's cell phone.

"Please don't let her see her mother now! That's just not good! Oh God my baby girl is gone!" Tye's mom cried out as the tears continued falling down her chubby soft cheeks.

William came out the door onto the backyard holding a big paper plate with 3 slices of bread pudding, eggs and turkey bacon on it. Slowly walking over to his aunt, he bent over and embraced her tightly.

"Oh, I didn't know Cousin William was here" Brenda

51

said as she finally got up off the rocking chair making her way inside the house towards the kitchen.

"At least now I know which Uncle is outside in front of the house with Jill and her daily temper tantrum" Joshua jokingly said.

"Yeah, that's my brother-in-law out there in front of the house playing referee. I'm not sure exactly where my husband Bucky is this morning. Usually, he's either at the bank conducting business for my restaurant or meeting with managers conducting business for his band. It's much too early for my husband Bucky's band to have rehearsal. However, he is aware of what has happened to our niece Debbie so I'm sure he will make his way over here to this house sometime today to see his brother" Rebecca spoke.

William finally let his aunt go, as tears also started to fall down his big cheeks. Slowly turning around and making his way over to the edge of the top steps on the backyard patio deck towards where Tye's father was standing in the yard. As William stopped, he dropped his head down resting his thick chin on top of his chest and cried.

"Thanks for coming nephew! It's, so good to see you!" Tye's father shouted as the dog brought the tennis ball back to him again from the other side of the yard.

"Listen sis, everything is going to be fine with our little Libbie. My son and his family are with Tye and Tanya as we speak. So, I'm sure together they will protect our baby girl and handle things in their best interest" Rebecca calmly said.

"Jimena and her baby are with them as well auntie. I overheard her comforting Cousin Tye while I was talking

with Tiny earlier when the Sheriff was at Cousin Tye's house explaining what happened to your daughter on the interstate yesterday" Bishop Joe said.

"Oh, now look at that! Sis! Everyone is with Tye. Look at how loving God is pastor! I happily rejoice! My nephew is not alone. God is awesome he will never leave us or forsake us as the bible says. That is why I said everything's going to be fine" Rebecca loudly shouted.

"That's our family auntie" Joshua loudly said as he continued tapping on Joes cell phone.

As the back door slowly swung open. A tall slim brown skin man stepped out onto the patio. Everyone's head turned towards him. He stopped, took off his cap, positioning the cap by his heart and then placing the cap onto his t-shirt standing still on the patio he said,

"Good morning my name is Jamie and I'm a close childhood friend of your daughter Debbie. Brenda let me into the house and told me Debbie's parents were back here. I simply came over this morning to give my condolences. To simply show Debbie's family my love. My heart is broken from the sad news I just recently received this morning. I'm sadly shocked! Like dumb founded and the whole neighborhood is absolutely crushed from what has happened. That's why I'm so weak this morning. On behalf of the neighborhood, we are truly sorry for your loss. Debbie was always full of life. She loved life and enjoyed living. I'm just weak and my heart is crushed. Everyone is terribly sorry for your loss" Jamie softly said.

William quickly turned around, wiped some of the tears off his face, put the plate of food down onto the rocking chair and quickly ran over towards Jamie.

Taking his left fist, he punched Jamie straight in the jaw knocking him backwards to the edge of the patio towards the back door he then quickly took his right fist and with an upper cut he struck Jamie in the left side of his face very hard knocking him over the banister off the backyard patio onto the grass in the backyard.

The dog started barking and growling as it ran over towards Jamie who was now lying on the grass next to the backyard patio slowly trying to sit himself up from being knocked off the patio by William. The Golden Retriever barking dashed towards Jamie grabbing near his ankle, the dog bit into the tongue of his high-top sneakers and started shaking his leg furiously.

"Ooh, my leg! Get this mut away from me!" Jamie yelled.

"Fight! Fight! Fight! Oh my God Williams fighting outside on the backyard patio!" Brenda screamed as she rushed through the back door onto the backyard patio deck.

Joshua and Joe together grabbed William who was trying to make his way down the patio steps to finish giving the stranger a beating that he felt Jamie deserved. Trying their best to stop William from further hitting the strange guest, Joshua and Joe began pushing William backward towards the house back door away from the patio steps which led to the green grass filled backyard that has now turned into fighting ring.

"What happened nephew? Who is this piece of crap in my yard?" Tye's father asked William as he slowly walked

towards his pet Golden Retriever that was growling and shaking Jamies leg furiously.

"William what up tho cousin? Why all the sudden hitting? What's going on with you Cuz?" Brenda screamed, still standing on the patio with a look of shock on her face from all the sudden commotion taking place on the patio while holding a small plate of her mom's freshly baked bread pudding on it.

"Yo, get this mut off my leg. Ahaa my shoe! Someone gets this mut off me!" Jamie continued to scream as he tried to kick the angry dog with his other foot, attempting to get the Golden retriever to let go of the tight grip while shaking his foot with the tongue of the sneaker.

"Stop kicking my dog!" Tye's mom yelled.

"Yo, get this crazy mut off my leg! Ahaa, my leg" Jamie continued to yell.

"Listen man, my cousin doesn't bother anyone. I don't know who you are or what you have done to piss him off but the disrespect in my aunt's house this morning is nothing but the works of the devil" Bishop Joe yelled out as he continued trying to restrain his cousin William who was determined to fight.

"Jamie, the Bishop is correct, my cousin doesn't even speak, and we don't know you! Whatever the meaning behind my cousin's hostility and anger towards you this morning warranted this butt whipping!" Joshua yelled as held Williams' arms, also trying his best to restrain him.

"Hope that dog rip his skinny leg off!" Rebecca hollered out as she quickly sat next to her sister-in-law.

"Mom! What happened?" Brenda yelled."

"Your cousin just tried to knock that boy out like a Champion boxer" Rebecca loudly replied.

"Get this dog off my leg! Ahaa!" Jamie continued to yell.

"Don't you hurt my dog boy!" Tye's mom continued to yell out as the tears continued falling down her soft cheeks.

Jill, her husband, William's father Willie James and Bucky came rushing out the back door from inside the house. After hearing all the yelling and loud barking coming from the dog in the backyard.

Jill's husband was originally from Florida. They met on a cruise to nowhere which departed out of the port of New York City where she was there for a bridal shower. He lied to her at first and told her he was a music executive who resided in a penthouse in the downtown area of Manhattan, New York. After hearing her vocals at the actual bridal event one of the cruise talent supervisors complimented Jill and booked her for 2 of the shows on that cruise. Her husband had promised to introduce her to top executives that would eventually grant her a recording contract when the ship returned to New York City. To his surprise the only phone call he would receive from Jill weeks later was that she was pregnant, and he was the father. To her surprise the only recording contract she would ever receive would be from her own hustle and hard work if she really wanted one. He was not a wealthy top executive but a resident in Florida and didn't have any plans of seeing her again once the ship docked at the port in New York City. Eventually they hooked up and 6 months later Bishop Joe married them in Joshua's living room.

CHAPTER 5

THE REASON WHY

"What the hell is going on out here in my brother's house!" Bucky yelled!

"Rafee yield! Down boy!" Tye's father yelled while grabbing the collar of his dog to pull him off the young man who was now laying on the grass in the backyard.

Rebecca helped Tye's mom to stand up from off the patio furniture as she continued to cry. Jill hurried over to Tye's mom and embraced her in a tight hug as both started crying loudly together.

"Who is this young punk laying in this yard Joshua?" Bucky yelled walking quickly towards the patio steps.

"Pops that's the dude! That's him Pop! I told you if I ever see him or catch him, I was going kill him!" William shouted out!

"Oh, that's him?" Willie James responded.

"Let my son go! Boy you right! I'm going to kick his butt

with you!" Willie James shouted as he reached down next to the patio furniture for a brick that had been sitting on the patio.

Bucky's wife Rebecca quickly jumped up off the patio furniture herself and quickly pushed the ladies towards the back door to go inside the house. Jill's husband, who already had quickly opened the door, assisted Rebecca in getting them into the house. Brenda moved herself back over towards the rocking chair and sat down now holding both plates in her lap.

"You heard your uncle boys let my cousin go. It's butt whipping time" Brenda loudly stated.

"Let me go Joe! I'm going to kill that piece of crap!" William screamed.

"No cousin it's not the time for this man! We are here for our uncle and aunt man!" Joshua yelled.

"That's him pop! I'm going to hurt him! That's definantly him pop" William said as he started to resist his cousins' restraints, trying to get to Jamie who remained on the grass.

"William, I need you to calm yourself! William, I know you can do it! You're stronger than this. You're stronger than him. You're a good guy. You're a family guy. Be strong for your family. Be a good example for your uncle and aunt. Be a loving cousin to Debbie who is now resting with God. Let her see how much you really love our family. Let our cousin Debbie sees that you have her brothers back and you won't allow any hostility or violent behavior taking place in their parent's home. Let heaven know that you have Debbie's back here on earth. We are all hurting right now. Cuz, I am in shock. To me it's

like a nightmare and I want to wake up and see my cousin's smiling face again. We are all terribly sad. Show everyone that you're the good family guy your father has raised you to be We need all this strength that you are displaying right now to comfort our aunt and her granddaughter" Bishop Joe calmly said.

As tears started falling down William's cheeks once again, he slowly took a deep breath then dropped his head down onto his chest. Joshua removed his hands off his cousin while backing up slowly away from William.

"Something going on here in my house! Cause I have never heard my nephew talk. He may have run off at the mouth in your house Bucky but never in years at my house! Now all sudden my nephew knocking bodies off my patio deck" Tye's father yelled while he held the dog who was still barking and growling at the stranger who now was trying to adjust his sneaker on the lawn.

"My nephew the real deal" Bucky said to Tye's father as he walked over to him embracing him in a bear hug.

"I didn't come over here for this. I just wanted to show my love and symphony to you sir. This is crazy! I didn't come over here this morning to start any trouble. I don't even know that dude. This is crazy. I had nothing but the up most respect for your daughter. Like I was trying to explain, the whole neighborhood is in real pain right now. Your loss is our loss. Debbie and I were always close. That sad news hit my heart hard sir. I had so much love for your daughter sir. She was a real one" Jamie said while finally lifting himself from off the grass while dusting off his shorts.

"Yeah, but like my brother said to you my nephew isn't

much of the talkative type. A man of no words! Always been like that as far back as we all can remember. Now I'm a grown man of many words that's why I perform every week and been doing so for more years than your young butt been alive. I am a talker Just like my pastor nephew over there who is holding back some serious vengeance coming from his cousin. Now I'm not sure what the trigger was or what sparked this anger in my nephew William. But in this peaceful loving family of talkers that you boldly put yourself amid this morning we are convinced that you are nothing but absolute trouble! And purposely stirred up rage in our peaceful loving family member" Bucky replied now standing directly in Jamies face.

"Joe, let my son go!" Willie James yelled!

"This isn't the time fellas! Nana didn't raise us to be disrespectful to our family. Cousin Debbie doesn't deserve this animalistic behavior. It's not fair to her parents and it isn't fair to our cousins. Like the pastor clearly stated!" Joshua loudly shouted as he continued slowly backing away from William despite what his uncle commanded them to do.

"I'm sorry Debbie! I love you and aunty so much" William muffled out softly while the tears of anger and grief continued to flow down his puffy cheeks.

"Yo, I'm leaving right now. I don't know why this dude just came at me; this whole attack is crazy. The dog is trying to rip apart my new sneakers. Yo, this is crazy. Sir, once again my condolences to you and your family." Jamie loudly said as he made his way to the patio steps to leave the backyard.

"Joshua, would you escort the boy out of my brother's house now?!" Bucky yelled.

Jamie walked up the steps onto the patio passing Brenda who was now seated back on the wooden rocking chair making his way to the backdoor of the house.

"You need to go home and put some ice on that face before everyone in the neighborhood knows that my cousin William tried to knock your skinny butt out. KO! And the winner is and remains the undisputed heavyweight champion, Big William!" Brenda yelled while rocking back and forth in the chair.

As Joshua and Jamie entered the house Tye's father picked up the tennis ball and returned to throwing the ball further into the backyard for the Golden Retriever to chase.

"I'm sorry about that but that little knucklehead had it coming to him" Willie James said as he walked up to his brother Bucky.

"Man, your son got a powerful punch there" Tye's father said while bending down to take the tennis ball out of the dog's mouth who came running back.

"At least we know he didn't get it from you Willie" Bucky jokingly said while putting his hands inside his slacks.

"That's why my little punk bother Willie had to go pick up one of my bricks I use to hold down my patio furniture when the winds start to pick up like that storm, we had yesterday afternoon" Tye's father replied.

"Hey Willie, what was you going to do with that brick? Stone him to death with your prehistoric self" Bucky jokingly said with his hands now in his slacks.

"*You gone to shatter your wrist keep swinging bricks, you old punk*" Tye's father said as he leaned against Bucky's shoulder.

"*Mess up dem ole joints in those ashy elbows with your Old Testament self*" Bucky jokingly said.

Bishop Joe and William sat down on the patio furniture. Brenda got up out of the rocking chair walking over to them and sat on the other side of her cousin William handing him his plate of food.

"*Both of you dusty old men need to shut up. You'll just jealous my boy has skills like his old man*" Willie James said while placing his right hand on Tye father's shoulder.

"*I have never seen that skill come from you before. You couldn't even swing or hit when we played stickball. "No eye coordination*" Bucky jokingly replied.

"*My nephew has the golden gloves moves. Like his uncle*" Tye's father said.

"*Yeah, how is Tye? Is he here? I know this is devastating to him*" Willie James asked.

"*Don't even try to change the subject punk. Why is my nephew dropping bodies on my brother's lawn?*" Bucky loudly asked.

"*Man, Willie, I haven't seen my son yet. Oh God! This is one day I wish to God never existed*" Tye's father said as tears filled his eyes. As Willie James quickly hugged his brother Tye's father, Jill and her husband came running back outside through the backdoor.

"*So, what was all that fighting about? I even saw you with the brick dad about to mess that man up. And why is my brother so upset?*" Jill asked.

63

"*I never heard my cousin talk that much*" Brenda said.

"*Diamond Jill! The Diamond!*" Willie James yelled out.

"Oh yeah the white Honda" Jill husbands said.

"*Wow big brother you are serious about your Diamond. You did keep your word. I remember that is what you said, that when you saw him, you were going to do real damage to him! I apologize everyone about my brother wilding out*" Jill loudly said.

"*You meant to say you apologize about your family's disrespectful behavior little gal! All of you'll have been arguing and fighting since you came over here. Just a bunch of wild asses*" Aunt Rebecca said as she came through the back door onto the backyard patio holding a plate with a slice of fresh baked hot apple pie on it.

"*Are you okay William?*" Jill's husband asked.

"*I really do apologize auntie about our behavior this morning. You know we love our cousin Debbie, and this is hitting our hearts hard. Pastor, I guess our emotions are getting the best of us early this morning*" Jill humbly said.

"*So, what is my cousins love over a diamond has him so angry this morning?*" Joe asked Jill.

"*Nephew, they been friends since Sophomore year in high school. I was very happy for my son since he always displayed behavior as an introvert as a little child so him having a friend even at that time was exciting news. They weren't dating each other throughout high school but William and the girl whose name is Diamond enjoyed each other's company very much. Now today they're young adults and are still very close. Isn't that right William?*" Willie James loudly asked.

"Yeah, he loves his Diamond" Jill's husband said.

"You are correct daddy. They've always been close. If anyone dares to mess with one, they are really messing with the other one. Now, when the incident happened that night to her white car. My brother was furious. He hung up his cell phone, grabbed a baseball bat and headed to her residential complex. I remember hearing that daddy was trying to calm my brother down but as you can see the issue is still not resolved" Jill said.

"Nope! I want to hurt him!" William yelled out.

"What happened to the car that night William?" Brenda asked.

"Someone totaled the car by throwing a chair over the balcony that landed on the roof crushing the driver side roof and bouncing onto the front windshield shattering the passenger side where the glass was all broken up all over the seats inside the white Honda. It was all captured on security surveillance cameras" Jill's husband said.

"I had told my son before he left my house to make sure they call the police" Willie James said.

"When I arrived at her building, and I saw the vehicle that together we worked very hard for I was so upset. Bishop, I was the one that coached her into buying a new car. She was dependent on her God sister who drives a Mercedes to get her around town. Her neighbor, who's a singer, always gave her a ride to work in his Posche. He's a nice guy but I felt she needed her own car. I constantly told her it was that time. Diamond was comfortable with her situation the way it was and admitted to me that she didn't have any money in the bank. No savings account and no sufficient checking account. She had enjoyed riding around town in a foreign. So, I helped her get the

money to buy a new car. We did it together. I got a part time job, down at the docks and she worked the two jobs. Monday through Thursday she worked at the supermarket, Friday and Saturday she worked down at the docks. On Sundays after church together we worked at Nelson's barn grooming their horses. That's how we saved the eighteen thousand dollars she had that day at the Honda dealership. But before the police arrived at her parking lot that night, she was angry because that was not the first incident with her white car that month. Diamond told me two weeks earlier someone slashed her front right tire in the parking lot which she discovered that Sunday morning as she left the building and approached the car. She didn't report it because it was only a flat tire. Tanya told her that it was deliberate while she was changing the tire after inspecting it. Cousin Tanya didn't replace it with a new tire but gave her a used one for fear it might happen again. Joe, when I heard that I got even angrier. Then when the police finally arrived at the parking lot in front of her building and asked her if she had any confrontations with any of the tenants in the apartment complex, she told the police officers no. However, one of the tenants had asked her out a few times but she repeatedly told him no and that she was in a committed relationship. Diamond then explained to the two police officers that she's not sure if he is an actual tenant. Because his face was new in the building and Diamond had never seen him since she'd been living there for so many years. He does own a Pitbull that he routinely walks the dog through the parking lot. Diamond told the officer that most of the tenants that own dogs regularly walk their pets around the grass areas not around the cars. So, his behavior was suspect. Right after the last time she *turned him down nicely every other day when she would leave her building and walk towards the car dog shit was by her car. Sometimes the dog shit was next to her neighbors Lexus jeep. Once again, she ignored it and didn't report it. Joe, my blood was boiling that night while I was standing out there. I didn't want to explode in a rage in front of the police officers, but if you would have taken a glance at my face it showed I was mad! Someone was deliberately trying to harm my Diamond girl. Bishop, I can't tell you if I was more upset about the events that had occurred or the fact, she never told me"* William said as tears continued falling down his cheeks.

Bucky, Willie James and Tye's father walked slowly up the steps onto the patio. Jill quickly ran over to Tye's father and threw her arms around him squeezing him in a bear hug.

"Diamond told the officers that she had not seen the guy in a while, but a darkskin rough looking woman was walking that same Pitbull dog all through the parking lot. Performing the same suspicious behavior. Her and the woman usually leave for work around the same time in the mornings. She explained to the cops that the woman looks a lot like him much older than him and it maybe his mother. However, she was unsure. The Management of the complex had assigned each of them a parking space which they paid monthly for. Diamond told the two officers that recently she's had problems with different BMW's parked in or around her space when she returned home from work. She did report those incidents to the complex management office. One morning a BMW stopped in front of the parking lot exit ramp blocking her from leaving as her car was about to exit the complex to let out a passenger who with

no acknowledgement proceeded to unpack their groceries from the trunk. The next day as she was returning home from work a white BMW was parked at the entrance of the complex parking lot blocking cars entering. Diamond told the police to avoid confrontation that both times she went around them driving her white car onto the sidewalk or walkway. She didn't know if it was the local drug dealers or a new gang on the premises that was trying to catch her attention. Diamond said whoever or whatever messages they were attempting to send she didn't want to be apart. The officers said they clearly understood. After taking her personal documents the cops started taking photos of the damage. They made the police report and told her that night that they would check the security cameras. The police officers told us because I was standing right next to her the whole time that the detectives would be contacting her in the morning and a police report would be available in three to four business days. Bishop, I didn't know Diamond was having issues with them bums!" William shouted!

"Nephew what did the detectives say?" Bucky asked.

"The detective called her the next night around nine o'clock. She told him in detail all the things that I just said. But the detective said to her that the complex management was giving them a little trouble with the surveillance footage and for her to send him copies of the photos that she took of the car that night if it was possible. That he would get back to her. The building management told her earlier that morning that they were going to check the cameras to see what exactly fell onto her car when Diamond called the office to report the incident" William said.

"Cousin, how do you know it was his skinny butt that

vandalized her car?" Brenda asked, still holding his plate while seated next to him.

"Well whatever issues you had with that boy nephew looks like it's not resolved." Rebecca said loudly.

"Nope it's not resolved, and I want to hurt him! I know!" William said.

CHAPTER 6

SHE HAS RETURNED

Joshua walked into his aunt's bedroom to check on her and make sure she was okay since he could hear her crying while he was in the kitchen. With all the commotion and arguments that was taking place in her house this morning from the family, her nephew was very concerned. Joshua sat down next to Tye's mom with a plate of hot apple pie in his hand that Rebecca had recently baked.

"Joshua, I really don't want Libbie to see her mom like that. I know I sound selfish, but I know what I am saying. Do you hear me, Joshua? I'm sending Tye over to the morgue because I know as hard as this is going to be on my baby boy I am confident my only son can handle this. Listen I'm not even strong enough to see my daughter right now. From what the Sherif said to us this morning I can only imagine the conditions of my only daughter that God gave to me twenty-seven years *ago"* Tye's mom said as she took the Kleenex tissue and blew her nose.

"Aunty, Georgia Mae is here" Joshua whispered.

"Here where boy?" Tye's mom asked lifting her head turning her eyes slightly to her nephew.

"I suspect she is probably with Tye now" Joshua quietly said as he continued eating the delicious hot apple pie.

"Oh really? And you're suspicious because?" Tye's mom asked as she placed her right hand on Joshua's knee.

"Tiny called me last night and told me things were going to heat up in town because Georgia Mae is back" Joshua said.

"I should have known that boy presenting himself this morning was nothing but an alarm to big trouble in Alabama."

"Auntie Tanya had a visitor yesterday at her workplace" Joshua said as he continued chewing on the delicious fresh baked apple pie.

"Oh, really, did she? Did she contact Blaire about her surprise guest?" Tye's mother asked.

"I guess she did which is probably the reason the family were all over at Tye's house for breakfast this morning" Josua answered.

"Joshua, one of those police officers looked very familiar standing in my house this morning. I know I was hysterical and as you can see my eyes are puffy because the tears can't stop coming. Joshua, I don't forget a face" Tye's mom quietly said.

"Aunty that's okay. You are allowed to cry. It's expected of you. What was not expected was the tragedy yesterday on the highway. We did not expect Debbie to leave us so soon. Your response to the horrific news is expected. That is why

Bishop is here Aunty. Our expression of love to your children. We love you" Joshua said.

"*Nephew, I don't forget a face out of uniform"* Tye's mom whispered.

"*Aunty is that the real reason you sent the Chief of police across town earlier this morning to see your son. Or is it the reason Tanya sent your nephew across town earlier this morning to see your son?"* Joshua asked quietly.

"*Oh, I see. Well, then Libbie, needs to be right next to her uncle now"* Tye's mom replied.

"*Aunty, my thoughts exactly"* Joshua said.

"*Honestly Williams whole behavior this morning raised my eyebrow, Joshua. It wasn't him finally talking in front of company even though I know my husband is probably going to talk about that for the rest of the day. I'm pretty sure William talks to whoever he chooses, probably just not in front of everybody. But that punch in a family member's house is what raised my brow to the company in my yard. Now Jill and her husband I'm used to their bickering! However, my brother in law's sudden appearance is what puzzles me"* Tye's mom softly whispered.

"*Aunty how did the whole neighborhood hear about a situation that is not confirmed? How did the neighborhood send a representative to comfort someone when no one has even talked to the son yet?* Joshua asked.

"*I wonder what Ms. Georgia Mae's up too?"* Tye's mom asked.

"*Has anyone talked to Assemblyman Roger?"* Joshua asked.

"*We haven't"* Tye's mom softly responded.

"The devil is busy in Alabama this week aunty! But we are going to pray to heaven and call on God to cancel all of Satan's evil assignments" Joshua shouted as he scooped up the last piece of pie on the plate.

"Does Bishop know?" Tye's mom asked as she removed her hand away from Joshua's knee.

"No Aunty!" Joshua said loudly as he looked into her eyes.

"Oh, I see. Then let Bucky tell your pastor that Georgia Mae is in town" Tye's mom said as she got up off the bed and proceeded to walk out of the bedroom towards the kitchen.

CHAPTER 7

THE TWISTERS DEVISTATION

"Lil-bit, come outside baby girl it's Uncle Tye seated inside the back of this white Chevrolet truck" Tye said to his niece Libbie who was in the house seated on the Livingroom sofa as he hung up his cell phone.

Libbie stayed at her grandparents' house on her father's side. Her father enlisted in the army, and he was on duty overseas. He and Debbie were junior high school sweethearts when they met and in her senior year, she ended up pregnant. They had plans to get married as seniors in high school after they graduated but Debbie started getting close to one of the local activists at the time who was interning in the state senator's office. When her daughter, who was now turning five years old at the time father had found out the young activist intern Roger and his baby mother Debbie were spending way too much time together,

74

he broke off the wedding engagement. He already graduated from high school because he ended up a year ahead of Debbie due to the whole pregnancy. A year later after the cancelation of the wedding he enlisted in the army and now only comes back to Alabama for short periods of stay. His parents were always there since the announcement of Debbie's pregnancy, he was their only child. Even though Debbie now lived with Assemblyman Roger the former state senator intern, her daughter stayed with the grandparents.

"Georgia Mae, who you keep texting? Seems like you been on that cell phone a lot since we got into your monster truck" Tiny asked.

"Why are you all in my business that has no concern of you" Georgia Mae replied.

"Because I can sexy" Tiny answered.

"With whose authority nosey?" Georgia Mae asked.

"I authorized myself to oversee all affairs around this family" Tiny replied.

"Well in my vehicle the queen is the only rule of authority that governs in here" Georgia Mae sarcastically stated.

"I hear that!" Tanya shouted from the back seat as she sat next to her cousin Tye.

"Hi everyone" Libbie, quietly whispered as she hoped up inside the back seat of the truck.

"Cousin I am very sorry for your loss this morning. I can't possibly imagine what you're feeling, and I know how much you loved your mother. Libbie, we all loved your mom. She wasn't just Tye's sister she was all our sister" Tiny loudly

said while turned around stretching his left hand out from the front seat as he rubbed Libbie shoulder.

"Baby girl, I'm at a loss for words. My heart is broken right now! I'm in serious pain" Tanya yelled out.

As Georgia Mae started up the truck and pulled out the driveway Tye noticed three BMW's quickly pass in front of the truck. Tye took his left knee and bumped Tanya's right knee cutting his eyes back and forth towards the front windshield as he turned his head directly to Tanya. Tanya took out her cell phone and started texting Blaire.

"Where is your grandparents baby girl?" Tye asked.

"Grandma took Grandpa to get his dialysis treatment. Tye she was devastated. Grandma was on her knees on my bedroom floor crying all morning. But we can't get in contact with dad. Grandpa was even calling some of his military contacts. Grandma kept saying hopefully somebody will eventually return the calls or locate dad. Grandpa felt she needed to get out of the house because everything was too overwhelming for her heart condition and get some fresh air. Grandma was devastated" Libbie said as the tears fell from her eyes while she laid her head on her uncles' chest.

"Where's the assemblyman? If he's not out somewhere protesting with some local union" Tiny asked.

"Cousin Tiny that's who called me this morning and told us about my mom. After I yelled, screamed and hung up on Roger a few times, eventually we talked for a long while. He assured me, with all his power, he was on the case, and he'd find out everything. That's why I kept saying to you Uncle

Tye, they did this to mommy. Because that's what Roger kept on saying to Grandpa over the phone" Libbie softly said.

"*Well, baby girl, we are on our way to the police department so I can find out everything that might have happened to my sister Debbie!*" Tye shouted out.

"*Uncle Tye, I called you right after I hung the phone up from Roger. It hurts me so bad. I'm so confused right now. I just want to see and talk to my mom right now*" Libbie said as Georgia Mae drove the truck onto the highway.

The morgue was located downstairs inside the general hospital in the downtown area. The police station was three blocks away from the hospital on the north side of the street. The Chief and the deputies had told us to come to the police station first to fill out paperwork. After we would go over to the Morgue together to confirm things concerning Debbie. Two exits up the highway the traffic was detoured off the highway because of the damaged road ahead. As we exited off the highway into that part of town there were dead cows literally still lying on the side of the road. Georgia Mae had to swerve off the road reducing her speed to slowly drive on the side of that local road because of the down wires and poles laying flat on there side across the road. There was a lot of huge debris and down trees scattered everywhere. As Georgia Mae continued to drive swerving the truck around everything, we saw flipped over vehicles and even a turned over school bus. That part of town was hit hard. We approached what looked like it was a community but because of the severe structure damage to those houses from the falling trees it was hard to tell. There were even dead horses still lying in the middle of the road. It was disastrous! Completely different from my neighborhood. We had no down trees from what I saw today as we drove throughout my side of town over to pick up Libbie. Even Libbie's neighborhood looked untouched compared to this section of town. Somethings were recognizable like a tractor trailer and other things were so badly damaged or dismantled you really couldn't identify the object. It almost felt like we were riding in circles because Georgia Mae constantly had to make right and left turns onto other routes because of all the constant road closure detours. That's one thing about the beautiful hills of sweet Alabama we do get Tornado's.

Arriving at the police station Tiny, Libbie and I went inside to meet with the Chief. Georgia Mae drove Tanya to work over at the auto repair shop. As horrific as this incident was to our family, I still needed to teach Libbie how to be tough just like her grandmother displayed with my sister. I even felt more compelled to implement that value because now she is motherless. Having Georgia Mae around the family again I felt was going to be helpful in that area because she was the embodiment of toughness and eloquence. In Debbie's absence Georgia Mae could instill a certain female sternness into Libbie I feel she was going to need as her days grow on down here in Alabama.

Entering the police station felt awkward because honestly, I always tried my best to be a law–abiding citizen. The only relief my nerves had at that moment was that my hands were not in cuffs. As we approached the reception desk it bothered me to see so many people walking around the station, talking on phones, even conversating among themselves as if I didn't just lose my sister. Personally, I felt everyone should be either standing in silence showing empathy for my niece Libbie who is in severe emotional pain or bowing their heads as if they're in a religious form of prayer paying respect to Debbie. A door behind the desk suddenly opened a jar as we waited for the officer who was sitting at the reception desk to finish talking on the phone. Tiny placed his hand on my shoulder. I automatically knew that meant he was in charge and was about to do all the talking on my behalf. Officer Davis who was at my house earlier stepped out the door accompanied with beautiful female police officer, and they came from around the long reception desk towards us.

"I see you'll made it downtown. Let me take you'll upstairs to the chief's office" Chaplain Davis calmly said.

"Good morning my name is officer Juanita Scott, and you must be Libbie young lady" The female officer politely said.

"Yes mam!" Libbie replied as she lifted her head off my shoulder and let go of my hand.

"Good morning to you sir, and you must be Tye" Officer Scott said as she looked directly into my eyes.

"I am deeply sorry for your loss, and I know this is a very stressful time for the family and we truly do understand your concern of the matter. Your assistance

79

in this investigation today is very much appreciated. Don't be hesitant to express any of your concerns or withhold any of your feelings. No matter what you are feeling. Our force is very much equipped to handle things. We truly do understand the pressure you may be experiencing right now. As I said anyway either of you can help us with this investigation on today is appreciated" Officer Scott said in a passionate but aggressive tone.

"With global warming it is so unfortunate that we here in this part of Alabama are seeing more of these disastrous storms" Chaplain Davis said.

"It looks as if that part of town a few exits back got hit hard man!" Tiny shouted.

"Yesterday certain areas were hit harder than others" Officer Scott replied.

"I mean they were carcasses laid out all over the road man. I feel for those farmers or whoever lost their precious livestock" Tiny said.

"As you can see it is still very busy in here a lot of emergencies" Officer Scott replied.

"It was busy out there! Man, everywhere we turned there was some kind of construction crew or team helping someone or something! Sheesh! Even around here I saw some places with window damage or something!" Tiny said loudly.

"With these storms you can never be sure of the wind damage. Most of the time it's not the actual twister or funnel itself that can bring a significant amount of damage. Simply high winds and large size hail can leave a path of destruction" Chaplain Davis said.

Tiny stepped back and moved directly behind me placing his hand on my shoulder. As Chaplain Davis escorted us to the elevator Libbie reached into her small pocketbook to pull out her cell phone.

"Are you okay baby girl?" Tiny asked.

"I want to let my bestie know that I'm here with the local authorities now and we're about to see my mama. She had told me earlier that she would be in the downtown area this morning and for me to give her a call if I felt like everything was going to be too much" Libbie replied

"Moral support is good Libbie. I have a few close friends outside my family who I cling to when I'm feeling awkward, upset, nervous or even when I am angry. Sometimes you need that extra support to keep you stable" Officer Scott said as we stepped onto the elevator together.

"That's my heart right there. My girl! My Ace! We truly rock together every day all day. That is why I said to myself let me text her now because I know she is going to be ringing my phone off the hook in a few. I don't need her calling my cell interrupting us in front of mommy" Libbie said as she continued texting on her cell phone.

"You are aware of the process Libbie? And why we are here at the precinct" Chaplain Davis said as the elevator door opened onto the floor for us to go on.

"She'll be fine officer" Tiny said abruptly.

Stepping off the elevator onto the third floor it was quieter than on the first floor, not as many people. We walked around the hallway and through a large glass door into a giant open space with what looked like three offices. As we approached the offices I could see the names clearer on the doors. Chaplain Davis walked towards the office door at the far right which had Chief Reginald's name on it. As he gently knocked and then opened the door, I heard what sounded like a man's voice crying on the other side of the door. Tiny stopped walking while Libbie, and I continued to slowly follow Chaplain Davis through the now opened door.

"Oh Libbie! I'm so glad to see you sweetheart" Assymblyman Roger said as he jumped up out a chair towards my niece with tears running down his face.

"Thank everyone for coming downtown" Sheriff Wesley said as he stood next to the Chief's desk.

"Tye, my big brother, man I am so glad to see you. This is unbelievable man how could this happen to someone so beautiful. She would never hurt anybody" Assemblyman Rogers said as the tears that were falling from his eyes dropped from off his chin while he embraced his stepdaughter Libbie in a tight hug.

Officer Scott came inside the room closing the door behind her leaving cousin Tiny, standing by himself outside in the large empty space. Walking over to Chief Reginald as he stood up from the chair that was behind his desk, Officer Scott handed him a few file folders. Sheriff Wesley, who had a tablet in his hands stepped up closer to the three of us Assemblyman Rogers, Libbie and me whose eyes were now filled with tears of grief.

I was a little puzzled Tho to see Roger here meeting with the Chief of police without us. Honestly, it did make sense being that him and my sister were together and have been since they were in school. But what puzzles my whole entire family is why they were never married. When Libbie finally let him go, he looked up at me and I placed my right hand on Assemblyman Rogers shoulder.

"Take all the time you'll need" Officer Scott calmly said.

I was always a jock; a rough playing kid and I love my basketball to this day. Some fellas were intimidated by my height, and for years I played on their fear. Yes, I fought, and I will fight for my family, but all this crying is not me. I never had this feeling of pain before. Honestly, I am in disbelief. I'm hoping that the person they are going to take me to identify lying in some refrigerated morgue is not my sister and Debbie is in a hospital being treated for a few cuts someplace else.

My cell phone began to ring, in haste I reached down into my shorts to answer without hesitation thinking it was my dad or even my sister Debbie so I could get the hell out of this police station. I answered my phone so quickly I didn't even have a chance to listen to the ring tone.

"Cousin I am here! I'm just pulling up in the hospital parking lot now! Jamena came home and told me what happened to Cousin Debbie! Exactly, where are you'll?" Quincy asked.

"Hey cousin, this is all so messed up right now man. We are over here still at the police station. We should be over there soon I guess" I answered as Officer Scott put a chair by Libbie.

"You need for me to come over there?" Quincy asked.

"No Doc. Stay where you at and I'll hit you up when were in that direction" I said while sitting down in the chair next to my niece. Hanging up the phone I looked at Roger to see if he was really alright. I knew my father sent these Officers to my house for a reason. It's the reason he is not here investigating the situation concerning his only daughter. I love my pops and when my pops give me a task I take it seriously. That's the reason I must make sure the Assemblyman is alright to handle my father's task. That's also the reason I'm a little puzzled Rogers crying butt, is even here. He was my sister's choice not my pop or mine.

"Is everything Ok Tye?" Sheriff Wesley asked as he also pulled up a chair sitting across from the three of us holding a tablet.

"That was my cousin Quincy he works there at the hospital. He was looking for us. His wife, my cousin Jemena who was the one consoling me earlier in my kitchen when you guys arrived at my house told him about the tragic accident of my sister Debbie" I said as I took the Kleenex tissue that Chaplain Davis had handed each of us to wipe the tears of grief from off my face.

"You have a very large family, Tye" Chief Reginald said.

"It seems that way huh" I replied.

"That's a good thing son. My observation this morning is that they all look to you as the leader of the family. In my professional opinion that says that you are an exceptional strong young man. There were a lot of trophies in your parents' house.

Are those yours or do they belong to your sister Debbie?" Chief Reginald asked.

"I won them sir. I am a ball player. Now I am a master chef here in Mobile, Alabama" I answered.

"There you go a multi-talented team leader" Chief Reginald replied.

"That's probably why your parents lean on you for assistance" Sheriff Wesley said as he begins typing on his tablet.

"I am positive of that! Tye's parents watched their strong handsome son led the team to victory wins game after game throughout the years! Now they're proudly seeing Tye supervise a kitchen yearly in fine dining" Chief Reginald said in a loud aggressive tone.

"That is a good thing Chief!" Chaplain Davis loudly spoke.

"My professional opinion this morning is that it is a great thing Chaplain Davis, Officer Scott and Sherif Deputy Highway State Trooper Wesley. A leader who is responsible. A strong individual who is dependable. Someone who demonstrates accountability. A young man who can execute teamwork under pressure.

And I do believe you have some questions for the family members. Am I correct Deputy Wesley?" Chief Reginald asked Sherif Wesley.

"Yes, I do sir. Tye for verification of identification purposes of this investigation I just need you to verify your sisters full name and the make and model of the car she drove" Deputy Highway State Trooper Wesley said to me.

"My sister's name is Debbie Vendridge she is my heart

we've always been close officers" I calmly replied as the tears of grief uncontrollably continued falling down my cheeks.

"Take your time young man. It's o.k. nobody is here to rush you. We need as much information from you as you can voluntarily give unto us this morning" Chaplain Davis interjected and spoke.

"This is so unreal man! One day I'm cooking preparing my grandfather's favorite meal. And the next day I'm in a Chief's office" I said, trying to wipe the tears from my eyes.

"It's O.K. Tye you're doing the right thing. Today you are the big brother. Right now, in the Chief's office you're helping your parents tremendously" Chaplain Davis replied.

"I hear you officer. Man, I love my family. Debbie was at almost all my home games when we played. When she was pregnant carrying my niece Libbie, she still loudly cheered me on outside at the basketball courts as my cousins along with my boys and I shot hoops with the local clowns. Debbie always had my back" I shouted as the tears continued to fall from my eyes!

Officer Scott and the Chief looked at each other.

"Tye that confirms what the Sheriff just said a minute or so ago about how you are executing teamwork under pressure. Sounds like you were the one that your sister looked up to as an example of good leadership" Chaplain Davis calmly said.

"Officer I'm so confused right now. I don't even feel like myself. This isn't me man. I'm a good guy. A hard worker like my pops. Debbie and I always did the noble thing. Either one of us is perfect but we did good for ourselves. Today is so unreal.

One day I'm in my favorite place, my sanctuary which is the kitchen. The next day I'm here in a police station. Officers, I heard the winds as they roared louder and louder, but I didn't hear any sirens. My house shook a little bit, but no power went out or anything significant. So, I thought everything was good. My girl shows up out the blue in a brand-new truck. Now law enforcement is literally standing in my sanctuary telling me Debbie may not be here with me anymore because of some wind that smashed up her car. This is Crazy" Tye shouted!

Officer Scott and the Sheriff slowly looked at each other again.

"What is the make and model of the car Debbie drives?" Sheriff Wesley asked again.

"My sister was like me we only rode in style. Everyone in town knows we will only drive a foreign. Now she might not be able to drive or afford the foreign that I have in my garage. But Debbie's red Lexus NX made Assemblyman Roger look good in these Alabama streets officers" Tye replied.

Officer Scott and the Chief slowly looked at each other once again. Sheriff Highway State Trooper Wesley turned the tablet around so that the display screen on the tablet was facing Tye and Libbie as she sat next to her uncle at the table.

"Does this look like the car?" Sherif Wesley asked Tye.

"Oh my God! Look at mommy's car! Look what they did to my mommy!" Libbie screamed as she dropped her head into Tye's chest while he wrapped his arm tightly around her, embracing his niece.

"Yes, officer that looks like Debbie's Lexus NX" Tye sadly answered as the Sherif turned the tablet back

around towards him and started typing information into the computer tablet. When he finished typing, he handed the tablet to Officer Juanita who scrolled through the computer tablet slowly with her fingers before handing the tablet back to Sherif Wesley.

CHAPTER 8

THE HOSPITAL WAIT

"Hi Quincy, it's been a while" Georgia Mae said as she set the car alarm on her truck in the hospital parking lot.

"Georgia Mae! Wow! This is a surprise" Quincy replied as he stopped from walking towards the hospital in the parking lot.

"Yes, I wish it could be a brighter visit, Quincy" Georgia Mae said.

"Is everything ok with you?" Quincy asked.

"It's all like a nightmare. I almost don't want to accept the news, but I know I must remain calm on today" Georgia Mae replied.

"You're here. You made it this far. Have you come to visit someone Georgia Mae?" Quincy asked.

"I just left Tanya at her job Quincy, and you know she's all messed up. So, I'm here for Tye" Georgia Mae responded.

"Soon as my girl came home and told me what had happened, I jumped in the BMW and drove straight back here." Quincy replied.

"She told us, this morning at Tye's house how busy you were yesterday here in the emergency room following the tornado. That was even before we all received the news about Debbie from the local authorities" Georgia Mae said as she started slowly walking towards the hospital.

"Oh, so you were at Tye's house this morning as well?" Quincy asked as he started walking alongside her towards the hospital.

"Jemena didn't mention to you that I was in the kitchen with her and your newborn baby?" Georgia Mae asked while gently removing the hair that covered her eyes.

"No, she didn't" Quincy loudly replied.

"With the sudden shock of bad news about Debbie from Brenda to Blaire and the intrusion of the Chief I think her cousin Tye was the only person on your wife Jemena's mind when she saw you at home" Georgia Mae said to Quincy as she walked slowly up the hospital entrance ramp.

"That's why I'm here!" Quincy shouted.

"That's why we are all here Quincy" Georgia Mae quickly replied.

"That's a very big truck you just parked in this lot. That's new?" Quincy asked.

"New to those who haven't seen me in it yet" Georgia Mae replied.

"What brings you back to Alabama if you don't mind me asking?" Quincy inquired as he stopped in front of the hospital door entrance.

"Your cousin Tye. I really did miss him" Georgia Mae calmly said.

"How long have you been back?" Quincy asked.

"I've been in town for a week. From the looks of some of that damage we passed coming downtown I was fortunate that I didn't get hit with that Twister on yesterday" Georgia Mae said.

"Cousin Debbie did! And so did dozens of others Georgia Mae" Quincy quickly replied.

"From some of the wreckage I just witnessed I can only imagine how chaotic this hospital was on yesterday" Geogia Mae said.

"So where were you exactly Georgia Mae when the storm came through on yesterday afternoon?" Quincy asked.

"I was with my brother taking care of business" Georgia Mae sharply answered.

"How is he these days?" Quincy asked.

"He is doing good. Keeping himself busy and connecting with the right people I can't be prouder of him" Georgia Mae answered.

"I haven't seen them around town in a while. But then I've been busy working long hours here at the hospital, so I pretty much don't see anyone except my girl" Quincy said.

"The two of you always seemed happy together so that statement doesn't shock me" Georgia Mae replied.

"I'm surprised you've been back in town a whole week and right now is the first time I'm hearing it. Not even my family has mentioned your return. But you have seen, my little girl" Quincy said.

"She is a bundle of joy Quincy with her little chubby

cheeks. *Earlier in Tye's kitchen I kept on pulling and tugging on her little clothes. She is adorable"* Georgia Mae replied.

"Yeah, my newborn is a healthy one" Quincy replied with a huge smile on his face.

"Quincy, honestly it feels like I never left Mobile, Alabama. This has been home for me so long that even when I'm away it is still a part of who I am. My family is here, and my man is here." Georgia Mae said.

"Jemena said Tye wasn't taking this news well at all" Quincy said.

"This was not the welcome home celebration I was anticipating for Tye and myself Quincy" Georgia Mae replied.

"It's his mom you're going to need to be more concerned about Georgia Mae" Quincy replied as he turned and walked inside the hospital entrance.

CHAPTER 9

FAMILY MATTERS

As Tiny stood by himself in the large air-conditioned open space upstairs inside the police station patiently waiting for his cousin Tye who was meeting in the Chiefs office with Debbie's daughter Libbie and Debbie's long time fiancé Assemblyman Rogers the hallway door that leads to the elevator swung open. Walking through the door being escorted from off the elevator by a police officer was Blaire.

"Hey man it's good to see you" Tiny said as the police officer closed the door behind him leaving the two of them alone in the large air-conditioned open space.

"Tanya text me while you guys were at Libbie's house about the unannounced BMW motorcade she had seen" Blaire calmly responded.

"I was just texting Bishop about that same unannounced escort. And then check this out cousin, when I asked Ms. Big

hip Sexy, why she continued to doodle on her cell phone instead of concentrating on her surroundings as the chauffer Tye wants her to be for us this morning she responded sarcastically" Tiny quietly replied.

"Tye is not seeing anything clearly right now Tiny! This is real bad man!" Blaire loudly replied.

"You see how fast I got up off that sofa when Bishop called my phone" Tiny replied.

"Wait cousin, you were texting Joe about the motorcade? Is he aware that Ms. Georgia Mae is back?" Blaire quietly asked.

"I know our cousins better than everyone gives me credit for. Definantly when it comes to them two. I'm talking about Joe and Joshua! He may be Joe's dependable assistant but as a faithful member of the best church in this town and even I know Joshua runs the church by himself. So, Cousin Blaire, I have no worries when I'm texting Joe, I already know who I'm really speaking with" Tiny loudly replied.

"Tiny, let me ask you, have you ever seen Joe carrying his own cell phone?" Blaire asked.

"No!" Tiny loudly answered.

"Joshua has Joe's cell phone he will know when the best time for Bishop is to handle the news of Georgia Mae" Blaire said.

"Joshua ought to let your dad Uncle Bucky report to Bishop that news" Tiny said while looking at his cell phone.

"Three officers came out to Cousin Tye's house. One of them is the Chief of police. I'm like Wow" Blaire loudly spoke.

"Thank God we were all over there this morning. However, it is still heartbreaking. That's why I kept my eyes on Tye because I didn't want him to go off. I know my cousin. Especially when he didn't want to pass his phone over to Tanya. I was feeling extremely nervous about his reaction to the sudden news of Cousin Debbie" Tiny said.

"What do you expect man? That's his heart! That's his little sister! This is real bad man!" Blaire loudly replied.

"Assemblyman Rogers is in there with them. He was in there before we arrived here" Tiny quietly said.

"Oh, was he? This is real bad man! Tanya texted and said Libbie couldn't find her father. This is going be the worst we've ever come across as a family" Blaire loudly said.

"Now Big Hip Sexy easing her way around our family tree isn't going to make anything easier" Tiny shouted.

"How many cars did you notice?" Blaire asked.

"I saw two BMW cars as we pulled away from Tye's house. It was hard for me to get a good look at the model or any of the plate numbers because of the police patrol cars that were maneuvering around us in his driveway. Then me watching Jamena's new car as she backed up in front of Georgia Mae's truck didn't help anything. You know her and Quincy are really doing good with themselves" Tiny said.

"Yeah, Quincy is a good dude. That's my guy!" Blaire shouted.

"Now as we pulled out of Libbie's grandparents' driveway there were three BMW's directly in front of us" Tiny said.

"Most likely her brothers" Blaire replied.

"Why you say that cousin?" Tiny asked.

"Because I just got off the phone with my mom and

Brenda before I came to the police station about Jamie being over there at Tye's mom's house earlier" Blaire answered.

"Wasn't we talking about that dude in Tye's kitchen before the Chief got there this morning?"

Tiny asked.

"Jamena and Tanya were debating back and forth whether or not he still worked at the Port warehouse" Blaire replied.

"Oh, that's why you rushed over here to the police station" Tiny said.

"Cousin Tiny this is really bad man!" Blaire loudly repeated.

"Yes, I agree, and that other guy Larry showing up at the auto shop yesterday is probably the reason Tanya had Georgia Mae drive her to work a little while ago" Tiny whispered.

"Oh, did she?" Blaire asked.

"Tanya didn't text you that one, huh, cobra ninja" Tiny sarcastically said.

"Georgia Mae's brothers!" Blaire loudly replied.

"Oh, I hear you. So, what did that dude Jamie say at the house today" Tiny asked.

"After William knocked him off the backyard patio, there was nothing much he could say" Blaire proudly answered his cousin.

"William who" Tiny loudly asked.

"Your blood cousin put the boxing gloves on this morning at your uncle's house" Blaire answered.

"William put his hands on the dude Jamie in front of our family" Tiny asked.

"My sister Delores told me Uncle Willie-James was going to hit that guy Jamie with a brick" Blaire shouted.

"*Now I'm nervous Cousin Blaire! When Tye finds out what took place at his parent's house today, he is going to blow a fuse man*" Tiny shouted.

"*That is what my mom kept on saying to me over the cell phone a little while ago! But Georgia Mae better be more concerned about Tye's mom rather than keeping company with Tanya at the auto repair shop*" Blaire loudly replied.

CHAPTER 10

THE POLICE REPORT

As the door of the Chief's office slowly opened officer Scott exited the office alongside Chaplain Davis. Immediately an office door on the left side of the large air-conditioned open space swung open. A tall grey-haired gentleman came quickly walking out of that office with a badge hanging from around his neck wearing blue jeans and a short-sleeved shirt. Officer Scott walked directly over to the tall grey-haired gentleman handed him a file folder and together the three of them exited through the door of the large air-conditioned open space headed towards the elevator.

Tye had a look of uncertainty on his face as he and Libbie came slowly walking out of the Chiefs office along with Sheriff Wesley.

"So, are you gentleman going along with us to the morgue?" Sheriff Wesly asked Tiny and Blaire.

"This is my family sir" Tiny strongly answered.

"That's fine with me. Will everyone come with me? There is a car waiting to transport us to the morgue for further identification verification concerning this accidental investigation" Sheriff Wesley clearly spoke as he began walking in the direction of the elevator.

"If you need anything Tye you now have my number don't hesitate to call son" Chief Reginald said while remaining inside his office as he closed the door.

"Roger, I hope they get in contact with her father today" Chief Reginald said as he walked back over to sit in the chair behind his desk.

"The armed forces are complicated chief in regards of their enlisted soldiers and usually when their officers are on duty in the field you cannot contact them directly. What concerns me Reggie is that

he was just here 2 weeks ago" Assemblyman Rogers replied.

"Well, I know she has a lot of love surrounding her now as we can clearly see. That is a very close-knit family. They clearly demonstrated that to me this morning so that eases the tensions somewhat on that part. She's going to receive a lot of love from all those grands of hers. But usually in cases where the victim involved is the parent the child or children gravitates to the closest remaining parent. As everyone knows her relationship with her father is revered" Chief Reginald loudly explained.

"Reggie what else is going on?" Assemblyman Rogers asked as he boldly sat on the Chiefs desk.

"There's no doubt that's Debbie. Derrick confirmed it

late last night when I took him over to the morgue to see his cousins' body. I took it that he didn't say anything to anybody because when the other officers and I went out to Tye's parents' house earlier this morning no one knew. Over at Tye's house the family members didn't have a clue. I did see Georgia Mae standing in his kitchen" Chief Reginald clearly said.

"Oh, it is true she is back here in Mobile," Assemblyman Rogers replied.

"Tanya called Derrick last night and told him about Georgia Mae's return. She also informed him on Larry inquiring about Tye at her job. He shared all this with me when he came home" Chief Reginald said.

"You know Chief Derrick and Debbie were tight ever since they were little kids. So how is he holding up Reggie?" Assemblyman Rogers asked.

"In the exact same grieving condition each of the members of the family are this morning. But Roger, how did you know what happened to your girlfriend Debbie" Chief Reginald asked?

"Derrick!" Assemblyman Rogers answered.

"Oh! Ok, I see" Chief Reginald replied as he leaned back in his seat.

"Reggie, Derrick is the one that told me they were bringing my daughter here to the police station to see you and it was extremely important for me to be present" Assemblyman Rogers said.

"Her father's presence is what's extremely important in Alabama right now. Roger, I understand what you are saying to me that the army does have its own rules and limitations on how they operate with their own personnel so the challenges

his family may face are noted. However, let me inform you Assemblyman that Larry has his eye on Tye. From the family gathering this morning in Tye's kitchen upon my arrival, if I can guess that was probably the discussion around the table. Now I did see Georgia Mae's brother parked outside Tye's house on our way off his property. However, I also saw Eric in his car parked out there too" Chief Reginald said.

"Now that's interesting Reggie" Assemblyman Rogers replied.

"What is even more interesting is the harassment to quiet Diamonds car at her place of Residence from Eric. Which had a lot to do with her close relationship with Shane" Chief Reginald clearly said.

"Who is Diamond and who is Shane?" Assemblyman Roger asked loudly.

"Shane is Bucky's lead singer and who happens to be my Derricks best friend. Diamond is Williams' best friend. All related to your now deceased wife Debbie" Chief Reinald answered.

"Oh!" Assemblyman Rogers said lifting himself from the Chiefs desk and slowly walking over to the small sofa in the office.

"Oh, is right Roger. Derrick called you to tell you to come down to my office because I suggested it to him as I was leaving Tyes parents' house" Chief Reginald said.

"The thing is Reggie; I have always loved Libbie as if she was my own daughter. Honestly speaking, I can't say she returns that love to me all the time. Mainly the reason the grands play an eminent role in her life. Specifically, the living situation. Debbie always insisted that we do things

together as a family unit but even that was difficult at times because Libbie lives so many exits away. Meaning we had to go through his parents in order for permission if her dad wasn't in town. Reggie, if her father was home our family plans would be cancelled immediately. No exceptions! I could never voice my concern because then I would have to face Tye. And Reggie, her brother, has never been a fan of mine. You kept me in your office while he goes over to view his sister's dead body is probably developing questions in his mind on my true intensions. I dare not come between Libbie and her father has always been a stigma attached to my role in that entire family" Assemblyman Rogers explained.

"Well then you agree with me that child needs her father in Alabama immediately?" Chief Reginald asked.

"I will go to my office now and make some phone calls before I do anything else today" Assemblyman Rogers said.

"You mean after you go over to Debbie's parents' house?" Chief Reginald asked.

"Reggie, you blocked that shot already man!" Assemblyman Rogers shouted.

"Roger, I didn't block anything" Chief Reginald replied as he leaned forward in his chair putting his hands on his desk.

"Reggie man, I thought that was the play when Tye and Libbie came into your office then together, we would see my wife's body. Who now everybody has seen but me. And how do you think that really makes me feel Reggie?" Assemblyman Rogers asked.

"Roger, I didn't block anything" Chief Reginald loudly replied as he stood up behind his desk from sitting in

the chair walking over to the mini refrigerator in the corner of his office.

"I said to myself this will be easier with all of us together going over to see my wife Debbie and collect her things then heading over to her father's house. Which is probably why Derrick called me again this morning for me to be here" Assemblyman Roger said.

"Look at this! All I'm seeing is Lemonade. Freshly squeezed. I just want a cold soda. Let me call downstairs and get someone to bring me something cold to drink that I like" Chief Reginald said as he slammed the small refrigerator door and quickly walked behind his desk pushing a button on his PC that was on the desk.

"Yes Chief" the male voice said.

"Tell Juanita it's hot and I am thirsty! Can she please come upstairs and bring me a cold soda right now!" Chief Reginal loudly said.

"Chief did you hear me?" Assemblyman Roger said crossing his leg as he sat comfortably on the small sofa in the office.

"Roger, I didn't block anything!" Chief Reginald answered as he sat back down in his seat behind his desk.

There were a quick two knocks at the door before the door opened and Officer Scott returned to the office carrying two sodas in her hands.

"What happened Chief you ran out of cold beverages sir?" Officer Scott asked as she handed the Chief the sodas.

"Juanita my dear you are a life saver. I very much thank you" Chief Reginald said as he started opening the soda.

"Would you like anything to drink Assemblyman?" Officer Scott politely asked as she slowly turned around.

"No thanks it's too early for me to drink any soda" Assemblyman answered.

"You sure Roger? Listen don't be shy man! It's extremely hot outside and officer Juanita Scott can assist you this morning! I'm sure this outstanding officer can help you beat the heat! No matter what team is playing! Isn't that correct officer Scott?" Chief Reginald asked loudly.

"Eric started harassing Diamond in her place of residence because of Shane. He could not attack her at her workplace, which is on the docks in my opinion that is what he originally desired to do. The ongoing feud between Larry and two of the companies' managers on site fueled Erics anger towards young Diamond. Their anger and erratic behavior spilled over towards the manager in the maintenance department in Diamonds residence. Which all started over a white minivan. The manager brought the minivan from Larry in cash. How do we know? Because the base of the feud is there are some payments still owed to Larry. Shane and Diamond, who are neighbors in the building, are friends with the manager in the maintenance department. One of the maintenance staff workers was having an intimate relationship with Shane. Eric didn't know until he sent Jamie onto the complex to stay with one of the female residences who the manager was also having a secret intimate relationship with as well. Apparently, Assemblyman not just to be intimate with the female tenant but to harass the maintenance staff during the day shift. The maintenance manager was the initial target of the harassment. What ignited Erics anger from Jamies report to him about the

intimate affair with the staff worker and Shane. Was because Eric and Shane had been intimate lovers for months." Officer Scott explained.

"My condolences to you Roger I am truly sorry for your loss today. Unfortunately, with tornadoes our advanced weather equipment can't even really predict the outcome of its destruction. Roger, this is an awful tragedy that has hit Mobile Alabama this week. Words can't express how deeply sorrowful I am about the loss of your girlfriend today. The two of you complimented each other well. Debbie brought out the best in you Roger. She played an intricate part in your rise as a respectful representative in this state. Debbie complimented your work in the community and positively represented her family well. I know this accidental death which was unexpected is going to be hard on your heart as well as your emotions Assemblyman. Debbie was very special to her family and her brother's heart. This is very unfortunate for your brother-in-law Tye. My investigation today Assemblyman Rogers leads me to suspect that in his most vulnerable state Tye is being preyed on as we speak" Chief Reginald clearly said as walked around his desk to stand next to Officer Scott.

"Roger, I need you to be the respected sibling that I believe you are and go be with your parents as they grieve the loss of their only daughter" Chief Reginald clearly said.

Assemblyman Rogers stood up from off the couch in the Chiefs office and shook Chief Reginald's hand. Turning towards officer Scott who was standing directly next to the Chief, Assemblyman Rogers folded up his right fist and gently placed it on his chest over his heart and spoke.

"*Thank you, Juanita, for looking after my family*" he clearly said.

"*Roger let their uncle Bucky be the one to tell the Bishop that Georgia Mae has returned to this community*" Chief Reginald lifted his voice and spoke.

Chapter 11

THE FAMILY'S HOSPITAL MEETING

As Quincy and Georgia Mae sat patiently in the receptionist waiting area inside the hospital awaiting Tye's arrival to collect his sister's body from the hands of the authorities. Quincy's cell phone started to ring. Quickly looking down at his cell phone caller Identification number he recognized that it was Bishop Joe.

"Hey Pastor," Quincy said answering his phone.

"Good morning cousin this is Joshua. Bishop and I are here at our uncle and aunt's house" Joshua said.

"O.K. that's good. Well cousin I'm still at the hospital waiting for Tye I'm not home with Jamena" Quincy loudly replied.

"So, they haven't arrived at the hospital with the Sherif as of yet?" Joshua calmly asked.

"No, I'm just sitting downstairs here by the hospital lobby entrance with *Georgia Mae*" Quincy replied.

"Bishop wanted me to inform you that he already contacted a very good friend of his who's funeral home is one of the best in the state. We discussed it with the parents, and they gave their consent. Bishop would like you to assist Tye in that matter regarding transferring the information on to whomever is in charge at the hospital since you're a medical professional that is employed there" Joshua clearly said.

"Ok cousin that is great news on such a sad day. That's definantly not a problem for me, I will oblige. After we hang up if you would kindly text me the funeral director's contact information when Tye arrives, I'll make it happen with the proper personnel" Quincy replied.

"Thank you very much cousin you're a gentleman and a scholar. I'm sure you're exhausted and as a family we appreciate you muscling up enough strength to be there for all of us at this time. Now If you don't mind Quincy let me speak to Ms. Georgia Mae" Joshua softly asked.

Handing the cell phone over to Georgia Mae who was seated right next to him in the hospital reception waiting area Quincy then sat back in the chair and crossed his leg.

"Hello this is *Georgia*" Georgia Mae softly spoke.

"I see you're back in the saddle with my cousin. I pray to God that this trail doesn't lead him into a dangerous path" Joshua spoke.

"Good to hear from you too Reverend. Our hearts are

broken this morning over Debbie. Rest assure Joshua I'm here for my man and it must be God ordained. No other explanation can be given looking at the timing of me being in Tye's house again when he would receive the worse possible news" Georgia Mae softly replied.

"Listen here Ms. Miracle wonder. If I get the slightest indignation that your presence at this time in this community is of no good. I will personally come for you. That's a promise Ms. Wanderer!" Joshua shouted over the phone.

"When Tye arrives here, I will let him know that we spoke Reverend" Georgia Mae replied.

"I'm here with his mama and the Bishop and I will not let them know that we spoke" Joshua shouted as he disconnected the call.

Georgia Mae handed the cell phone back to Quincy and quickly stood up as Sheriff Wesley, Tye, Libbie, Tiny and Blaire entered the hospital lobby doors.

"Hey there Quincy" Tiny said as they all turned and approached the hospital waiting area.

"This is such a shock family. I'm speechless" Quincy loudly said as he stood up with the cell phone in his hand.

"Good day sir I'm Deputy Wesley and I'm here to continue the investigation" Sheriff Wesley said as he extended his hand towards Quincy.

"Excuse the scrubs officer I had just arrived home from a long night here at work when my wife gave me the bad news. So, I'm back here to be of support for our cousin" Quincy said while extending his right hand to shake the Sheriff's hand.

"*Understood*" Sheriff Wesley calmly replied.

"*Hey cousin, my eyes are all full of tears right now man. This is like a nightmare Quincy*" Tye spoke as he embraced Quincy in a hug.

"*Understood*" Quincy said.

"*I'm surprised to see you here with us Blaire. I thought you and the family would be over at your aunt's house if anything*" Georgia Mae loudly said.

"*Maybe you don't know this family as well as you think you know Georgia Mae*" Blaire replied.

"*Cousin Tye, your parents and Bishop Joe have text me contact information for the arrangements of Debbie's body*" Quincy loudly said.

"*If you all don't mind waiting here in the lobby while Tye, Libbie and I go downstairs to see Debbie and verify some important information that would be helpful*" Sheriff Wesley said.

"*That's not a problem officer*" Tiny lifted his voice and responded as the three of them Sherif Wesley, Tye and Libbie walked towards the hospital elevator.

"*My mom and sister told me Cousin William was over at Tye's father's house fighting this morning*" Blaire said.

"*William who?*" Quincy asked as he sat back down in the hospital lobby waiting area chair.

"*That was my response man. I asked Blaire the same exact question*" Tiny lifted his voice and spoke as he sat down next to Quincy in the hospital lobby waiting area chair.

"*Apparently quiet William knocked the guy off the backyard patio*" Blaire said.

"You are kidding me?" Quincy replied.

"Hey, Big Hip, sexy, don't get quiet now. You have an explanation of why there's boxing matches happening at your, man's parents' house?" Tiny loudly asked Georgia Mae.

"Is that why Joshua wanted to speak to you on my cell phone a minute ago" Quincy asked.

"Wait who speaking to who? Does Pastor know you're here sexy? Tiny loudly asked.

"Does Tye know his cousin was fighting at his dad's house is the main question? Quincy loudly asked.

"Okay you guys need to chill. I really think all of you'll need to fall back. I've been with my man all morning. I only know what Tye knows" Georgia Mae softly replied as she pulled a fingernail file out of her pocketbook.

"That's right she's the chauffer of that white monster truck parked outside in the hospital parking lot!" Tiny yelled.

"Quiet cousin William got it rocking with the fist at Tye's dad's house today! Man, my cousin going to go all the way off when he finds out what took place in front of his parents" Quincy replied.

"Who is the guy, Georgia Mae?" Blaire asked.

"This is the first time I'm hearing about it" Georgia Mae replied as she continued filing her long fingernails.

"She's the chauffer everyone. You'll fall back off the driver. She only knows how to text and drive. You may need to ask who she was texting if her man was in the car with us. Because she sure was not texting him" Tiny loudly said.

"Does not sound like a law-abiding citizen to me" Quincy replied.

"Definantly criminal behavior. And I do believe in safety.

So, who was more important than my cousin Tye that you had to keep looking at your phone and responding to them while you were chauffeuring us Ms. Big Hip Sexy" Tiny said.

"Are we having this conversation again?" Georgia Mae softly asked.

"Now I'm in the conversation. I was the missing link from the conversation earlier. Who was the guy in my uncle and aunt's house this morning? I'm sure you know Georgia Mae." Blaire spoke.

"Now I'm in the conversation. Who did Joshua say was in my uncle and aunt's house that was causing mischief?" Quincy asked.

"Why are you teaming up on, me? I already asked you guys nicely to fallback. This isn't the time for any false accusations. We are in the hospital lobby for God sakes. My heart has been crushed. My man needs me. I'm here and have been here with him all morning. This is not the time or place for us as a family to fall apart. Debbie was like a little sister to me. My niece Libbie is devastated this morning. Plus, we still must survey the wreckage with Tye. Wherever they towed the car. Personally, I feel that's why her dad and mom sent Tye because that is a site even, they couldn't handle. Right now, I feel better you'll are here because he has family shoulders to cry on. I saw how puffy and red his eyes were when he walked into this hospital some minutes ago. We all know Tye is not a crybaby. The whole state of Alabama knows he is a team leader. An all-star gladiator. Those puffy eyes were a sign of pain. I know my man! I love my man! I need my man! I'm here for my man! Most of all my man needs all of us to be together not apart. We can accomplish more on today as a

family unit for our uncle and aunt" Georgia Mae said as she crossed her thick legs filing her long fingernails.

"We know our role Ms. Big Hip Sexy! We have always been here for our cousin! Even when you weren't" Tiny replied.

"Even when you disappeared" Quincy said.

"Even when you left him" Blaire added.

"I always been there for my uncle and aunt. The real question this morning is does my aunt know you're here at the hospital with her son" Tiny asked.

"Does my aunt even know Georgia Mae is back in town" Blaire added.

"Like I told Tye last night before you bullies showed up in our faces today. I'm back here in Alabama because I have always loved Tye. Yes, I may have made some ugly decisions in the past that may have broken some hearts, but nothing has ever stopped me from loving Tye. My maneuvers may have even displayed abandonment, but my man and I are as tight as ever. Now this here today concerning my little sister is a tragedy. And you bullies are not helping the situation by interrogating me about any unfortunate situations in your families lives on today. Tiny who I talk to in my vehicle is my business and I'm not going to repeat myself" Georgia Mae said as she put her fingernail file back into her pocketbook while pulling out her cell phone.

"Your maneuvers? So that's how you justify your selfish actions as maneuvering. I don't think my aunt would call your despicable moves justified maneuvers. On today as my aunt's heart is in severe pain because she has now lost her

only daughter your maneuvers may not be condoned" Tiny replied.

"Who was maneuvering in your tailgate party on the way to Libbie's house this morning?" Blaire asked.

"Car chasing! Your brother and his goons are harassing my family, Georgia?" Quincy asked.

"Is that the business your family has been conducting since you have returned to Alabama?" Quincy loudly asked.

"Wait a minute. Her brothers? There's a family business in operation? Let me call my pastor. I see everyone is working in families this morning. I need to team up with God! Link up with a higher source for this family reunion. Connect with the man of God for that almighty power to get our family through this unforeseen hour!" Tiny shouted.

"Hey Quincy, I'm surprised to see you still here" a nurse who was exiting the hospital said to him as she slowly walked past the waiting area where Quincy, Georgia Mae and Tiny were seated. Blaire had remained standing with his arms folded.

As Quincy stood up to walk over towards the nurse to hold a light conversation, the lobby doors opened, the tall grey-haired gentleman wearing blue jeans and short sleeved dress shirt from the floor of the Chiefs office at the police station quickly came walking in. Blaire and Tiny looked at each other both remembering where they saw him last. As Tiny watched the tall grey-haired gentleman who at this time wasn't wearing the badge around his neck get into the elevator, Georgia Mae made a call on her cell phone. The hospital lobby doors opened once again, and Tanya came running in the lobby.

"Tye called me, we must get to him quickly. He was distraught! Seeing his sisters, dead body in that condition was too much. Libbie was overcome as well, and she is laid out on the floor! Where's the elevator?" Tanya loudly asked.

Tiny and Georgia Mae jumped up out of their chairs and started running towards the elevators along with Blaire. Quincy was running towards the elevators behind them.

CHAPTER 12

THE CARS

As Assemblyman Rogers pulled up at the docks in Mobile Alabama, he purposely parked his car next to a black BMW. He quickly pulled out his cell phone to make a personal call to Libbie's grandparents.

"Good afternoon, hi mama Whitehead it's the Assemblyman. I was just calling to check in on you two.

"Hi there son, I am glad to hear your voice. We are just devastated! This is awful, son, just very sad. Our hearts are broken. How's my Libbie holding up?" The grandmother asked.

"She's taking this very hard mama Whitehead. Her world has been shattered" The Assemblyman replied.

"That's what I'm saying son. This is awful! We are so worried for her. Not sure how this is going to affect her schoolwork or her behavior. Libbie is such a sweet young girl with a bright southern future. Every week she makes her father

proud. She pushes herself to do the right things for her mother and father. She kept herself in a positive mindset. Now, I just don't know" The grandmother softly said.

"That is also why I'm calling you. Have you heard from your son at all today? And has he been notified about the death of his baby's mother? The Assemblyman asked.

"We just returned home from the clinic a little while ago. My husband had his routine dialysis appointment this morning and we haven't heard from him. We left messages but my son has not returned our calls yet" The grandmother softly answered.

"Mama Whitehead it is extremely important he comes home today. There is trouble stepping in high heels parked outside on your lawn" The Assemblyman said.

"Oh really, walking across the freshly cut grass in my front yard?" The grandmother politely asked.

"Yes mam! Very dangerously!" The Assemblyman sharply replied.

"Son, you got mama's attention start running them gums and speak up so I can hear it all clearly" the grandmother spoke.

"Mama Whitehead seems like the prison did our clean community of Mobile, Alabama a disservice by dumping their trash out into our neighborhoods. Street scum named Larry is our new local problem. Everyone knows gambling can get sticky even if you are always on its lucky side. But not everyone is comfortable with one's record of wins. Even if your sister is sleeping with the lucky winner. Now my wife's uncle's band member may have been creeping with the trash, but the target has always been the winner" the Assemblyman said.

"Oh, I hear you loud and clear son. Very discomforting news about the new arrival in the area. Sounds like revenge. I must say his mom was always worried about him playing them cards. From what I'm hearing now is that thug might have his eyes on these cars specifically her son. Sounds like someone may have returned to protect her son and Libbie from the eyes of her brother. You might need to find out what the brothers' eyes are really fixed on" the grandmother softly replied.

"I'm on it now Ma as we speak" the Assemblyman replied.

"That's good Assemblyman. And I'll make sure my son is here in Alabama by tomorrow to mow my lawn" the grandmother replied as she disconnected the phone from the Assemblyman.

Assemblyman Rogers exited his Cadillac Truck. Walking slowly over to the docks he noticed a silver Hyundai with Kentucky license plates parked directly next to one of the containers from off a ship. What caught his eye wasn't that the car was not parked in the parking lot with the rest of the cars. Or that it was stationed next to a large container. It could be an upper-rank employee with special access to the docks. For the Assemblyman it was the license plate. He had seen that Kentucky authorized vehicle a few times in his circle.

Entering one of the offices at the Mobile Alabama docks, the Assemblyman asked the pretty middle-aged receptionist for a gentleman who is named Waley. She escorted him out of that office, and they walked a little way down the pier onto the entrance of a huge ship. After walking up some stairs and then some more stairs they entered another office. There was a very large, bearded man standing by a water cooler with some papers in his hand.

"Hey Gus, this is Assemblyman Rogers and he's here to speak to Waley" the middle-aged receptionist said.

"He's in there just knock hard on the door" Gus, the very large, bearded man answered.

"Go ahead and knock Assemblyman he's inside the office" the receptionist said as she exited walking back towards the steps to return to one of the main offices on the docks.

As the assemblyman proceeded towards the door to knock the very large, bearded man dropped his papers on the floor.

"Oh darn, look what I did now. How's my fat butt gone pick up this mess. Hey Assemblyman, can you please help me sir?" Gus, the very large, bearded man requested.

"That's not a problem man" Assemblyman Roges replied.

Turning around to head towards the water cooler where the papers that were now on the floor beneath the water cooler where the very large, bearded man was standing the Assemblyman reached down to gather the papers together before picking them up.

"I really appreciate this boy! After you finish you can have some of this cold water" Gus, the very large, bearded man shouted.

Assemblyman Rogers proceeded to gather the papers together and afterwards he stood up with the papers in his hand.

"What did you just say to me?" Assemblyman Rogers asked Gus.

"I believe the papers in your hands belong to me boy" Gus replied.

"When you see a boy, you address a boy and when you see this government official standing in front you then you address me by my correct official government adult name" the Assemblyman said.

"Yes sir, nigga boy! I would like my papers that's in your hands" Gus, the very large, bearded man responded.

"Listen, what's your problem? You know me?" The Assemblyman asked.

"I don't have a problem boy! You will if I don't get those papers that you picked up into my hands! Nigga, it seems you maybe a little slow so I'm going to help you out this afternoon. Put the papers in my hands boy and I'll reward you dumb nigga by giving you some of this cold water" Gus, responded as he leaned on the water cooler.

"Man, I just lost my wife yesterday by that deadly tornado and looks like I'm about to lose my freedom as a law-abiding government official modeled citizen by bashing your skull in with this water cooler. Pick up your own damn paper's you maggot" the Assemblyman said as he dropped the papers back onto the floor and walked back towards the office door.

"You better watch yourself around here boy" Gus, the very large, bearded man said as he remained standing by the water cooler.

"Seems as if you're a little slow this afternoon so I'm going to help you out. Everyone who's in authority watches me

around here, you, large piece of trash now bend- ova and pick up your own crap maggot!" Assemblyman Rogers shouted, as he knocked hard on the office door. A skinny white gentleman wearing a suit was talking on his cell phone opened the door.

"Hi Assemblyman, didn't expect to see you out here" the skinny man spoke.

"Waley, may I come in we have to talk?" Assemblyman Roges requested as he walked into the cargo ships office. Shutting the door behind the Assemblyman, Waley disconnected the call on his cell phone.

"You have to excuse me bro, I'm really surprised to see you and in one of my offices is everything ok?" Waley asked.

"Debbie was killed while driving in her car yesterday in that storm" Assembly Rogers replied.

"Aww, Bro. I'm sorry. Aww man, come have a seat" Waley suggested.

"No, Waley I can't sit anymore. My whole body is numb, and I really don't feel like standing up either. I can hardly breathe at times. My nerves have my hands shaking and I didn't sleep at all last night. Honestly, Waley, I really don't know where my head is right now. Because of circumstances I can't even stay here long, and you know that. Waley, I want to see my wife and kiss Debbie goodnight something which I couldn't do at home last night" Assemblyman Rogers said.

Waley reached out and hugged The Assemblyman in a tight squeeze.

"I love you Bro. always have baby and always will" Waley said as he kissed the assemblyman on his cheek.

"Everything happened suddenly! I'm talking with Debbie around noon about what she was planning to eat for lunch and before midnight I'm receiving a call from her cousin that my wife is dead. I even had to go downtown to the police station" the Assemblyman explained.

"What are the authorities saying to you that happened to Debbie?" Waley inquired.

"Your messed up staff you have working out here" Assemblyman Rogers replied.

"Oh, I see bro. Does mom know what happened to you yesterday?" Waley asked.

"No, I haven't had a chance to call her yet. You are the first one I came to. All morning, I was on the phone with Debbie's daughter Libbie after they discovered her body. It's a really bad situation. I was at the precinct with Debbie's family a little while ago which prompted me to come see you. Debbie's family don't even know about mom. As a matter of fact, everyone thinks Ms. Nesfield is my mother and I never corrected anyone. Waley I just left it as is. Honestly, as our maid growing up, Ms. Nesfield was more of our mother than mom is. As a politician, since she always came around to my house for every function that was given, or she even participated in many of my public engagements and banquets I left it as yes Ms. Nesfield is my mother if anyone asked why I called her mom" Assemblyman rogers replied.

"That's because she's black like you brother! Pick up the phone and call your real mother!" Waley lifted his voice and spoke.

"I am I promise" The Assemblyman whispered.

"So, what in that meeting prompted you to come all the

way out here aboard this huge vessel and see me publicly, Mr. future Alabama governor whom I'm personally voting for?" Waley inquired.

"The police investigation of you" Assemblyman Rogers replied.

"Well, their report must not be all that accurate if no one knows you and I have the same mother. I sure can't recall seeing Debbie over here at the docks. And brother by the way you have my deepest condolences. She was a beauty queen, and I know her daughter is in shock right now. The emotional pain of losing her mother. Lot like what you're probably experiencing. These storms come in and they have no regard for human life. Such a tragedy. I can only imagine the emotional pain and grief you're experiencing right now because of the absence of your wife Debbie. If there's anything you need from me don't hesitate to ask. I don't care what it is. Emotional support, a friend, financial, food, even if you need someplace to sleep, my house is always open to you bro. I love you! We are family. However, I'm a little puzzled on why I would be on any local authorities hit list" Waley said.

"Apparently, you've been collecting community undesirables amongst your cargo. The consistent contention amongst rivalry family members around your freight has captured the authority's attention. And brother I've loved Debbie ever since when, so her daughter is like my child. Anything that endangers the welfare of a child in my sight needs to be dismantled by law officials. Anyone that dares to bring a threat to the safety of my daughter needs to be in the eyes of the law" Assemblyman Rogers said.

"So, the police are checking my cargo" Waley said.

"*More like the Mobile, police department is shaking your ships. With a unit attempting to sink them*" the Assemblyman replied.

"*How does that connect to your daughter Libbie?*" Waley asked.

"*Debbie's older brother Tye has captured the attention of Larry who is part of your cargo here at the Mobile, docks*" Assemblyman Rogers responded.

"*Now that sounds like a sticky situation someone may have there*" Waley replied.

"*Then big brother I'm all ears and I want to hear this volume of weight that involves my daughter's safety*" The Assembly said.

"*Bro. he's a piece of work. If anything, I'm suspecting Larry has his eyes on a car. I run a respectful business despite others' opinions of my work ethics or supervisory abilities. At the end of a quarter the job gets done. No major complaints about this end or any losses have ever been filed here. Heads of business operations have been pleased since I moved up to this position and changed some things around. That's not to say everyone is excited about changes because the two companies which corporate headquarters have merged now function under one main umbrella and down here, I'm in charge. Yes, I was a warehouse worker for years, yes, I was a forklift driver loading and unloading trucks at the warehouse for years. Yes, I loaded and unloaded freight here at this dock a few seasons, but I still worked. Even when I was high on cocaine. Or hung over from drinking and partying with my buddies all night at the local pub. However, you cut the check on my background and the results will reveal I know the operation of business in this field*" *of work. I'm not a racist how could I be with a deceased African American stepfather. Now that's our personal business, little brother. Compared to the few other companies that run their respectable businesses along this pier I seem to be less interested in my staff's backgrounds and more impressed with their work skills. So here at this site there's a mixture of everyone and every kind of background. It doesn't bother me, I'm all about getting the job done but at times it seems to bother some. Which is why I set up this office here aboard this ship to lessen some of the internal tension brewing by being present on site. Now I will have your back if you don't have me out there looking like a fool. Which is what Larry and Jamie purposely were doing to me. Then got some kind of goons to try and sabotage my business. I had to fire Jamie over repeated theft infractions. Larry got pissed at me about that and came full force with some punk named Eric. I just promoted my good friend Bill to combat that crap"* Waley explained.

"Who's Bill?" The assemblyman asked.

"My personal assistant we nicknamed Gus, that you just met outside my office" Waley answered.

"Besides your ugly bigot bulldog, who else do I need to be aware of running around loose in your junkyard?" The Assemblyman asked his brother Waley.

"Like I said Larry brought aboard some goons who were causing a lot of internal trouble amongst the workers. Bunch of loudmouth rebel rousers! But what disgusted me was the war he was stirring up against me with another manager on the east side of the dock. Now over on that site they handle only car shipments, so I figured out his game in that freight. And

from your presence today the managers must have gotten law enforcement involved" Waley explained.

"You're being watched Waley!" Assemblyman Rogers shouted.

"Eric was the one who brought in the eyes of the law with his fetish for auto racing and side hustling right here around the docks. Ushered in crooked crowds from hoods all over the dirty South. A few men and women were busted and booked some nights on several different occasions. Several of my workers were even involved and charged who I never fired. That's where my reputation went sour around the ships. None of it was done during working time or during my billing hours. Out of my sight out of my mind. Not actually on my site not actually on my mind. Which is also why you're standing on my floating site right now. That was just some of the light drama that occurred. The secret burglary, which also involved Jamie that I could not cover up was the main bout" Waley explained.

"Seems like that heavy weight match is still ongoing. Let me ask you about Diamond. What's significant about her?" Assemblyman Rogers inquired.

"A real princess. She was very special! Extremely unique, hard worker, dedicated, fast learner evident that she didn't belong here compared to her colleagues. I was upset when she and another good girl named Juanita quit" Waley replied.

"Juanita? Really? Long honey blond hair with dimples?" Assemblyman Rogers asked.

"Yeah, Bro. Another unique beauty on board working these docks. They both left at the same time. Heard it was after one of my workers got into an argument with Eric in the parking lot over something small. Then that altercation

126

escalated into a big thing. The problem was the worker was Diamonds friend. I'm telling you Larry's a piece of work" Waley answered.

"You have been helpful to me today. Let me go to the house and see her parents. I'll keep you updated with the arrangements we establish for Debbie. I love you forever brother" Assemblyman Rogers said as he embraced Waley in a hug inside the office.

"I love you even more, little bro. I always have baby, and I always will" Waley said as he kissed him on his cheek.

"This is a real heavy blow to my household Waley" Assemblyman Rogers said as he walked towards the office door.

"I'm sure you're strong enough to handle any sibling rivalry and sneaky revenge that races up your street little brother. Come, let me walk you back to our main office on the docks. I don't need you to get bitten by my watchdog" Waley replied as they exited the office.

As the Assemblyman walked outside of the main office towards the parking lot, he noticed the silver Hyundai with the Kentucky license plate was not parked by the container. Strolling back to his car the Assemblyman begin looking over as many cars parked in the docks parking lot and the plates as he could to see if anything stood out or looked somewhat suspicious.

As the noonday sun stood brightly unclouded unbothered over the city of Mobile, Alabama Assemblyman Rogers turned on his Cadillac trucks air conditioner as he remained parked in the docks parking lot. Taking out his cell phone to check his messages he noticed the slogan "we built it, and God blessed it" on an orange and yellow bumper sticker on the back of a red pickup truck two vehicles down directly across parking lot rows from his Cadillac truck. Calling the Chief the assemblyman took out a small notepad from his glove compartment.

"*Good day this is Chief speaking*" Chief Reginald answered the phone call.

"*Hey buddy this is Rogers, listen if you don't mind me asking Chief. Have you noticed a Kentucky licensed silver vehicle riding around in the downtown area over the past few weeks*" assemblyman Rogers asked.

"*What type of vehicle Rogers?*" The Chief asked.

"*I believe it's a Hyundai with an out of state license plate*" the Assemblyman answered.

"*Not sure Rogers, you know with yesterday's storm hitting us the way that it did, and sections of the highway closed this entire area has been congested with all kinds of vehicles. My entire department is swamped with calls needing assistance. But if I see something I'll definantly keep you in mind*" the Chief replied.

"*Thanks Chief!*" Assemblyman Rogers said as he hung up the phone with the Chief of police. Calling over to the Greenlit Lounge the Assemblyman made another call while sitting in his air-conditioned truck.

"*Good afternoon Greenlit Lounge this is Marcy who do I have the pleasure of speaking with?*" The female voice over the phone asked.

"*Afternoon their pretty lady it's the Assemblyman*" he answered.

128

"Hi Assemblyman Rogers, how are you today" Marcy asked.

"Not good at all Marcy. That tornado that blew through here yesterday killed my wife on the highway as she was driving in her car" the Assemblyman replied.

"Oh my God! I'm truly sorry to hear this Assemblyman Rogers. That is heartbreaking news you just shared. Hope you're not alone at this horrible time sir?" Marcy asked.

"No, I'm with family pretty lady. However, let me ask you about my uncle Bucky. Has Georgia Mae been to the lounge this past week to hear his band perform?" The Assemblyman asked Marcy.

"No, she has not come by here. But Assemblyman Rogers she is presently in town. Your cousin Derrick has been here a lot recently. I figure that's to support his buddy Shane but even the jury on that is still out in deliberation" Marcy replied.

"Okay, perhaps a split decision between friendship?" The Assemblyman quickly asked.

"No whether or not he's here for Shane or Eric?" Marcy quickly replied.

"Oh, so you know about their love relationship" the Assemblyman asked.

"If Derrick happened to be now coming around here for that handsome heart throb ladies' man Eric, then Georgia Mae's baby making brother has his eyes also on that hot little booty hole" Marcy responded.

"Thank you so much Marcy I appreciate your time and for taking my call" Assemblyman Rogers said.

"My pleasure Assemblyman Rogers and my condolences

to your entire family such a tragedy" Marcy spoke as she disconnected the call from the Assemblyman.

Pulling out of the docks parking lot driving his Cadillac truck, Assemblyman Rogers took one last look over as many cars as he could while passing them on his way to the ramp that led out onto the state route. Driving slowly down the state route, on route to the highway the Assemblyman begin checking out some of the tractor trailers hauling cargo into the docks that were either driving on the opposite side of the road or was parked on the side of the road. Looking into the cabs as they passed seeing if he recognized any of the local drivers by their faces and reading some of the company logos on the sides of the big trucks as he drove by them. Assemblyman Rogers cell phone started to ring and as he connected the call to his Cadillacs Bluetooth, he answered the phone call.

"Good afternoon, this is the Assemblyman who's calling" Assemblyman Rogers asked.

"Oh my God little brother Waley just told me. How horrifying your night and day must have been. Where is you now?" Sally, Assemblyman Rogers older sister inquired.

"I'm driving on the state route headed to mom's house. Can you meet their Sally?" Assemblyman Rogers asked.

"Sure, I'm leaving work right at this minute. I'll take a half day" Sally said.

"I appreciate you Sally" Assemblyman Rogers replied.

"You don't need to be alone, during this time little brother. I don't care what office title you are holding. You are not invincible" Sally said.

"I'm not alone Sally. Remember I still have my daughter Libbie who needs me" the Assemblyman replied.

"On my way to mom's house! See you there!" Sally yelled as she disconnected the phone call.

As the Assemblyman proceeded to drive his Cadillac truck northwest up the state route towards the highway while increasing his speed, he quickly dialed his mom's houseline.

"Hello" soft voice answered.

"Mom it's me" the Assemblyman replied.

"Well, what an amazing surprise today it's my son" she remarked.

"Mom, Sally and I are on our way to your house I hope you're not busy today. But my wife Debbie died yesterday afternoon as she was driving in that twister" the Assemblyman explained.

"Dear Lord son. Oh God! Aww baby" she sadly replied.

"Mom, I can't eat, I couldn't sleep I'm so angry and upset right now" the Assemblyman explained.

"Oh, I know you are son. I'm here. I'll be here when you get here" the soft voice spoke.

"Love you mom!" the Assemblyman shouted as he disconnected the phone call from his mother.

Approaching the entrance ramp to the highway the Assemblyman's cell phone began to ring again, connecting it to the blue tooth he answered the phone call.

"Good afternoon, Kyle what happened?" the Assemblyman asked his assistant.

"*Good day sir, I know that you said unto me this morning that you wouldn't be taking any calls this week. I did relay your messages to the state assembly as well as to certain committee members you advised me to. Many send their condolences to you and your family sir. However, Assemblyman, I received an odd message from a man named Keith a few minutes ago*" Kyle the Assemblyman's assistant and long-time high school friend relayed to him over the phone.

"*Keith! I'm not familiar with Keith. Who is he Kyle?*" The Assemblyman loudly asked.

"*Sir, that's what I'm relaying to you that was particularly odd about this message. There was no last name. Someone who I'm unfamiliar with myself and it came from a voice who I didn't recognize. Usually any calls, voicemails or emails that you may receive where I'm unsure of the person than I treat it as spam or junk mail. But this message caught my attention Assemblyman. The gentleman named Keith said it's not revenge on the Bentley's I'm after. The turbo parked next to it in the garage is my collateral that is owed. So sweet little brown skin Libbie can leave the keys with me*" Kyle relayed.

"*Text me the phone number from the caller ID Kyle thanks very much for your keen perception. Listen I'm on my way to see my immediate family I will check in with you later*" Assembly Rogers said as he disconnected the call with his longtime assistant Kyle.

Chapter 13

THE UNMARKED VEHICLES

As Quincy, Blaire, Tiny, and Tanya escorted their cousin Tye who was crying hysterically out of the hospital to Quincy's vehicle Georgia Mae who was holding up Debbie's only daughter Libbie who was also hysterical stopped in the hospital lobby waiting area. Taking out her cell phone as if she was about to make a phone call the tall grey-haired gentleman with blue jeans that had his badge around his neck and a short-sleeved shirt from the Chief's office floor walked up to Georgia Mae and grabbed her elbow.

"I advise you not to call him Georgia Mae. Take Libbie to see Debbie's mom now. I will be your only escort this afternoon" the plain clothe officer said.

"Sir don't put your hands on me as if you knew me!" Georgia Mae shouted.

"*You are lucky I'm not putting you in hand cuffs Ms. Georgia Mae*" the plain clothe officer replied.

"*Like I said, don't touch me stranger!*" Georgia Mae shouted.

"*I haven't begun to handle you authoritatively the way your family needs to be dealt with. Keep it swiftly moving and take Libby to see her grandmother now*" the plain clothe officer said.

"*Listen stranger don't tell me what to do! I advise you to swiftly move away from me! I will call whoever I feel like talking with!*" Georgia Mae shouted as she slowly picked Libby up from off the seat in the hospital waiting area and they walked out the lobby doors.

Quincy, Blaire, Tiny, and Tanya drove their cousin Tye whose body became numb while hysterically crying after viewing his now dead sisters' body over to the funeral chapel that their cousin Bishop Joe had connected them with to plan for Debbie's body to be released from the morgue. As Georgia Mae slowly walked over to her white truck with Libby still hysterically crying wrapped in her arms the tall grey haired plain clothe officer stopped directly in front of the hospital to talk with a doctor that was about to enter the lobby. Georgia Mae slowly turned around to see who the person was that the plain clothe officer was talking with and then she glanced over halfway at some of the cars that were exiting the lot to see if Quincy's car was one of them.

"*Libby! Oh my God! I'm here*" a strange voice yelled out from across the parking lot. As Georgia Mae slowly turned back around in the direction of her truck a chubby bright skinned girl came running through the parking lot up to them out of breath.

"Libby poo bear I'm here! I can't believe our mom is gone" Libby's bestie said as she ran up to them and grabbed Libby. Georgia Mae released her as the two girls hugged screamed and cried in the hospital parking lot.

"Robin! What am I going to do now? Not my mama Robin! Why did it happen like this" Libby screamed hysterically as they hugged each other.

"I know Libby! I can't believe mommy has gone from us! Not like this" Robin replied as Georgia Mae proceeded to slowly wiggle her hour shaped figured body to her truck. Starting the engine and glancing her eyes out her driver side window, Georgia Mae watched the plain clothe officer with his badge hanging around his neck continue to talk to the doctor directly in front of the hospital entrance while his eyes were looking directly back at Georgia Mae sitting inside her air-conditioned vehicle. Slowly moving the big white Suburban out of the parking space and up to where Libby and her best girlfriend was huddled Georgia Mae begin to dial a number on her cellphone. As the call connected to the blue tooth inside the Suburban truck Shane answered the call.

"Hey Georgia girl" Shane said.

"Hey boo, I know by now you have heard what happened" Georgia Mae said.

"Girl I'm here with Derick now, he's in the bathroom Tho. I believe he's trying to take a shower, but you know

he's gone girl Just done! I don't know Georgia girl how his comeback gone to be ever since he saw his cousin Debbie's dead body last night at that cold place. We finished eating brunch thirty minutes ago and he didn't lose his appetite. So, I'm here now crying with him Georgia girl" Shane replied.

"Boo I hear you. I'm here at that cold place you are speaking of now with Debbie's daughter Libby and she's a mess. Totally devastated. Her older cousin Tanya along with the Highway state trooper had to help us scoop her slender body up off the floor. Boo, it was so sad. My man is no better. That being his baby and only sister him seeing her lifeless body took him all the way-out boo" Georgia Mae explained.

"I can believe it Georgia girl. Derrick kept repeating how scared he was of his cousin Tye's reaction. He kept on saying how this incident was going to crush your man's heart. He really, hoped that somehow you may be able to ease the burden of pain of Debbie's death from off him Georgia girl" Shane replied.

"Boo, if I'm here now and the family is just seeing Debbie's body then explain to me when and how did her favorite cousin already view her dead body" Georgia Mae politely asked Shane.

"The Chief, Georgia girl. Late last night he drove Derrick over to where you're at now to confirm if that was Debbie's body that the emergency Hurricane, Tornado & Storm response crews discovered in the woodlands to match the wreckage of her vehicle they had already identified from on the highway. But the Chief is not here now" Shane replied.

"Of course, he's not there we just left his office at the precinct Boo. I'm now staring eye to eye at one of his k-9 units.

Thanks Boo. You have been such a tremendous help today. I was also calling to perhaps speak to Eric. Obviously, he's not with you'll but do you happen to know where he may be this afternoon?" Georgia Mae softly asked as she leaned over towards the passenger side door attempting to push it open for the girls to make their way inside of her truck.

"Georgia girl, no I'm not sure I've been here with Derrick all morning" Shane replied.

"When he comes out of the bathroom are you'll heading over to Tye's parents' house?" Georgia Mae asked Shane.

"Georgia girl no I don't think we are. He's expecting folks to come over here at any minute to have a meeting in regards of that big benefit fashion show that is still planning to be held in the downtown area tonight. Anyway, we already saw Bucky earlier this morning Georgia girl. That's how we got to enjoy the delicious chicken and waffles it was just that we didn't sit ourselves down to taste it until a little while ago" Shane softly replied.

"Downtown area tonight, Boo. Good luck with that showcase. All these detours around town because of the down lines of wires and huge amounts of debris that is still scattered across these Alabama roads. But causes do continually need money to be raised so sweety I understand the extra efforts to keep them cameras flashing on tonight's fashion event. You both take care and be safe driving around Alabama today" Georgia Mae said.

"Georgia, girl make sure you do not get yourself bit by that trained dog out there eyeing your sexy steps right now" Shane said as he hung up the cellphone call from Georgia Mae.

Quickly stepping out of her Big white Suburban

truck Georgia Mae wiggled her hips around to the passenger side to assist Robin with laying Libby who was still hysterically crying and loudly screaming across the back seat of her big white vehicle. Together as they laid Libby's slender body inside the huge truck as Georgia Mae stepped back quickly turning her head towards the hospital to see if the plain-clothes undercover officer was still watching them. To her surprise he had disappeared. As she then quickly wiggled her hourglass shaped body back around her white truck, she glanced one last time around the hospital parking lot to see if Quincy and the fellas were having the same type of dramatic challenges with her man Tye that she seemed to be having with his niece Libby. The fellas in Quincy's car Georgia Mae didn't see neither did she see the plain clothes officer. Quickly closing her door Libby's best friend Robin jumped up in the front passenger seat and started to fasten her seat belt. As Georgia Mae put her feet on the brake to switch the auto gear shift unto drive at the same time a navy-blue Kia Sorento Lx that sped from around the other end of the hospital parking lot pulled up head on directly in front of them and completely stopped. The driver side door slowly opened and a tall grey-haired woman wearing a badge around her neck slowly got up from out of the driver's seat. With her right-hand remaining holding onto the top rubber seal of the car door as she slowly bent over to pull down her blue jean's pants legs all the way down to touch the tongues of her black sneakers. Georgia Mae taking her foot off the brake kept her auto gear in park. As the tall grey-haired woman slowly straightened herself up then begin to slowly dust off her blue jeans with her left hand, she quickly turned her head to the right and looked through the white Suburban front windshield directly into the eyes of Georgia Mae.

"Is she a friend of yours, mam?" Robin asked Georgia Mae as she watched the undercover officer.

The tall grey-haired woman then walked over to the passenger side of the vehicle. As Georgia Mae slowly rolled her window down.

"In Which direction are we headed towards Ms. Georgia Mae?" The tall grey-haired woman with a badge hanging from around her neck boldly asked.

"You are allowing all my refreshing cold air to escape out from my truck! Ms. Can you please remove your car from in front of mine" Georgia Mae loudly requested.

"You watch out for my vehicle there Ms. Lady! Don't you go hitting my vehicle now! I don't want to have to arrest you today. Just make sure we take Libby directly to her grandparent's house" the plain clothes officer replied as she turned away from Georgia Mae's driver side window and slowly walked back to her navy-blue Kia Sorento Lx.

"No Robin that law enforcement K-9 unit here now, is no friend of mines" Georgia Mae loudly spoke.

CHAPTER 14

THE DELIVERY MAN

As the hot humid sun shined heavily sending its southern heat over Mobile, Alabama, at Tye's parents' house aunt Rebecca, Tye's mother, Jill and Brenda were in the kitchen cutting up lots of greens, fresh carrots, and slicing up tomatoes picked out of the garden located at the other end of the backyard as they begin to prepare lunch. Bishop Joe and Joshua took William outside for a little stroll around the neighborhood in hopes he would calm down emotionally before their cousin Tye arrived at the house. As Willie James, Bucky, Jills baby father and Tye's father sat comfortably in the living room, the dog started barking loudly outside the house in the backyard.

"The Parcel delivery man must have parked outside in the front of the house" Tye's father said as he got up to walk over to the front door.

"Are you expecting a package today uncle?" Jills husband asked as he munched on a slice of apple pie.

"No, but sometimes Tye has things delivered here for him" Tye's father explained as he peaked out the hallway window to see what activity his dog was responding to.

"Wait a minute here comes my beautiful queen carrying baby number two in her fitness fit belly walking up to the house along with the Parcel Delivery driver carrying a small box" Tye's father loudly spoke as he opened his front door.

"Hi uncle, I'm truly sorry for our loss today" Delores lifted her voice and said as she got closer to the door before, she hugged Tye's father.

"Yeah, I'm still shocked about my baby girl Debbie. My nerves are all bad today. This is unbelievable, my beautiful queen Delores. So, where's my karate kid?" Tye's father asked Delores.

"After I dropped Blaire off at the precinct to be there for your son. I took my son over to his godparent's house. Their identical twins and him get along great and play well together" Delores explained.

"I'm glad you did that my beautiful queen, because Libby does not to be there! I don't like that at all! Your aunt is very upset about that decision to include her in that identifying the body process. Tye isn't thinking straight! Libbie's too young! I'm glad my nephew Blaire is there with them" Tye's father loudly replied as he walked over to the Parcel Delivery man.

"Afternoon buddy you have something for me?" Tye's father asked the young Parcel delivery worker.

"Yes, sir another package for Tye. And my condolences to

you and your entire family today sir for your sudden loss. I went to school with your daughter Debbie. The news of her passing is shocking sir. Even though Debbie and the Assemblyman were two and three grades ahead of me we were all still cool with one another" The young Parcel delivery worker said.

"Is that right young man. Well, I appreciate all you just said to me that meant a lot. It's a small world you never know who may pull up to your door" Tye's father replied as he signed for Tye's package.

Going back inside into his air-conditioned house Tye's father quickly shut and purposely locked his front door. Returning into the cool living room with his pregnant niece Delores, he called for his wife to come from the kitchen to join them in the living room.

"What happened brother?" Bucky asked Tye's father as Rebecca and Tye's mother hurried into the living room.

"Something isn't right under our roof.! Something doesn't feel quite right!" Tye's father shouted.

"Queen Delores, let me ask you something, do you know that young man that was just here at my doorstep in that Parcel delivery uniform?" Tye's father asked his niece as he stood up in front of the flat screen television mounted on their living room wall.

"No Uncle! I may have seen him around town, even though I'm not sure. It could just be a brother in a Parcel delivery uniform that looks familiar to me. He's never delivered any packages to our door. At the Martial Arts school across town, we have another regularly scheduled Parcel delivery man. And our Parcel Delivery man is white" Delores responded

as she took a seat on the comfortable sofa next to Willie James as they embraced in a hug.

"What's this all about?" Rebecca asked as she handed her daughter-in-law Delores, her glass of cold freshly squeezed lemonade.

"The Parcel delivery man was just here delivering at the same time Delores arrived" Jill's husband explained as he ate another slice of the fresh baked apple pie their Aunt Rebecca baked.

"So why do you feel uneasy in your own home" Tye's mother asked.

"All these unsavory characters that keep dropping by unannounced is what's bothering my brother! You saw earlier on how I was about to knock that other skinny character upside his head with a brick" Willie James shouted.

"My point exactly brother. I'm hurting and I'm angry because I found out this morning that I lost my little girl. But that's the thing Rebecca! We found out this morning because the deputies came out here to my house. I haven't been able to tell anyone yet. My wife hasn't been able to notify anyone yet. We were shocked! We've cried and as you can see my wife is still crying. We are just devastated! I even feel bad that we didn't call our only son Tye. I'm his father and I'm sure my son didn't like the fact that we didn't notify him of his sister Debbie's death in that tornado yesterday. I know that boy is going to come for me, with that one question in his mouth. That question is why I didn't call him about his sister Debbie. I'll handle my son whenever I see him! My only concern was my daughter Libby! That is still my only concern. Libby is too young and way too vulnerable to cope with this devastation

even if it is due to a natural disaster. Her mama is gone! Her mother has died less than twenty-four hours ago! Libby's moms body found in only God knows whatever kind of condition. Now her two daddies must come together and be a parental unit if there's any such thing. But you'll know what I mean! From today on they are going to have to parent Debbie's child. My wife said she didn't want Libby to see our daughter's body yet, and I agree. We haven't even gone to see her yet. I sent her big brother with the deputies because I felt at the time that was a wise decision. But that's what is troubling me right now. If we haven't even seen Debbie or notify anyone except our pastor and few of our church members who is here at the house with us now as a family waiting to hear confirmation from Tye that it is my daughter's body. Then how do these young men showing up at my doorstep know about Debbie? Like you said brother, how did that skinny boy named Jamie show up here earlier knowing? How did that young man who comes by here periodically bringing packages for Tye a few minutes ago know about my daughter's death" Tye's father loudly and frantically asked.

"This community isn't all that small" Jill said as she came out from the kitchen along with Brenda who handed her sister-in-law Debbie a plate of fresh baked apple pie to go with the lemonade she was sipping on.

"I never seen my cousin William go off like that! That's what I told my brother Blaire over the cell phone when I chatted with him earlier" Brenda shouted.

"Exactly sis. That's why I had to drive my husband to the precinct, and then he insisted for me to leave him there when I dropped him off! Blaire didn't like the sound of William *having to fight at all. Plus, Tanya was texting him that they were being followed by several BMW's as they went to pick up Libby"* Delores lifted her voice and spoke.

"It's Georgia Mae she's returned" Tye's mother said.

"Auntie, you are correct. That's why I left my son at his godparents. Tanya called us last night about certain visitors at her shop and their inquiries concerning your son Tye. She also told us about Georgia Mae being back in town. That's why we all went over to his house early this morning knowing of course she would most likely be staying in Tye's house once they reunited. Not even knowing what had happened yesterday afternoon to Cousin Debbie in that deadly Twister on the highway" Delores explained while eating a slice of the fresh baked apple pie.

"Talking about being in the right place at the right time" Jill lifted her voice and spoke.

"Cousin Jill, you are correct. I was like how Auntie is now totally devastated. When Brenda texted me the news about Cousin Debbie, I lost it, right in Tye's house. I hollered and screamed so much my son took the cell phone away from me in Tye's living room and gave it to his father. But Auntie, so did your son Tye when the Chief of police arrived at his house. It was because Libby called him at the exact same time the Chief came into his house. Uncle that name Jamie you just mentioned was your son Tye's only concern in his kitchen earlier this morning. He along with some guy named Larry was partying together at Candice's 30th birthday party and Cousin Jemena overheard their conversation about the work they do at the docks. Cousin Tanya was trying to persuade Tye that he had been terminated since she's been his only mechanic for

years. Cousin Tye's whole disposition had changed when he heard those names way before the shocking news of Debbie's death from Libbie and the Chief of police" Delores explained as she sat comfortably in the sofa eating the fresh baked apple pie.

"It's gambling! That's the problem! Talking about "yeah mom, I'm a card shark. I'm unbeatable! Yeah, Ma, they can't touch me in Poker I'm unstoppable! Mom, I always get the lucky hand." It's all those late night and weekend trips of gambling! Driving around in very expensive cars because you beat somebody in a game. Celebrating a lucky hand. That has been my son's problem since I could remember" Tye's mom yelled out as she stood next to Rebecca in her living room.

"Auntie, you are correct! I may be viewed as a queen in your husband's house, but Georgia Mae is viewed as his queen in your son's house! She has always enjoyed showing off them lucky hands" Delores loudly replied.

"All that gambling that boy did and she never helped" Tye's mother loudly spoke.

"She helped him spend them winnings when they were together that's exactly what she helped Auntie!" Brenda loudly replied.

"Then she wanted to invest my money in some mess. Girl bye! You are no broker! You're a joker! And my son is a fool to be all caught up in mess fooling around with you. Get out of my face with your get rich schemes chic!" Tye's mother loudly spoke.

"What my wife is saying about Tye is that he's a gladiator. I raised him up to be in that frame of mind. Setting goals and

going after them. Winning is your goal. Be a champ! I instilled that drive into my son. But betting valuables and people's personal possessions is a lot more dangerous than shooting hoops with a basketball. My wife talked to him many times about her concern of him playing them cards with certain street type individuals. But his nose has always been opened wide for that street girl Georgia Mae. He wouldn't hear anyone else's advice. Her trying to swindle some of our hard earn money was Just crazy!" Tye's father explained.

"The chic had the nerve to go behind my back after I told her no, to ask my husband to invest our money" Tye's mother loudly explained.

"Wow Aunty, now that's crazy! However, she was always selfish in a lot of her ways" Jill loudly spoke.

"That's why she is slithering around my nephew's house now. And I had never seen my nephew William so angry! Your brother took me by surprise this morning Jill with that left hook right off the patio! Look at it here now. Gladiator, champion mind set. I'm just saying. I even said to myself well damn nephew has you been boxing much!" Rebecca loudly spoke as she chuckled.

"Does pastor know Georgia Mae is back here in town?" Jill softly asked.

"Joshua knows because he is the one that told me earlier. No, Joe doesn't know Georgia Mae is staying with Tye" Tye's mother softly replied.

"With all this street interference in my brother's house today I feel I should be the one to tell him. I owe it to my nephew. I'm very proud of him and his accomplishments as a Reverend. What he has done with his church is phenomenal.

I heard that the live band he brought into the church is just as good as my band, even though I have two of the best singers in town" Bucky said.

"Watch yourself Uncle Bucky don't start tooting your own horn as of yet" Jill said.

"My singers are far better than your tender pipes Jill" Bucky jokingly said.

"With that new band Uncle Bucky, they been chirping on beat better and better" Jills husband jokingly said.

As everyone in the room started laughing the doorbell rang. Rebecca quickly walked over to the front door to open it up for Bishop Joe, Joshua and William who have returned from there walk around the neighborhood.

"The champ is here!" Jills husband yelled out as he lifted his fist up into the air.

Everyone started laughing again. As Bishop Joe, Joshua and William made their way into the living room Bucky rose up off the small sofa and asked his nephew Bishop Joe if he could speak to him privately. The two of them went out the back door onto the backyard patio. Joshua, looking into Tye's mother's sadden puffy eyes instantly he knew what that conversation was going to be about.

Standing outside on his backyard patio along with his nephew pastor Bishop Joe Bucky kept one hand in his pocket and placed his other hand on Joe's shoulder. *"Bishop, I'm proud of what you've done for our family, the community and this state as a leader. Your new band I hear sounds great. I hope it brings into your church the kind of* members you've been asking God for and the type of members that is needed in that church house. But your cousin Tye's house has a returned resident that we know you don't want in your church house. Georgia Mae has come home to play with Tye" Bucky calmly said.

CHAPTER 15

MURDER IN BROAD DAYLIGHT

As the humidity continued to swarm the energetic area of Mobile, Alabama clean-up crews continued working through the heat effortlessly in those areas that were hit hard from the tornado. Even though Williams' longtime friend Diamond was in her own car driving home from work yesterday afternoon when the Tornado came spiraling through Mobile, Alabama she and so many other motorists missed its path of destruction. William had texted Diamond early in the morning about the sad news of his cousin Debbie's fatal car accident due to the deadly twister while he was on his way to his uncle and aunt's house. Even though Diamond and Debbie were not close friends Diamond still felt in some way sorrowfully connected to her very close friend William's pain because of their long-time friendship. Having a feeling of urgency in wanting to help any victims that

were displaced because of the storm as fire safety and
firefighters use their trained methods to the disposal
of debris, Diamond contacted one of her friends who
specialized in equipment setup and labor supervision
for guidance on how she can be of any assistance. Her
friend gave her the name of an organization that was
collecting groceries in a designated site to which she
can contribute. Rushing out of her apartment in shorts
and sneakers Diamond hurried to the elevator to go
around the corner from her apartment complex to the
local neighborhood supermarket. When the elevator
door opened Jamie was standing in the front of the
elevator car and a young dark skin woman was at the
rear of the elevator car. As awkward as that moment was
for Diamond because of her prior acquaintance with
Eric at the docks, she was more committed to the cause
of disaster relief than the recent consistent harassment of
events at her place of resident. Knowing that Jamie and
Eric were close friends themselves she never associated
herself with him. Pushing past her own fears Diamond
stepped onto the elevator car in boldness and spoke.
"Good afternoon" Diamond said boldly. *"Afternoon"*
Jamie and the unidentified woman responded while
Diamond moved her lovely, shaped body to the left
of the elevator pushing the lobby button located on
the elevator landing panel. As the elevator door closed
Diamond staired at the buttons on the elevator landing
panel to avoid any eye contact. Not knowing what had
gone down earlier that day with her best friend William
and Jamie at Tye's parents' house, Diamond did notice

the dark shades Jamie was wearing to hide his eyes from what she thought was the blazing hot sun. Jamie was on his way to the emergency room downtown at the hospital to have his face looked at by a professional physician. Stepping off the elevator first into the apartment complex lobby Diamond continued her state of boldness by leaving everyone in the elevator with her expression of good wishes by turning around and saying *"goodbye have a great day"* with her soft sounding voice. *"You do the same"* the unidentified woman in the rear of the elevator responded back to Diamond. Quickly walking to one of the side exits of the building that led to the parking lot Diamond saw Kareem handling the buffing machine shining the lobby floors. *"Hi Kareem, is it hot enough for you outside"* Diamond asked him as she stood by the buffing machine. *"It's like being trapped inside of a sauna out their Diamond"* Kareem answered with a smile on his face. Diamond noticed how Kareem watched Jamie, and the woman walk out the front lobby doors. Putting her head down, checking inside her purse, making sure she had everything she needed, Diamond felt the urge to say something about Jamie. *"Kareem I never saw that woman before, is she a new tenant"* Diamond asked. Pushing the heavy Buffing machine slowly across that side of the large apartment building lobby floor while flexing his muscles in his short sleeve maintenance uniform shirt Kareem answered, *"who you referring to Jamie's girlfriend she's your neighbor Diamond."*

"Oh, Jamie is his name. I've seen him plenty of times but never knew his name" Diamond responded as she zipped

up her purse. *"Yeah, he's a character Tho! He likes to create a lot of drama with her for the building staff"* Kareem shouted. Diamond looking up at Kareem into his bedroom eyes clearly said, *"so she's been here for a while?"* Stopping the buffing machine from moving across the floor and taking his hands off the handles Kareem responded *"it's her apartment Jamie moved into. Their apartment windows face the back of the building overlooking that whole area, including the parking lot where your car is parked and that side of the road where those crowds of fellas like to stand and hang around"* Kareem loudly explained. Diamond put her hand onto Kareem's muscular shoulder *"Oh, Jamie is affiliated with that crowd"* she softly responded. *"Don't let his gang star theatrics get you fired Kareem"* Diamond continued to say as she turned and hurried out the side lobby door exit. Kareem responded with an outburst of laughter as he continued to shine the apartment complex lobby floors with the buffing machine.

Walking through the parking lot Diamond glanced over to that side of the road Kareem was speaking about but there was no one outside yet it was too early and too much hot sun for anyone to be standing around outside talking and joking on that road in front of the apartment complex parking lot. As Diamond exited her residential parking lot quickly walking to the local grocery store, she also glanced at her shiny brand-new car making sure her ride had no visible marks. The money she received from the insurance company from the accident which Diamond reported to the insurance company that occurred in the parking lot of her residential complex Diamond used towards getting the brand-new car since the auto collision repair shop along with the insurance company agents deemed her other car as a total loss. Devastated but still relieved, Diamond was rewarded the money which she quickly went across town along with her best friend William to another car dealership to get another new car. The impact of the accident and police investigation with the cameras left Diamond with an uneasy feeling around her apartment complex. It was friends like Kareem who works in her building and her neighbor Shane who lives next door that gave her somewhat of a feeling of protection. Though nobody physically attacked her the damage to the roof of that car, broken front windshield and sporadic harassment left her with a nervous feeling when it comes to her safety in her neighborhood. William promised that he would never let anything happen to her and that helped ease Diamonds nerves a whole lot. The men in Williams family are all strong in physique and personality including their sisters which gave Diamond a bold sense of security when she walked her neighborhood streets of Mobile, Alabama.

As the afternoon sun continued to blaze its hot rays over everyone Diamond turned the corner in the humid hot weather a block away from her apartment complex power walking east on the road. A block and a half away from the grocery store that Diamond had chosen for her Tornado relief efforts there was a navy-blue Dodge Charger with tinted windows parked 15 feet in front on her side of the road. Walking quickly

Diamond glanced to the other side of the road to see if someone was standing on the opposite side, but Diamond didn't see anyone. Power walking, her lovely, shaped body up the street quickly approaching the navy-blue charger the trunk slowly opened. Ignoring the sudden opening of the trunk, Diamond kept her pace. As Diamond proceeded to pass the car the driver of the tinted windows rolled his window all the way down while blowing smoke from out of the car. *"You too pretty to be walking alone"* the deep voice spoke.

Diamond begins to speed up her pace ignoring the humidity from the sun and the strange voice from the car.

"Pretty girl you got a beautiful future behind you" the deep voice spoke again as Diamond sped up her pace walking away from the parked navy-blue Dodge Charger.

Crossing the street that led to a neighborhood of houses Diamond glanced quickly to her left to see if anyone else was outside their house or perhaps someone was walking from their house getting into their car. Diamond did see in the distance a police car slowly rolling up the neighborhood of that street which brought a sigh of relief to her shaky uneasy nerves.

When Diamond finally approached the door of the local grocery store, she quickly turned around to see if that Dodge Charger had followed her but the stranger with the deep voice didn't move his parked car from that spot. Entering the very small grocery store Diamond looked around to see if there were any people that looked suspect or resembled the strange driver of that navy-blue charger. Seeing five other adult customers in several of the isles who looked average like herself Diamond walked over to the cashier that was talking on her cell phone from her hands-free headset device. *"Hey Diamond girl I didn't expect to see you this early in the day"* the petite big booty cashier shouted out. As Diamond reached down towards the floor to pick up a shopping basket to assist her in carrying the groceries Diamond replied in loud *tone "Hey big booty Argentina I'm out on missions this afternoon girl."*

"What kind of mission is your quiet, self-outside on in all of this Alabama heat" Argentina politely asked.

"That deadly twister we had yesterday claimed the life of Williams cousin. I feel so bad, big booty Argentina that I made some phone calls, that directed me to an organization where I can contribute and be a blessing to people effected by the tornado helping in disaster relief" Diamond softly explained.

"Are we talking about perishable items or fruits and vegetables?" Argentina politely asked. Diamond opening her small purse she pulled out her Gucci wallet and placed it on the grocery store register counter *"I would like to purchase a little bit of everything because this is definitely for a worthy cause I'm feeling very strong about"* Diamond sweetly replied.

"Diamond I truly sympathize with you and personally I understand. All afternoon I've been on the phone with my new boo while she's at work downtown in an auto repair shop who is going through the very same thing as your compadre

William. Diamond her heart is broken, and I can feel my girlfriend's pain. The shock of the loss of her cousin who was thrown from their car on the highway by the tornadoes funnel cloud in that storm yesterday has her really feeling sick right now" Argentina loudly said.

Diamond quickly put her Gucci wallet back in her purse as two tall white police officers entered the grocery store. The sound of loud talking over their police radios alerted Diamond of the policemen sudden entrance. Argentina shifted her tearful eyes from off Diamond onto the police officer's slow movement in her workplace. *"Good afternoon officers everything ok?"* Argentina loudly asked.

"Yes, mam just patrolling the area" one of the policemen loudly responded.

Diamond turned away from the register while slowly glancing at the police officers and walked toward the juice and beverage isle. Not recognizing their faces for they weren't the police officers that assisted her that night her car had been vandalized in the parking lot, but their presence now still gave Diamond a comfortable sense of security.

"Let me assist you Diamond girl" Argentina loudly said as she quickly came from around the counter following Diamond to the juice isle.

"Thanks so much big booty! I really appreciate this today. However, your new boo is William's cousin Argentina" Diamond quietly whispered.

"No! Really Diamond! Oh my God what a small world we live in. Yeah, I met her at the park three months ago where

I conduct my fitness classes on the weekends. She was there playing basketball along with three of her cousins" Argentina replied as she was placing bottled juices and small packaged drink boxes in Diamonds basket.

"One of those cousins she plays basketball with is the brother to the young lady who was killed by the tornado yesterday" Diamond softly spoke as she slowly begins to walk towards the crackers and chips shelves.

"No way Diamond! My boo is so good to me it hurts my heart to hear her crying today over the phone" Argentina whispered as she begins putting cans of soup in Diamonds basket.

"Argentina, can you please call your girlfriend now for me I'm sure she is with her cousin William. It would really make me feel better to hear his voice and know how my friend is feeling" Diamond quietly asked as she continued putting the boxes of crackers into her basket. Argentina pulled out her cell phone from out of her back pocket while resting one of her hands around Argentina's extra wide hips to dial her girlfriend's cellphone number. Handing the cellphone to Diamond so they could talk Argentina walked away returning to the register counter located at the front of the grocery store where the police officers were posted.

"Hello Tanya, this is Diamond, your cousin Williams childhood friend. My condolences to your family for the loss of your favorite cousin Debbie. I asked my good friend Argentina to hit you up so I can possibly speak with William I have something urgent to share" Diamond clearly spoke on the cell phone while putting fresh bananas into

her basket. As the policemen exited the grocery store big booty Argentina walked up the produce isle to where Diamond was standing with her filled basket of groceries.

"Is that my boo on the phone you are talking too Diamond" Argentina shouted!

"Hi Diamond, pleasure to meet you and thank you for your kind words of sympathy. My cousin is not with me. He's at our uncle's house probably with his father and sister" Tanya replied as Argentina quickly walked over to Diamond putting her left hand onto Diamonds shoulder leaning her ear to listen to their conversation.

"Hi, boo missing you" Argentina softly whispered into the cellphone that was in Diamonds hand.

"I'm terribly sorry Tanya I didn't mean to interrupt you at work" Diamond immediately apologized as she reached for a package of large plastic cups that was on one of the store shelves.

"No need to apologize Diamond you are so sweet. My cousin William is lucky to have a beautiful friend like you. Hi, boo I'm very sad and missing you deeply too. Ladies, I'm here with my cousins at the funeral parlor. We just finished making all the arrangements for our cousin Debbie. The funeral is going to be Sunday afternoon at my cousin Bishop Joe's church. Can't wait to see you ladies there" Tanya softly spoke.

"Boo you know we'll be there for you! Today is just a sad day in Mobile" Argentina loudly replied to her girlfriend Tanya's invite while grabbing the basket of groceries from Diamonds hands *"I think you collected enough items to donate towards the Tornado relief"* Argentina whispered.

"*Diamond, I think you need to make your way over to my uncle's house to be with William*" Tanya loudly suggested over the cellphone. "*Some punk named Jamie was at their house earlier today and my cousins are telling me your buddy William knocked him clear off My uncle's backyard patio. My cousin Brenda told her brother that the left side of Jamie's face has William's fist print engraved in it*" Tanya clearly spoke.

"*What!! Oh No! Tanya is Jamie close to your family*" Diamond loudly asked as the two girls headed back towards the front of the grocery store where an older couple with a baby in stroller had just entered inside the store.

"*No Diamond Jamie's not part of the family! It's crazy! Damn Georgia Mae brought the heat back to Alabama*" Tanya clearly spoke.

"*Tanya, I just saw Jamie on the elevator with his girlfriend who he's staying with around the corner from this store at my apartment complex. Tanya, coincidentally I saw the dark black shades that he was wearing hiding his eyes from the outside world. I was even a little nervous about being on the same elevator with him because their whole crew has been harassing William and I for some time now*" Diamond honestly confessed.

"*What! So, Larry and his boys have been intimidating you and my cousin?*" Tanya asked while Diamond began to take some of the groceries out of the basket and placing the items on the store register counter.

"*Yes, this neighborhood has been changing recently in the last year girl. You see the police just left the store minutes ago. There's been a lot of incidents in this neighborhood that*

160

we didn't have before. Lots of criminal activity around your complex Diamond, especially at night. Which is why, I always work the morning and day shifts" Argentina loudly said as she started ringing up the items that Diamond had taken out of the basket.

"No, the police followed me inside here because of the dark tinted navy-blue Dodge Charger that was parked block and half from the grocery store. The strange deep voice guy that was sitting in the driver seat who I don't know kept complimenting me as he blew smoke from whatever he was smoking. I just picked up my pace and walked faster until I arrived here. I felt so much better when I heard the police officers come inside the store. I saw them patrolling as I crossed the street. They had to have seen me high tailing it away from that car" Diamond loudly explained as she placed the bottle of juices on the register counter from the grocery store basket.

"The cops are probably why he didn't pursue to chase you over to that store" Tanya replied as she listened over the cell phone.

"Where's your car Diamond? I feel safer if you were driving it right now. Plus, there are a lot of grocery items you are purchasing for the disaster relief project. I think you'll need your brand-new car Diamond to make it easier for you to carry all these groceries to be delivered to the place the organization has set up. And like my boo Tanya just told you it would be wise for you to drive over to the uncle's house to see your compadre William" Argentina loudly spoke.

"No, she going to stay right there with you boo until I get there!" Tanya interrupted and shouted over the cell phone. *"We are heading over there now. My cousin Tye is*

here hurting, and he is devastated. But he is also an angry man. Your safety over there, which is important, warrant, us to come. I'm confident my cousin Tye will understand even if it requires kicking some punk's butts trust me in my cousin's condition, he will be glad to do it and release a lot of his anger. We are coming through Diamond to get you" Tanya said as she quickly disconnected the call.

The toddler that was in the stroller of the old couple who were shopping in the frozen section of the grocery store by the ice cream freezer started to cry. As the older woman picked up the crying child out of the stroller into her arms two young males walked into the grocery store laughing together as they headed to the candy section which is located next to the refrigerators in the frozen section of the local grocery store. One of the young ladies who was already in the grocery store shopping walked over from the paper goods isle towards the two young men with her grocery basket in her arms and she joined in on their laughter.

Suddenly a fat man wearing a shirt and jeans carrying a shot gun ran into the store and yelled *"Diamonds are definantly a girl's best friend!"* pointed his shotgun directly at Argentina who was holding in her hand a bottle of the juices that Damond had put on the register counter and fired his gun striking Argentina directly into her forehead. As the blood splattered from her skull that was just hit with the bullets onto the counter and onto Diamond who dropped to the floor screaming the fat man then hurried to the candy isle where the two young men were and fired a shot killing one of the young men who was already down on the floor. The fat gunman quickly exited the grocery store as a white large SUV truck screeching its wheels pulled up in front of the store. As the fat gunman jumped into the front passenger side of the white large SUV truck it sped off down the street screeching its wheels as the white truck rode off into the distance.

The other two store employees who had been in the back stockroom, came quickly running up to the front counter where Diamond was lying on the floor as she continued to scream and yell. One of the employees had his cell phone to his face as he talked to the 911 emergency operator reporting the shooting.

"My baby is shot! Oh God! My baby is shot there is blood Oh God! Help Please" the older woman who was crying yelled out loud as she held the toddler in her arms while lying on the floor leaning up against the cold refrigerator glass door. The older gentleman who had been shopping beside her along with a slim Spanish woman who was athletic built both ran towards the front door of the grocery store screaming *"call the police! Please call for help we need the paramedics my baby shot my baby is shot"* the older gentleman cried out loud as he and the athletic built Spanish woman both exited the grocery store door. A police car that had been patrolling the area pulled up.

"Oh, my God officers help us please my baby is shot" the older gentleman yelled as he ran to the police car. Another police vehicle pulled up to the store from

the opposite direction which happened to be the same policemen that was patrolling the store earlier.

"*A very tall fat man came into the store, started shooting at people before he and a driver sped off! They went that way*" the athletic built Spanish woman yelled to the police officers as she pointed in the direction of the vehicle. As the police officers who had jumped out of their vehicles quickly walked up to the older gentleman one of the store employees came running out the grocery store yelling *"There's people dead in here officers!"* Three of the police officers then moved quickly towards the front door of the grocery store that's when the other store employee who was on his cell phone with 911 emergency operator also came running out the store yelling *"there are bodies everywhere officers!"*

While three of the officers proceeded to enter the grocery store to further investigate the shooting one of police officers remained outside in front of the store with the older gentleman and the Spanish woman trying to gather as much information as he could. Grabbing his radio the police officer listened to them both as they described the shooting.

"*We have a possible multiple homicide at the supermarket location. Witnesses claim the unidentified gunman has left the premises in a large white SUV truck speeding South in the direction of the apartment complex. Witness claims there was only one shooter a large black male. Officers are on site now and we need medical assistance for victims with shot wounds including a child*" the policeman loudly said. Two other police cars pulled up to the grocery store along with an unmarked vehicle.

As the older gentleman escorted the police officers inside the grocery store to where his family was to see his child that had possibly been shot the unmarked vehicle and one of the police cars sped off in the direction of the white SUV truck. Diamond was still lying on the grocery store floor crying because those bullets barely missed her but hit and killed her friend the store employee Argentina right in front of her. One of the police officers kneeled to Diamond to check and see her status. *"Mam, it's OK it's the police we are here. Mam have you been shot, or do you need medical attention"* the kind police officer asked Diamond. Diamond reacted by putting her hands over her ears as she continued to cry. As three more police officers came walking quickly into the store one of the policemen came out from one of the isles walking up to one of the senior police officers with his gun in his hand *"sergeant looks to be a homicide not a robbery. Execution style perhaps the gunman knew the victims. We have two victims shot dead, one female behind the register counter identified as an employee and another male in the isle by the freezers. One male unconscious probably in shock there seems to be no shot wounds, and he is lying directly next to the deceased male shot victim. There is another victim a child who seems to have been shot and is in the arms of female relative in the freezer isle"* the policeman said in a loud clear voice to the senior officer. As the sergeant slowly walked over in the direction of Diamond to speak to the police officer that had kneeled to inquire on her status the EMS quickly rushed inside the grocery store wheeling a stretcher and carrying their medical equipment. One of the police officers directed the EMS workers to the freezer isle where the old couple with the toddler was still lying and both were crying with a plea of help. Another team of EMS entered the store with their stretcher and the Sergeant turned to them *"hey guys there's no active shooter on site just a bloody mess he cowardly left for us deal with! Follow them up that same isle cause there's another male victim unconscious possibly an shock victim positioned directly next to the deceased victim in the refrigerated section"* the Sergeant loudly said. Turning back towards Diamond with a look of concern on his face *"has she been shot as well"* the Sergeant asked the policeman that kneeled by Diamond. *"I'm not sure sir she's not complaining of pain I do see a lot of blood on her clothing but I'm thinking it belonged to the deceased female victim that is lying covered in blood from the gunshot to the female victims head behind the cashier register counter"* the policeman explained.

"What an afternoon of horror" the Sergeant loudly replied as he walked behind the cashier register counter where Argentina's dead body was lying.

As Quincy slowly pulled his BMW up to the block where the local grocery store was that was now filled with flashing lights coming from a dozen police vehicles, unmarked vehicles and several EMS vehicles Tanya started to get nervous rolling down the backseat window as she sat next to her cousin Tye.

"Big booty boo won't pick up her cell phone I don't like

this at all. I'm getting a bad feeling something is not right. Look at all this madness! I've been texting and she's not replying to me" Tanya said while sticking her head out the window to see a clearer view of what was taking place in front of the grocery store. As two female officers started taking the yellow tape and surrounding the store which is now deemed a crime scene.

"That yellow tape in those police officer's hands doesn't look good at all Tanya. If something bad did go down inside that store, the police might be detaining your girlfriend for questioning since that is her place of employment" Tiny replied. *"I'll walk with you to the store cousin to help you locate your girlfriend and Cousin Williams best friend Diamond"* Blaire loudly said as he opened the back door of the BMW because he was seated on the opposite side of his cousin Tye stepping out into the hot sun. Tanya without any hesitation quickly jumped out of the backseat of Quincy's BMW, hurrying up the street in the hot high temperature walking around the police and EMS vehicles in her attempt to get into the store.

"I hope we're not too late guys" Tiny shouted! *"Tanya kept on saying on the ride over here that she had a gut feeling that bum Larry is going to try something on William's friend Diamond. But that's a lot of ambulances for one little person in my opinion. I'm going to hit up Bishop on his cell phone and let him know our status so your parents will not be too worried about us Cousin Tye. This is one horrible day"* Tiny loudly said as Quincy slowly backed his BMW up off the main road bringing his vehicle closer to the curb of the sidewalk.

"It just keeps getting horribly worse as the hours approach" Tye sadly replied as he pulled out his cell phone to check on his niece Libbie to see if she had reached his parents' house.

Though I will honestly admit I'm weak when it comes to Georgia Mae, I'm still aware of her criminal presence. Her dishonest associates and hoodlum family members. The BMW's zipping in front of us this morning as we pulled out of my niece's house already alerted me that she's involved in something. Yes, I'm weak for her passionate affection that she gives to me it makes my penis hard just thinking about her lips all over me. Yes, I miss her when she's not around. Yes, I missed her when she left town. But last night her sudden appearance in my driveway with that brand new white truck didn't fool me one bit. Even my family and their children showing up for breakfast at my house and in my kitchen, I knew they wanted to protect me from her troubled hoodlum associates. I know personally that bum Larry has a devious mind! A quiet block now full of loud sirens and flashing lights from police vehicles in the early afternoon of Mobile, Alabama is that jail bird Larry's handywork.

"Hey Tiny, ask Bishop did my niece arrive yet because she's not responding to any of my texts now either. Seeing my sister's dead body today may have traumatized Libbie. My call just went straight to voicemail so she's not even answering her cell phone and tell him we are on our way to the house with the information regarding Debbie's funeral arrangements" Tye said.

Chapter 16

MISSING HER DEEPLY

As Assemblyman Rogers entered his natural mother's house, he kept his eyes on the house across the road checking the driveway for any cars to see if someone perhaps was home.

"Oh, my baby boy it's so good to see you" his mother said as she threw her elderly arms around his neck. *"I have missed you tremendously boy"* she loudly said. Removing her arms from around his neck she looked into his eyes with tears slowly rolling down her rosy cheeks and grabbed his hands *"you have my deepest sympathy I am truly sorry about your loss son, on today"* his mother softly said unto him.

"I love you mother, and I loved Debbie since I first laid eyes on her beautiful smiling face in high school. How I wish I could see her smile again is my only desire right now mother" Assemblyman Rogers softly replied.

"*You will son in Gods time. Debbie will always be smiling in your heart Assemblyman. Heaven has received another angel, and every day Debbie will let you know she's right with you*" his mother softly whispered as she embraced her son in a hug.

Assemblyman Rogers cell phone started to ring. Listening to the ringtone he knew it wasn't his office assistant. Pulling out his cell phone from his pants pocket he saw on the caller ID that it was Derrick Debbie's favorite cousin calling him. "*Hello, Derrick I'm glad to hear from you*" Assembly Rogers quickly answered his cell phone and said as his mother then turned and walked towards the kitchen area of her house.

"*Cousin, listen, the Chief just called me and told me there was a shooting at the grocery store by Diamonds apartment complex! People are dead and Diamond is one of the victims in the store. He did inform me that he briefed you on some of the investigations they were doing regarding her and my cousin William this morning in his office*" Derrick shouted over the cell phone.

"*D., that's why I'm glad you called me. Because of you I found out a lot of things that I had no idea was taken place around me here in Mobile, Alaba*ma" Assemblyman Rogers loudly replied.

"*Cousin, listen to me, one of the detectives just informed him that Tanya and Cousin Blaire just showed up to the grocery store at the crime scene. Chief was calling me to ask if I had an inquiry of why my cousins would be on the premises of a crime scene when we just lost our cousin Debbie*" Derrick shouted.

"I'm not sure why they are there. I'm not with them D. I only saw them at the precent in the Chief's office and that was because of you which once again I personally thank you" Assemblyman Rogers loudly replied.

"I know you're not with them! I was the one that told him to tell you everything he could concerning that investigation! Are you at my uncle and aunt's house yet Assemblyman Rogers" Derrick loudly asked.

"NO, D. I'm with my own mother" Assemblyman Rogers loudly replied.

"Get to the damn house with Libbie and my uncle now" Derrick hollered as he hung up the phone.

Walking to the kitchen to be with his natural mother Assemblyman Rogers put away his cell phone back into his pants pocket calmly ignoring the urgent phone call from Debbie's favorite cousin Derrick.

"Mother the house looks really clean have you hired new help?" Assemblyman Rogers politely asked.

"Believe it or not my grandchildren pitch in on weekends and help out your older sister and very handsome black brother-in-law in cleaning my house from top to bottom" his mother replied.

"We are now called African Americans mother if you have been informed" Assemblyman Rogers sarcastically said as he pulled out a chair from under the kitchen table to sit down in.

"They were called African Americans when I laid down in my queen size bed and we created you" his mother sarcastically replied as she scooped the chocolate ice cream out of the carton and placing the scoop into a

bowl. *"We all love and miss you around here very much son"* his mother continued to say. *"Is everything else o.k. son? Did something from that phone call you just received trouble you"* his mother softly asked as she took a spoon out from the dish rack located by the sink.

"Mother the Chief wants me to be with Debbie's parents as we speak. But I also know him a little too well" Assemblyman Rogers loudly spoke as his mother put the bowl of chocolate ice cream in front of him. Quickly getting up from the chair at the table in the kitchen the Assemblyman walked towards the first-floor bathroom to wash his hands. The doorbell rang twice then the sound of keys started unlocking the front door of his mother's house. As Assemblyman Rogers slowly walked out of the first-floor bathroom his older sister Sally came in quickly through the front door jingling a set of keys. *"Little bro. oh God it is so good to see you"* Sally softly said running towards Assemblyman Rogers as she gave him a big hug. *"I'm truly sorry to hear about the loss of your wife Debbie"* she continued to say.

"Guess I'm thankful our brother Waley told you Sally. It just happened so suddenly yesterday, Sally! When Debbie didn't call me last night, I automatically knew something was wrong. She was not even home when I arrived. She didn't respond to any of my texts. I kept looking at the clock checking the time to see how the hour kept on getting later but then I remembered sometimes she would meet up with her cousin and they would hang out together at one of his late-night events. Then her cousin Derrick finally called me after he went downtown to the morgue to confirm that it was her body

the authorities had found in the woods after the Tornado came through and ejected her from the car that she was driving on the highway." Assemblyman Rogers loudly spoke as tears began to fall down his cheeks. Sally grabbed him again in an even tighter hug as their mother slowly entered the hallway.

"What a tragedy son. Such a young vibrant innocent girl whose life was taken from her because of global warming. Mother nature's fury has no exceptions and there are no excuses for her treacherous destructive behavior. However, heaven's golden gates of unconditional love and mercy have enough room for such a beautiful, delightful heart like Debbie. Your wife is in a far better place today son" his mother calmly said as she leaned against the wall of her house.

"It's o.k. little bro. your family is here for you now" Sally said as she continued hugging her brother.

"You both come on into this kitchen and eat some cool refreshing chocolate ice cream because I know this heat were experiencing today from the warm temperature has, everyone hot and uncomfortable" their mother loudly spoke as she walked back into her kitchen.

Walking into the kitchen of the mother's 3 story house together they all sat around the kitchen table.

"I can understand protocol for I am a professional government employee so notifying Debbie's parents is justifiable they are next of kin. However, it was her favorite cousin that eased some of my burden when I didn't hear from Debbie at all last night. Her favorite cousin Derrick called, and he informed me of what had happened to her. Not Chief Reginald! Who's supposed to be my friend. That bothers me even now more

173

than it did earlier after that phone call that I just received from Derrick urging me to be with Debbie's parents I assume to help protect our daughter Libbie after a grocery store shooting which occurred a little while ago. All this criminal mess that is now escalating around me, how could Chief Reginald not consider my worries and concern that I had over the possible missing of my wife last night. Mother I still haven't seen her body yet on today and look what time it is" Assemblyman Rogers screamed out as he slammed the spoon on the kitchen table. *"I miss the love of my life. Why can't anyone understand that I loved her with all my heart. I just want to see Debbie's face again I have never been this cold towards my wife or my family"* Assembly Rogers shouted as he dropped his head down towards his chest and cried. Sally quickly jumped up out her chair running over to the kitchen cabinets pulling out a roll of paper towel for Assemblyman Rogers to wipe the tears that fell from his face.

"This is why our brother Walley called me because he saw the pain that you are currently feeling in your eyes. He listened to you with his heart, and Walley is very concerned about your well-being little bro." Sally quietly spoke.

"Have you spoken to her parents anytime today son" Assemblyman Rogers mother quietly asked as she sipped on a cold glass of homemade iced tea.

"Mother they sent their only son Tye to identify the body this morning. We were all in Chief Reginald's office together, including Libbie along with a few deputies. Some of their nephews traveled downtown to the precinct along with Tye. I always knew Tye's feelings for me were not brotherly because

of his respect for Libbie's father who hopefully will return from his military service on tonight to be there for his daughter Libbie" Assemblyman Rogers replied as he took a piece of the paper towel that Sally had handed him and begin wiping his face from the tears that had fallen from his eyes. Assemblyman Rogers then picked up the large silver spoon that was next to the bowl of chocolate ice cream and he started eating at his natural mother's table. *"I know Derrick is only looking out for me and I love him like my wife always did but I'm not sure if he's very much aware of his uncle Bucky's addiction to playing poker. I know the family is familiar with Tye's gambling habits, but I don't think they're aware of Bucky's love for the game."* Assemblyman Rogers said while licking the chocolate ice cream from off the spoon.

"You *just mentioned there was a shooting at a store that prompt him to call you. Do you think whatever took place there involved his uncle?"* Sally quietly asked.

"I personally feel his uncle's hand may not be as lucky as his nephew Debbie's big brother Tye's hand has always been down here in Mobile, Alabama" Assemblyman Rogers replied as he stood up walking over to the Television switching it on to watch the local news.

Chapter 17

CAME TO PICKUP DIAMOND

Sirens filled the hot humid atmosphere as the street surrounding the grocery store started to get even more crowded with more police vehicles, another ambulance, police vans, crime unit trucks, Crime Scene Response Unit walking around with clip boards, medical examiners, coroners' vans and more unmarked vehicles. Tiny had his eye on one unmarked vehicle when it pulled up because that same tall grey-haired gentleman wearing blue jeans and a short-sleeved shirt with a badge around his neck had stepped out among all the traffic of local authorities.

"Guys that tall salt pepper haired gentleman walking to the right headed towards the grocery store is the same detective that was on the Chief's floor when Tye was in the office with those deputies. He was also at the hospital before we rushed downstairs in the elevator to pick Tye up off the floor" Tiny

loudly spoke as he communicated by text to Joshua of their current location.

"Look at the situation here. As you can see the coroner's van is on the scene this is not looking good now there must be some concern from the police department of our involvement somehow because we are here at what appears to be a crime scene as well" Quincy replied.

As the helicopter hovered circling the area a news van pulled up. Unable to get into the street of where the actual grocery store was located the camera man and anchorwoman quickly jumped out of the van rushing towards the now official crime scene. Another news van pulled alongside Quincy's vehicle and that media team hurried out of their vehicle rushing down the street trying to get as close as possible to the crime scene. One of the EMS trucks which was one of the first team to respond on the scene was now loudly making its way back up the street carrying one of the young male victims to the hospital. It was reported from an eyewitness that he had passed out when the gunman had twice fatally shot his young male friend that was in the candy isle next to him. The female that had been laughing with them in the candy isle was being counseled by crime unit investigators who were now on the scene she had escaped unharmed. The toddler that was with the old couple had been hit with bullet fragments from the gunman's shotgun which had caused the bleeding. The toddler was being treated by EMS paramedics. Diamond was still hysterically crying, now seated in the EMS stair chair as she was in a state of shock but in the care of other medical professional teams that had arrived on the scene. Because Tanya nor Blaire were next of kin, direct relatives to anyone that was being contained in the grocery store by the police and investigative units, they were not allowed to pass the yellow tape which was set up directly outside the store. Frustrated as they stood outside the grocery store because her girlfriend Argentina was not responding to any of Tanya's emergency text. None of the police officers or detectives that was canvasing the street was giving her any information about what really had happened inside the grocery store where her girlfriend had faithfully worked. Angry and upset because Tanya watched two stretchers exit the grocery store. Her boo was lying on neither of the stretchers, she then started to harass the police officers that were posted outside the grocery store as she noticed the medical examiners from the coroner's van walk slowly inside the store. As the second ambulance finally made its way back up the street blaring its loud siren Tanya then made her way towards the news cameras that had set themselves up near the large window of the store outside of the yellow tape with her cousin Blaire marching right behind her. As the news anchorwoman spoke with the lieutenant on the scene Tanya stood up close to the camera man attempting to ease drop so that she could hear what had happened. As the other news anchorman from the other channel joined in on the conversation Tanya overheard that channel news anchorman say that it was confirmed a female employee had been fatally shot. Tanya ran up to the high-ranking police officer yelling, *"Argentina! Are you talking about my Argentina? Is that the employee"* she loudly asked.

"Mam, please we need you to step back and clear this area now" another police officer loudly shouted with his hands extended out towards Tanya and Blaire.

"Is Argentina the female you are talking about is all we need to know officers" Blaire shouted as he moved in towards the other police officer. The Lieutenant stopped talking to the news media and addressed them politely. *"Are you related to her"* the Lieutenant asked.

"That's her wife! That is why we are here! Officer, we have been calling and calling her with no response. Not even a text. That's not like Argentina and nobody is giving us an answer" Blaire loudly replied.

The Lieutenant stuck his fingers up in the air signaling for two of the detectives who were posted in front of the store to come over to him. One of the detectives was the tall grey-haired gentleman that Tiny had been seeing now all day. Whispering something to them the detectives walked over to Tanya and slowly ushered her and Blaire inside the grocery store where Diamond was seated.

"I believe she's been waiting for you guys" the other detective said as they approached Diamond.

"Are you Diamond?" Tanya loudly asked.

"Yes" Diamond softly replied as her hands were still shaking.

"Diamond where's my big booty boo" Tanya frantically asked.

Diamond pointed to the other store employee who was nervously standing there with his hands on his head looking around at the crowd of local law enforcement inside the store. He was the store manager and in the event of an emergency he was trained to call 911, which he did. They were waiting for the store owner to arrive since the authorities had notified her. Turning to the store manager Tanya shouted, *"Where is Argentina?"* The store manager whose name is Freddy pointed to the cashier register where a white sheet covering perhaps a body was sticking out on the floor from behind the counter. Without hesitation Tanya ran over to the sheet as three officers tried to stop her by grabbing Tanya as she lifted the sheet only to see the bloody disfigured face of her deceased girlfriend Argentina, forcibly pulling her back away from the cold dead body so she wouldn't contaminate the crime scene with her prints or DNA any further. The two detectives who brought them inside the store for Diamond because during questioning by investigators Diamond informed the homicide detectives that her main reason for still being at the store after she made the purchase was that she was waiting for her ride which had been them. It was also so the homicide detectives could observe and get a full scope of the relations with the victims.

Blaire quickly grabbed his cell phone from out of his front pocket calling Tiny to tell him what they just discovered and a full update of the actual murder scene inside the store. As Tanya wrestled with the police officers for a minute angry and upset because she just saw her girlfriends lifeless body Tanya then dropped to her knees as Blaire moved in quickly grabbing his cousin with one arm and signaling for Diamond to arise out of the EMS chair to assist him in taking Tanya back outside of the store towards the car. Seeing how aggressive and upsetting the situation was making Tanya, the tall grey-haired detective encouraged Blaire to remove her from the store immediately.

"I must get you to your parents' house Cousin Tye. Looking at what time of the day it is I know your mother is in dire need of seeing her pride and joy" Quincy said while texting his wife Jimena to inform her of the shooting and for Jimena to tune into the local news so she could get a better understanding of what had occurred at the grocery store.

"Blaire just said over the phone it's a blood bath inside, so we don't need to be out here either. My gut feeling also tells me as a family we are already on the detectives' list. Hopefully our cousins are on the way back up the street to the car so we can get out of here" Tiny clearly spoke as he continued texting Bishop the update with his cell phone.

"Today has not shown our family any kindness whatsoever it has surely not been a good day for us" Quincy replied.

I've always been a good son to my pops. I loved my grandfather like I was his son, and I enjoyed watching the interaction between the two of them. I never competed with my sister Debbie for my pops attention because the smile she kept on her face was evident from both my parents' attention they lovingly gave to my sister. The family interaction between my grandfather and my pops growing up is what kept me doing the right thing when it came to pleasing my pops. Mainly it was winning a game on the basketball court. Mastering the kitchen and becoming a great chef, which I felt gave our grandfather honor. Our name is respected due to hard work. Labor and sweat have given our family name validity. Not murder, violence and brutality. I admit I have a real tender soft spot for Georgia Mae but her family's way of proving themselves is not in my eye anymore the respectful way of doing things. Right now, I don't feel proud she's even back in my life. I'm hurting in a way I've never hurt before. This loss is very painful. I just lost my baby sister, my friend, my niece's mom and I'm not even seeing the respect for my loss. Now from what my tearing eyes is seeing is everyone around me is in as much pain as I am, and Georgia Mae really thinks her hourglass figure is going to be able to get over on me. Her family involvement sickens me today even if it had nothing to do with my baby sister Debbie's death.

Rolling down the backseat window allowing the hot humid air to now invade my cousin Quincy's car I stuck my head out of the window to see if I could see Blaire or Tanya amidst the crowd of police officers in the street of the grocery store. *"I think I see Blaire's shirt slowly walking this way"* I yelled. Cousin Tiny stepped out of Quincy's BMW onto the sidewalk to get a better view of the crowded street that was full of local authorities and news media. *"YUP, that's them walking this way now"* Tiny loudly replied. *"Listen Tye, Bishop Joe said your niece has not arrived yet. This may be the wrong time to share this with you, but I must let you know what took place at your parents' house this morning while we were on route to the police station. Jamie showed up to the house and Cousin William apparently started beating on the guy. That's why Blaire quickly made his way downtown to the precent to hook up with us."* Tiny said to his cousin Tye as he walked towards the back of Quincy's BMW sticking his head into the vehicle's back window looking directly at him.

CHAPTER 18

THE FAMILY BUSINESS

After making a quick stop at Robin Libbie's bestie's house to pick up her travel bag which she had already packed before leaving her house earlier that morning so she can stay with Libbie for a couple of days Georgia Mae finally made it to Tye's parents' house. Slowly pulling up to their house, Georgia Mae was shocked that she didn't see Quincy's BMW parked in their driveway. Looking down at her Cartier watch on her arm to check the time for she estimated that the fellas should have been done by now with making the final arrangements for Debbie's body with the funeral Director. As Joshua, Lisa and Bishop Joe came out of Tye's parents, house together Georgia Mae's cell phone started to ring. Hoping that it was Tye calling to check on her, or give her an update on their status Georgia

Mae quickly answered her cell phone without checking the caller ID.

"Georgia, oh my God! Ron was just shot and killed at the grocery store and his friend Jermaine is in critical condition. He's been transported to the hospital" the caller on the phone had yelled out.

"What Orange oh God no! Who shot my nephew Orange?" Georgia Mae loudly replied.

"We don't know yet. I just received the call from the homicide detectives who have my son's wallet and ID in their possession. I'm on my way to the grocery store now. I spoke to Jermaine's Godmother who is on the route to the hospital. They killed my baby Georgia my man" Orange yelled as she hung up the phone and disconnected the phone call. Georgia Mae dropped the cell phone onto her lap and started hitting the steering wheel in anger with her soft hands.

"Ms. Georgia Mae are you okay?" Robin softly asked.

"No, I'm not Robin! Someone just murdered my nephew in a grocery store" Georgia Mae loudly replied. "To be perfectly honest with you Robin I had a bad feeling about the watch party this morning outside of Tye's driveway. I saw the BMW's circling around us from the time we left Tye's house until that detour off the highway in that part of town where the Tornado must have touched down and did most of its damage. The police presence in Tye's driveway this morning, even the deputy vehicles parked around my truck must have alarmed them idiots! Now another young man is clinging to his life in the hospital that was with my

nephew who has probably also been shot. I must get to my sister-in-law Orange right now. Robin, please help take Libbie into her grandparents' house. I will see you young ladies later." Georgia Mae loudly spoke.

"The BMW's presence in front of my uncle's driveway must have alarmed the undercover police officers in the parking lot of the hospital where my mother's body is now laying lady" Libbie loudly shouted in anger as she jumped out of the large Suburban truck leaving the door open and quickly ran into the arms of her older cousin Bishop Joe who was standing in the house doorway. Robin slowly hoped out of the truck walking to the trunk grabbing her travel bag quickly walking back she closed the back door before going back over to the passenger side of Georgia Mae's vehicle where she had been sitting *"I'm truly sorry about the loss of your nephew Ms. Georgia Mae no one deserves to die by the hands of a gunman. I hope they catch the coward who took it upon themself to end an innocent life of a black man. You are very pretty. I'm sure your nephew was very handsome. Thank you for taking me to my house to pick up my things. Once again, my condolences to you and your brother Ms. Georgia Mae for the tragic death of his son"* Robin softly spoke as she closed the Suburban trucks door. Making her way to the front door to be with her best friend Libbie and Debbie's immediate family, Robin observed the parcel delivery truck parked three houses down. Walking up to the pastor as Robin placed her hand into Libbie's hand so they could hold hands she turned around again to stare at the parked parcel delivery truck. *"Afternoon everyone Ms. Georgia Mae has*

a family emergency that is why she couldn't stay. If you don't mind, may I ask you all how long that parcel delivery truck has been parked on this block?" Robin inquisitively asked.

"It was parked in front of that same house when we arrived back a little while ago" Joshua answered as he opened the house door for everyone to return inside the house.

Chapter 19

THE SUSPICIOUS NEIGHBOR

Finishing up the bowl of delicious cold chocolate ice cream Assemblyman Rogers reached into his pants pocket to pull out his cell phone. After seeing the breaking news story on the fatal shooting which took place at the grocery store Assemblyman Rogers started thinking about the message that his longtime school friend and assistant Kyle retrieved for him earlier in the name of Keith. Remembering the silver Hyundai with Kentucky license plate parked in the lot at his older brother's job that mysteriously disappeared from the docks Assemblyman Rogers called Mama Whitehead again to see if she had heard from her son Libbie's father.

"Mama Whitehead, have you watched the news this afternoon" Assemblyman Rogers asked as she softly answered the phone call.

"Yes, I have, you were correct Assemblyman; the trash is

outside and its stinking! I finally spoke to my son, and he'll be home as soon as he can. How's Libbie doing" Mama Whitehead softly responded.

"I was getting ready to call her now. I'll let her know I spoke with you and that her father is on his way home" Assemblyman Rogers replied as they ended the call. Quickly getting out of the chair, walking over to his mother's living room window to observe the house driveway directly across the street checking again to see if anyone had arrived home yet. He slowly pulled back the beautiful blinds.

"Is everything ok little bro." Sally asked as she came walking behind him into the living room.

"The Brady's that live across the street do they still own their jewelry store business" Assemblyman Rogers asked.

"As far I know they still do. Why what's bothering you about them" Sally asked as she located a comfortable spot to sit on her mother's sofa.

"Exactly sis.! As far back as I can remember their family business flourished. Growing up we all knew they had quite a bit of money. Even with bad investments, which sometimes does happen in business, I personally don't think it would have sunk their Jewelry business entirely because of the longevity of its operation here in Mobile, Alabama. Even the Brady children which are now young adults like us wouldn't be struggling. As a matter of fact, they should have benefited greatly or be in the business themselves trying to make a fortune" Assemblyman Rogers loudly spoke as he slowly backed away from the window.

"I agree that family has been in the jewels business ever

since I can remember. But little bro. why is that any of your concern" Sally Politely asked as their mother slowly entered the living room.

"Sally, that orange and yellow colored slogan of theirs has been on display down here in Alabama ever since I can remember. And today I observed a vehicle with that slogan on its bumper parked in the lot at our brother's job. Listening to Wally earlier with some of his staff troubles I'm really wondering why there would be a honey blond hair dimpled undercover officer that I personally met today posted in our brother's office. Why are detectives secretly investigating Wally?" Assemblyman Rogers loudly replied sitting down on one of the living room chairs *"Don't the Brady's have a beautiful blond-haired daughter?"* Assemblyman Rogers asked.

"She never spoke to me little bro. Matter of fact the whole family never really associated with any of us too much" Sally quickly replied.

"Yes, they do son. She drives a red pickup truck. But if anyone asks me, she's a rough little thing. If it serves me correctly, I do believe she's into auto racing with them wild guys down at the mud parks. She always has a lot of guy friends around for her to be such a pretty blond" his natural mother loudly responded.

"I know I'm not a law enforcement officer, but I do have my suspicions concerning your neighbors' children's money laundering hands on my brothers docks mother" Assemblyman Rogers loudly said.

CHAPTER 20

THE FAMILY DISCUSSION

Sitting down in the comfortable chair inside Tye's parents' large living room as the cool air blowing from the central air system vents inside their spacious house Robin felt somewhat relieved looking at all of Libbie's mom's immediate family members that lovingly came together on such a sad occasion. As Rebecca handed Robin a small plate with a slice of warm baked apple and a scoop of vanilla ice cream on top Jill's husband also handed Robin a chilled glass of freshly squeezed lemonade from the kitchen.

"Robin why does that Parcel delivery truck parked in front my uncles' neighbor's house concern you. Are you familiar with that driver?" Bishop Joe in a clear tone politely asked.

"Here we go again talking about this Parcel delivery driver this afternoon" Willie James loudly shouted. *"Nephew don't*

let my brother's paranoia get your Holy collar all nervous and bothered" Willie James continued to say.

"You see Georgia Mae didn't come inside the house with us Uncle Willie and the look on Robins face did display a look of concern as she walked away from that giant white truck" Lisa replied.

As Libbie gently lifted her head up from off her crying grandmothers' bosom, she turned to her great uncle Bucky and asked to use his cell phone to call Assemblyman Rogers apparently her cell phone battery had died. Brenda quickly leaped up from out of her seat and handed her cousin Libbie her cell phone to make the call to Assemblyman Rogers.

"I'm very thankful that Ms. Georgia Mae gave us a lift here to this house and she also drove us to my house so I can have a change of clothes. She is a very pretty woman. That's very sad what just happened to her young family member being shot and killed at the grocery store a little while ago" Robin said as she licked the ice cream off the spoon.

"That is where Tye and our cousins are now." Joshua shouted out! *"Tiny has been texting Bishop apparently, Cousin Tanya knows someone that was somehow involved in the shooting. He said they're swarmed with law enforcement agents all around them and they will be over here at the house as soon as they can"* Joshua continued as he sat next to Robin.

"Wasn't we just talking about this you'll. That lady isn't nothing but trouble!" Brenda shouted as she crossed her thick legs sitting back in the chair.

"I'm so glad my husband is now with Cousin Tye he

doesn't need this kind of drama around him. Especially on today of all days. Like I said from this morning as we were in Cousin Tye's kitchen you can see he is already emotionally upset from the shocking news of what happened to Debbie in that tornado yesterday" Delores loudly responded.

"They had to pick my uncle Tye up from off the floor as we viewed mom's body." Libbie shouted out! *"I never saw my uncle break down like that. Cousin Blaire also helped that Georgia Mae lady carry me back to the morgue's elevators because I couldn't contain myself either. You are right he was a great help today"* Libbie weepingly said as she started to dial Assemblyman Rogers cell phone number. Bucky slowly stood up from off the sofa walking over to Libbie *"That's your dad Assemblyman Rogers on the phone? Let me talk with him Libbie"* Bucky said as he reached for Brenda's cell phone out of Libbie's hand.

"Hey there nephew its Bucky and we are all here at my brother's house along with your beautiful daughter Libbie. Listen man, we are terribly sorry for your loss on today. There are no words that can express what our hearts are truly feeling right now. My brother and sister are devastated Assemblyman. Such a tragic way of death. Debbie was a beautiful young lady. My nieces smile could light up the room. Her charming glow would melt your heart which she had ever since I first laid eyes on her in the maternity ward when my niece Debbie was born. Not only was she pretty but Debbie was extremely smart. Assemblyman we all love you and feel the pain of her absence with us this afternoon" Bucky said as he walked towards the front door to take the remainder of the call outside of Tye's parent's house. Closing the front dooby

behind him Bucky walked towards the driveway by the front lawn. *"Assemblyman we are so blessed that Debbie brought you into our family and you have shown nothing but respect demonstrating nothing but absolute love for your family. Don't shy away from us now. We have always accepted you as Debbie wanted us to. My brother and my sister need you to remain an active part of their lives now, the same as you did before. I'm sure my nephew Tye is going through a difficult time and in my opinion, his behavior will probably get worse before it gets even better but don't let, you'll distant relationship distance you from your father and mother-in-law."* Bucky clearly said as he continued strolling down the driveway talking on his niece Brenda's cell phone.

"I love you Uncle Bucky, truly love you man. Thanks for the expression of sympathy. I always loved Debbie and did my best to make her happy Uncle Bucky" Assemblyman Rogers clearly spoke as the tears started to slowly fall again from his eyes as he, his older sister Sally and his natural mother sat in the living room together. "I'm a hard-working man and did my hardest to exemplify good work ethics in front of Libbie. I know I could never replace her father, who is also active in her life, but I still showed fatherly love to Libbie even now. Bucky, I'm glad you'll called me because I just hung up the phone with mama Whitehead who informed me her son will be home as soon as possible." Assemblyman Rogers continued to say clearly.

"That's good news man! From what seems to be going down around town here today I feel her father's presence can be beneficial to us all." Bucky said as he exited the driveway

194

and slowly started strolling down the street in the direction of the parked Parcel delivery truck.

"Yes, Uncle there has been a lot going on seems to me it's been going down for a while all around me and I was unaware until this morning in a meeting in the Chief's office" Assemblyman Rogers lifted his voice and explained.

"Libbie's adorable little friend who is here with her just informed all of us that Georgia Mae's nephew was killed in the grocery store a little while ago" Bucky said as he continued slowly walking up the street towards the Parcel delivery truck.

"Your nephew Derrick just called me to inform me that your other nephew Wiliam's friend Diamond was in the store when the gunman opened fire as well. But watching the breaking news report some minutes ago the anchorwoman said it was only two people that was shot and killed. So, the other person killed must have been the female employee they mentioned not your nephew's Diamond" Assemblyman Rogers clearly said while wiping his check off from the watery tear with his hand.

"She was there too! Sheesh man. William was just telling us about the love he has for his Diamond. This day is turning out to be very bad nephew" Bucky said as he observed the house across the street from where he was standing staring at the parked parcel delivery van out in front.

"Georgia Mae's nephew being killed may have just turned everything bad to even worse for us all Uncle Bucky" Assemblyman Rogers loudly said.

"That's why I took the cell phone from Libbie to speak with you Assemblyman because there have been unwelcomed *visitors showing up at the house here all day one of them as soon as I arrived who Diamonds friend William put his hands on while my brothers both tried to attack him"* Bucky said.

"Oh God! Oh No! Cousin Tye doesn't need any of this additional mess added onto his already stress" Assemblyman Rogers replied.

"I'm going to let you go so you can get back to handling things nephew I know your plate is probably full now. Be glad to see you, Assemblyman Rogers whenever you get enough strength to come around and say hi to us" Bucky said as they ended the call, and he quickly turned around to walk back towards Tye's parents' house.

"Wow mother as if this day couldn't have gotten any worse. One of the victims in that grocery shooting is blood related to a notorious crime family down here in Mobile Alabama that is connected to Debbie's older brother Tye. It's starting to sound like it's more than revenge" Assemblyman Rogers loudly said to his mother as they sat in the cool air-conditioned living room.

"So that's why that phone of yours keeps on ringing son" Assemblyman Rogers mother loudly responded.

"Speaking of phone calls, my personal assistant Kyle retrieved a message to me from someone who we don't know. That is why I'm now convinced a lot of what is happening to Debbie's family today involves her uncle Bucky who I was just speaking with. The culprits are after something valuable, and he didn't let me speak to my daughter Libbie because the messages they are sending him is probably starting to make Bucky nervous because he knows the value of whatever it is they are after" Assemblyman Rogers said as he scrolled

through his contact list on his cell phone to call his brother-in-law Tye.

"I'm sure the villain didn't start sending messages today little bro. Especially if there are agents on our brother Wally's job" Sally loudly replied.

"That was why I didn't go over to Debbie's parents' house as was suggested for me to go. Like I said I personally know Chief Reginald. The information he shared with me was revealing but it would be vital to my brother-in-law! My reasons for conducting my own little investigation today. Yes, I love Debbie with all my heart, but I love my brothers more than they ever expected. My brothers are my family's heart" Assemblyman Rogers loudly said as he dialed Tye's cell phone.

"Hey Tye, I'm so glad you answered your cell phone man" Assemblyman Rogers calmly said as he stood up slowly walking over to his mother's large living room window again.

"I knew it was you I saved your number. Man, it's Debbie. Her body looked badly bruised from the accident. I couldn't contain myself man. Today is just unbelievable. I never would have imagined my baby sister would be gone before me. Man, I know you miss her too, but I've known Debbie her whole life and this can't really be happening" Tye clearly said to Assemblyman Rogers as he opened the back door of Quincy's BMW.

"Tye this is difficult on both of us. Honestly, I just want to see Debbie smile at me again. I fell in love with her smile in high school and even today I still yearn for that same smile. However, Tye I know where you are at right now and I know

what happened in that grocery store" Assemblyman Rogers loudly spoke over the cell phone.

"Hey, man, are you at my parents' house with Libbie right now" Tye loudly asked purposely cutting Assemblyman Rogers off by changing the direction of the telephone conversation.

"Tye please listen to me clearly. Derrick called me because the detectives who are watching you informed him that Tanya, Blaire and you are out there now at the crime site. I even know that you're upset about what went down at your parents' house concerning William, but Diamond is not the only victim in the grocery store. Your girlfriend Georgia Mae's nephew is one of victims the gunman shot and killed inside that grocery store. Libbie is safe at your parents' house now. I'm safe at my own parent's house now. But in the eyes of those cops that are surrounding you none of us are safe. That's why Chief Reginald detained me when you walked out of his office. Tye, I think who Larry is working for probably wants all your uncle Bucky's family dead" Assemblyman Rogers said as Tye remained silent and then angrily hung up the cell phone call on him.

"I didn't think he would take hearing that well. Tye hanging the phone call up on me Sally is understandable. That is the emotional anger what his uncle was just warning me that I may encounter with him. But I had to let my brother know who the big deal really is" Assemblyman Rogers calmy said as he walked back over to the chair and sat down in the living room of his natural mother's large house along with his older sister Sally who was comfortably sitting on the sofa.

CHAPTER 21

CHAOS IN FRONT OF THE GROCERY STORE

After angrily hanging up the phone on Assemblyman Rogers Tye threw his cell phone directly through the opened back window and then angrily started hitting the roof of Quincy's BMW with his big hands. His cousin Quincy quickly jumped out of the driver seat of the car even though Tye is much taller than Quincy, he didn't want Tye to make a serious dent in the aluminum roof of his car. Tiny quickly ran around the car placing himself in front of Tye's tall athletic muscular body in a defense position as if they were on the basketball court trying to block the player from getting close to the hoop to score a point by making a shot. Tye staringly looked at his cousin Tiny and then backed off not only because of the brotherly type love he had towards his first cousin, but they've been ball players and playing together since they were kids.

"What happened now Cousin Tye" Quincy loudly asked.

"One of the dead victims in that grocery store happens to be Georgia Mae's nephew!" Tye shouted.

"Oh no! Okay we got to get you out of here now Cousin Tye! I told you that the detective has been tailing us since the meeting this morning at the Chief's office" Tiny said as he leaned up against Quincy's BMW.

"That's what Assemblyman Rogers was just warning me about over the cell phone. This situation here is why chief Reginald kept him in his office this morning" Tye loudly replied.

"Well, it's now late afternoon and we are parked here at a murder scene which means homicide detectives are not only investigating but they are out here in this hot sun working with crime units to find the killer or suspects. I'm walking over to the store now to get Blaire and Tanya so I can drive us out of here" Quincy said as he proceeded to walk towards the store. As Quincy walked around a law enforcement SUV that was parked diagonal on the street, he saw his cousin Blaire consoling Tanya who was throwing her hands up hysterically in front of two police officers. Speedily turning back towards his BMW Quincy yelled to Tiny and Tye that their cousin Tanya was having some kind of altercation with the cops. All three of the cousins hurried down the street as fast as they could towards Blaire, Tanya and Diamond to see what really happened. Approaching the crime scene Tiny observed

that tall grey-haired detective talking to Blaire and a young woman. Tanya was still acting aggressive towards the police like the way her cousin Tye was acting in the kitchen as his niece unfolded the bad news of what had recently happened to her mother over the cell phone. Tiny quickly grabbed Quincy stopping him from interfering with the commotion in front of the grocery store. Allowing Tye to jog ahead of them to assist his cousin Tanya as she released her anger and frustration out at the cops. As the news anchorman who was still posted outside in front of the small local grocery store along with his camera man begin filming clips of the fiasco Tye immediately snatched Tanya's arm pulling her closer to him as Tye attempted to give her a hug. *"Her girlfriend was a victim, Quincy. She's dead!"* Tiny loudly shouted out. *"You were correct cousin this day got a whole lot worse"* Tiny loudly said as he stopped walking familiar with both his cousin's behavior patterns and if anyone had a clue of what would set both off in an angry response like what is being displayed it would be their cousin Tiny. Blaire started walking away from the detective along with Diamond towards Tiny and Quincy introducing them to Diamond as he explained everything that had occurred inside the small local grocery store. The news anchorman ran up to them trying to catch an eyewitness report. Tye didn't need an explanation because he remembered the conversation he and Tanya had over the phone yesterday evening when Georgia Mae was in the bathroom at his house. Assuming that the visit to her shop was a warning of these events that would even affect her. Now that Tiny shared the news with him regarding the commotion with his cousin William at his parent's house Tye automatically knew the loss of his cousin Tanya's girlfriend's shot up bloody body in that small local grocery store was her only reason for acting erratic to this event. Quickly with his arm around his cousin's neck, Tye escorted Tanya back up the street in the direction towards Quincy's BMW. Tye motioned to the fellas and Diamond to speedily follow him back up the street. As they proceeded to follow Tiny called Bishop Joe's cell phone not only to briefly explain to him a few minor details of who had been shot and killed inside the grocery store but for Bishop Joe to inform their cousin William of why Diamond would be returning with them to Tye's parents' house. Quincy called his wife Jimena on his cell phone as they walked back up the crowded street to update Jimena of everything that is transpiring with her family on this day and to also let Jimena know which direction they were now heading in case she wanted to meet them over at Tye's parents' house. That decision would be solely up to Jimena because of their newborn child. The tall grey-haired gentleman detective telephoned Officer Juanita to inform her of all who had been involved in this execution style murder which took place at the local grocery store blocks away from Diamond's apartment complex. The lieutenant telephoned Chief Reginald to give him a very extensive detailed report of all the events that had occurred at the crime scene. The estimated time the shootings occurred. The names of the dead victims as well as the names of all the survivors. The EMS report and the location of the hospital where the victims were taken. The witnesses' reports and possible positive description of the gunman. The leads that the investigating units currently have and what occurred inside the store with Tanya. As Tye opened the back door of Quincy's car, he finally removed his arms from around his cousin Tanya's neck and quickly retrieved his cell phone from the back seat of the BMW to give Georgia Mae a call so Tye can get a detailed report of why her nephew was just shot and executed inside the small local grocery store.

CHAPTER 22

THE CAR CONVERSATION

Pulling her white Chevrolet Silverado 1500 truck back into the hospital parking lot, returning now to visit Jermaine's godmother who is in the hospital emergency room while the qualified nursing staff treated his injury Georgia Mae's cell phone started to ring. Looking at the caller ID this time making sure she was aware of who it was that was calling her Georgia Mae answered her cell phone for Tye.

"Tye, I was so worried when I didn't hear from you. How are you baby" Georgia Mae softly asked answering his phone call.

"I'm not good! Where is lil-bit Georgia?" Tye shouted.

"Tye, I miss you so much right now baby" Georgia Mae softly repeated herself.

"Where is Lil-bit Georgia Mae?" Tye loudly repeated himself.

"I left her and Robin in front of your parents' house with your cousin Bishop Joe" Georgia Mae softly replied as she parked her white truck in a parking space close to the emergency entrance.

"Why are you not with all of them and tell me the honest truth Georgia!" Tye loudly replied as he, Blaire, Diamond and Tanya squeezed tightly seated together in the back seat of Quincy's BMW.

"Baby something horrible has happened to my family on today and I don't want to trouble you with this problem because your heart has already been severed" Georgia Mae replied as she turned off the engine of her vehicle.

"Where are you now?" Tye shouted as Quincy pulled his BMW away from the curb trying to make a U turn so they could leave the vicinity of the crime scene and get on the highway.

"Tye, my nephew Ron was gunned down this afternoon in a grocery store. My sister-in-law Orange called me when Libbie was here in the truck with me. Baby don't worry about my problems. Tye, you have enough to worry about. Take care of your heart as best as you can. I loved Debbie like a sister. I'm here for you Tye. I promise I'll be back at your parent's house to see you baby as soon as I possibly can" Georgia Mae softly replied.

"Where the hell are you, Georgia!" Tye loudly shouted over cell phone as everyone seated in Quincy's BMW remained silent eagerly listening to his phone conversation while Quincy sped away from that neighborhood heading towards the highway.

"Baby I'm back at the hospital to see my nephew's best

friend Jermain's Godmother apparently, he survived, and we don't know all the details concerning his condition or what took place at that store. Better believe I'm going to find out before I leave this emergency room" Georgia Mae loudly responded as she went inside her purse to pull out her lipstick.

"Diamond, what happened to the other young man who the EMS took out of the store to the hospital" Tye loudly asked.

Diamond, whose head was down in the back seat sitting in between Blaire and Tanya as the tears continually fell from her eyes slowly lifted her head to answer Tye. *"I heard the police officer mention someone was unconscious probably in shock, but he was not shot. I'm sorry I was too busy on the floor crying when the medical personnel arrived to even check me. Only two people were dead, I guess"* Diamond answered as she started to cry again. Tanya lifted her muscular basketball athletic shoulders to wrap her arms around Diamond consoling her as they both wept.

"Tye who are you talking to? Who the hell is Diamond? And where are you guys now?" Georgia Mae asked as she looked out her windows for any possible undercover officers or unmarked vehicles circling the hospital premises while applying the lipstick to her lips.

"We were at the grocery store that your nephew Ron was just killed in. Tanya's girlfriend was also murdered in that store. Diamond is Williams best friend that's why she is here in Quincy's BMW with us. She survived the shooting earlier" Tye clearly explained as Quincy drove onto the highway entrance.

"Her nephew was the other murder victim. Oh man Tye! This is personal cousin" Blaire shouted out listening to his cousin's conversation as he put his right hand over his face to rub his eyes. *"Georgia Mae's nephew Oh man Tye! Definantly personal"* Blaire continued to say.

"Yes, this is personal! That's why we all came over to your house this morning, Tye. Soon as Larry came to my job talking that unnecessary chatter, I just knew man. Ooh big booty Argentina they didn't have to do you like that Tho" Tanya shouted sniffling her nose. *"Damn Tye I knew Larry was coming with some dumb crap Cousin"* Tanya continued to say.

Diamond lifted her head from off Tanya's chest *"Larry and Jamie were both problems during the time when your cousin William and I were working down at the docks. Eric really was my biggest problem while I was down there. After a while my coworker Juanita and I just quit working at that job. William felt they were harassing me because they probably wanted to sleep with me, but I knew that wasn't the reason. My neighbor Shane already told me about him and Eric, but I never shared that part with William"* Diamond continued to say.

"I didn't know Cousin William worked at the docks" Tiny loudly replied as he turned his body turning his head towards the backseat.

"We both did! We both worked hard for that new vehicle that the thugs Jamie being one of them wrecked in my apartment parking lot! Your cousin was pissed! And if you'll know William like I have known William all these years the parking lot incident is the reason why he punched Jamie

in the face today at your parent's house Tye. But Jamie and that woman in the elevator to me looked suspicious as I was going to the store before the gunman opened fire on Argentina" Diamond loudly explained as she started to cry. *"The fat gunman called out my name pointed the gun directly at, Argentina and shot her but not me. All I heard was screaming and more gun shots as I laid on the store floor screaming"* Diamond continued to explain as she continued to cry laying her head on Tanya's chest.

"Wow Tye! I swear to you baby I didn't know about any of this. Now my nephew is dead. But my older brother is not going to rest until" Georgia Mae loudly spoke. *"Wow Tye! I honestly didn't know about any of that. It's my younger brother who sent me here to the hospital to see about Jermaine"* Georgia Mae confessed as she sat still in her white Suburban truck.

Diamond lifted her head off Tanya's chest *"The detective was telling me outside of the store that they will be calling me to come into the office for further questioning. They have more investigating to do there at the grocery store to track down the killer before we left and got into this car"* Diamond loudly spoke.

"Your neighbor Shane where he works?" Tiny asked, trying to get more information about what is possibly happening to his cousins in Mobile, from Diamond.

"He's a singer with that popular band, The Brown Bucky Blues Band over at the Greenlit lounge" Diamond honestly answered.

"Our Uncles group? He recorded with Uncle Bucky "Oh, Diamond girl please don't stop. Tell us some more" Tiny

seriously replied turning his body even further around towards the back seat of the BMW.

"Larry is a real bum like I said unto you last night at my kitchen table Georgia! You link up with trashy trouble has serious consequences attached" Tye shouted. *"I'm terribly sorry to hear about your nephew on today Georgia. My heart goes out to your younger brother. Like how I'm feeling now Georgia the pain of loss seriously hurts! Your nephew Ron might not have deserved that. Go and continue to handle your aunt's family business as I continue taking care of my family's business"* Tye loudly said as he disconnected the phone from Georgia Mae.

"Her nephew! Oh Man this is ugly!" Blaire loudly said. "While I was in that store little while ago looking at all those officers taking pictures along with the detectives pointing, discussing things with crime unit investigators, I said to myself a deadly shooting this time of day at this location is a deliberate message" Blaire continued to say as he shook his head from side to side.

"The message is to your father. That's why the Chief of police was at my house standing in my kitchen this morning. Your father called me from my parents' house on your sister's cell phone while you were outside in front of the crime scene. Uncle Bucky is the one that informed me that it was her nephew who was murdered in that grocery store along with Tanya's girl." Tye said as he started to scroll his contact list on his cell phone. *"But it was Assemblyman Rogers who called me on his cell phone minutes before your father had*

called telling me that it's your father's hand that we are dealing with on today" Tye clearly spoke.

"Uncle Bucky, wow Cousin Blaire I just lost my appetite for Aunt Rebecca's sweet potato pie which I know your mom has baked, at our uncle and aunts house" Tiny loudly replied as he finally turned back around in his seat looking out the front window while Quincy sped the BMW up on the highway that was now filling up with after work rush hour traffic.

Diamond once again lifted her head from off Tanya's chest *"Tye, I'm terribly sorry to hear about your sister Debbie. William always talked about her warm smile and extremely cool personality. William always compares our close relationship to your sister Debbie and your cousin Derrick close blood relationship. This morning when William called my cell phone to share with me about how that severe storm on yesterday formed a deadly tornado with terrifying winds hitting Debbie's car ejecting her body killing Debbie instantly I felt so bad that I simply wanted to contribute some kind of assistance to those impacted by the tornado. I didn't realize my decision to donate groceries to the Tornado victims would involve me being an eyewitness in Argentina's murder"* Diamond said.

"Diamond, I know your emotionally confused by all this sudden loss of life surrounding you on today but let me ask you what exactly your job responsibilities at the docks were?" Quincy asked as he slowed the speed of his vehicle down, easing his foot off the gas pedal because of the traffic of vehicles on the highway.

"William was and still is my coach" Diamond calmly replied wiping away the tears from off her face. *"I owe*

your cousin big time for constantly motivating me to become more responsible in handling my business affairs. There were lots of times I may have wanted things but financially I didn't have or couldn't phantom the possibility that it can be achieved. William just boldly says we're going to do it like this and next week I will have what I want. He's my gentile giant. Your cousin is my purpose pusher. William shared with me that there was a company at Mobile's docks which had some weekend positions open, and I was going to apply. That next week I was a Material Handler along with William and another cool friend Juanita working for that company. Waley our company supervisor himself taught me how to operate the forklift and I received my certification through him." Diamond replied.

"Earlier this morning preparing to eat a gourmet breakfast Tanya, and I were laughing and joking around on your front porch. Now everyone is heartbroken and crying in the backseat of a BMW!" Blaire loudly spoke.

Tye turned his head slightly to the right to look at Diamond as she was seated tightly next to his cousin Blaire *"Cousin Quincy drive us over to my job now man"* Tye demanded putting his phone to his ear as he made a call to his good friend Jason on the cell phone.

Tiny slightly turned his body around in the front seat looking towards the back seat at Blaire *"the answers to the messages was seated in the front seat driving those BMW'S circling around Georgia Mae's shiny new white Chevrolet Silverado this morning"* Tiny spoke.

CHAPTER 23

TRUTH IN THE HOSPITAL

Entering the hospital emergency room waiting area the hospital security officer that was on post by the entrance door stopped Georgia Mae and handed her a brown file folder. As Georgia Mae slowly opened the brown file folder a nurse wearing pink scrubs quickly came walking over to the security desk from out of one the screening rooms signaling for the hospital security officer to direct Georgia Mae towards her. Tossing her natural long black hair back from hanging off her shoulders Georgia Mae followed the young nurse down the hallway pass the reception desk, through the double locked doors, passing the other hospital security guard that was posted seated in a tall chair on the very busy emergency room floor where the patients that were individually laying on a gurney was being treated by qualified doctors. An EKG nurse came from behind a curtain signaling them to walk in her direction where she was stationed. Approaching that section that was isolated by the long, tall curtain the EKG nurse handed Georgia Mae a stack of printed out papers that she then gently placed inside of the brown folder. As the young nurse turned around walking away from Georgia Mae back in the direction of the crowded emergency room waiting area, the EKG pointed to the freight elevators. When Georgia Mae stepped on the freight elevator, she calmly pushed the third-floor button on the elevator landing panel because that number was the only thing written on a white sheet of paper inside the brown file folder. Stepping off the elevator on the third-floor Georgia Mae slowly walked around the floor quietly looking for Jermaine's godmother. Remembering how her older brother had described his godmothers features over the cell phone prior to her arrival at the downtown hospital Georgia Mae slowly looked in room to room over the woman as she passed who were visiting their sick loved ones. Spotting a woman with those similar features sitting outside a room with isolated glass doors Georgia Mae walked over towards her. Introducing herself as Oranges older sister his godmother shared with Georgia Mae that Jermaine had suffered a severe case of shock. He was going to need psychological counseling medicine more than any oral medications after surviving that deadly shooting. Jermaine's godmother told her that they had him heavily sedated on medications because he did fall and hit his head which caused the mild concussion, but she assured her that her only son was going to be fine.

"The gunman gave my baby a serious headache that I'm going to have to deal with tomorrow and beyond" Jermaine's godmother angrily said as she got up out of the chair and walked away.

Knowing that homicide detectives would soon be arriving at the hospital to interview the witness in search of finding the suspect as quickly as possible Georgia Mae pulled out her cell phone to text her younger brother all the information that was shared. Officer Juanita slowly walked up to the glass door with her hands in her pants pockets staring into the room at Jermaine where he quietly lay on the gurney. Georgia Mae seeing her standing there purposefully ignored officer Juanita as she continued to text her brother Jermaine's update.

"He's a good ball player you know. His godfather did an excellent job coaching him since he was a toddler. I'm surprised Jermaine stayed with basketball all these years. Personally, I felt your nephew Ron was a much better basketball player than him Georgia" officer Juanita calmly spoke.

Georgia Mae continued ignoring Officer Juanita not lifting her head from texting on her cell phone *"I'm sorry do you think you know me lady"* Georgia Mae responded.

"I do know that even you know better at this point. I'm aware you know what the right thing is to do now Georgia Mae. Even you know this has gotten way too ugly even for your well-known pretty skin self. Real blood has been innocently

shed and now delivered by the hands of law enforcement on the doorsteps" Officer Juanita clearly responded.

"Lady, I don't have the foggiest idea of what steps you are referring to. I guess you're a cop" Georgia Mae sarcastically responded.

"Yes, I'm an undercover detective who was responsible for that team of agents in the hospital parking lot earlier today when Libbie, who was hysterical, was seated inside your vehicle. I'm also the one who gave the order for the agent to pull up in front of your vehicle" Officer Juanita clearly spoke.

"Listen here Ms. Orders, I hope they're not outside in the hospital parking lot now waiting to block my Chevrolet Silverado again as I exit the hospital grounds. Not after what has happened to my nephew today Detective Orders" Georgia Mae sarcastically responded as she stood up turning to face Officer Juanita.

"Don't stand there and act like you didn't see this type of bloodshed coming Georgia. You and I both know the reason why you wiggled that gym fit hourglass figure of yours back into Mobile, Alabama in that stolen Chevrolet Silverado was for protection. It was not just to lay up with Tye as some happy bride but to protect the man you have always loved not from the dangerous hands of those street thugs Eric, Jamie and Larry. But from the capable hands of your own dangerous brother!" Officer Juanita clearly spoke as she took a step closer to Georgia Mae staring directly into her eyes.

As Georgia Mae stared right back directly into officer Juanita's eyes placing her right hand on her hip *"Like I said Detective Orders I don't have the foggiest idea of what you are referring to. What I suggest you and your plain clothe wearing rough looking undercover chicks need to do is stay out of my vehicle's way"* Georgia Mae said.

"My name is Officer Juanita. What I suggest you need to do chick is remove yourself away from my sons' heavily guarded room. You see Georgia Mae not only am I an outstanding officer that directs orders but I'm a proud parent. At this moment I'm also a concerned parent. Yes, the investigators are going to do their job speedily because you don't know the mindset of the suspect. Who may intend to kill again. Our job is to look out for the safety of the citizens of Mobile, Alabama" Officer Juanita clearly responded.

"Jermaine is your son chick?" Georgia Mae asked.

"Who do you think named him. You're standing here looking at the proud parent who chose his godparents. Born and raised in Baton Rouge Louisiana is where I'm originally from. Jermaine was conceived in New Orleans when I met your older brother at Mardi Gras" Officer Juanita said as she took a seat crossing her legs in the chair that was in front of Jermaine's room. *"I love my child. Loved Jermaine since my water broke and I gave birth to him. Holding his tiny, closed eyes, self tightly wrapped in my arms. I promised him then as I whispered softly into my babies' ears long as I'm alive with breath in my southern body that I would never take him out of my sight. His father knows that fact. And he has kept both of his sons together under his watchful eye. I'm not sure if Orange would take knowing this truth too well definitely not after what has happened to her own baby boy Ron on today"* Officer Juanita continued to say. *"Yes, you are pretty Georgia Mae, I'll give you that. Tye is a good athletic catch I'll even applaud you on staying with that. But the real queen in this family*

has been in Mobile, Alabama and I never left my son or have taken him out of my sight. So, I encourage you to do what you know is the right thing to do for the best of the family. The bull crap meetings you have been creeping around town attending are baloney. I may be employed on the opposite side but even I know the godmother never fools around with rubbish. Her legendary respect has always been because of zero tolerance of nonsense. Now get from out of my face and go protect my baby daddy chick" Officer Juanita clearly said.

Tossing her long black hair off her shoulders Georgia Mae took a step closer to Officer Juanita almost stepping on her shoes *"floozy, you have some nerve to come out your mouth with any kind of demands to me. Obviously, you don't have any respect for royalty. Talking all this gibberish to me today as if I'm supposed to have a feeling of sympathy for your dirty butt. Check your vision chick I'm a dime a whole lick while you're still the side piece. You are nothing but a dirty cop thinking she got royal status over me because my brother loves his sons. No, my brother just handled his mess so his aunt wouldn't whip his butt for his dirty hands at the table. Broad you hear what I'm about to say unto you and listen to this good because I'm only going to tell you this once. I'm the queen in this family and your baby daddy ushered me down here in front of your son so that you will be reminded of the weight on my crown. This respect is not only given but even the citizens of Mobile, Alabama knows these jewels have been earned"* Georgia Mae clearly responded as she turned around tossing her long black hair off her shoulders and slowly walked away wiggling her hips towards the main elevators on the third floor of the hospital.

Getting up off the chair Officer Juanita turned

around facing the Glassdoor of the Intensive Care Unit where her son Jermaine was in the room by himself quietly sleeping on the gurney, she pulled her small cell phone from out of her pants pocket calling the unit who was strategically posted outside inside their cars around the hospital parking lot *"all units suspect now leaving the hospital stand down. All units stand down to further instruction is given"* Officer Juanita clearly spoke.

As Georgia Mae slowly wiggled her hourglass frame of body down the hospital parking lot steps onto the parking lot driveway, she looked around checking to see if there were any noticeable unmarked law enforcement vehicles in the vicinity. Pacing her stride as she walked to her Chevrolet Silverado, she stuck her hand into her purse pulling out her compact size cell phone to immediately call her eldest brother. Assuming he wouldn't answer the call when the voicemail answering service came on the line Georgia Mae quickly disconnected the call. Arriving at her parked white truck as she opened the driver side door Georgia Mae immediately selected her sister-in-law Oranges name from off her cellphone contacts list to speak with her knowing that Orange and her Eldest brother were more likely together somewhere around the vicinity of that grocery store where their son had just been murdered. Orange didn't answer her phone either. As Georgia Mae pulled her white Chevrolet Silverado out of the hospital parking lot her cell phone began to ring, and it was her youngest brother with further instructions after receiving the detailed text Georgia Mae sent him.

CHAPTER 24

THE REVEREND'S PLAN

Joshua, feeling a little uneasy about all the negative tension in his aunt's house, made a couple of phone calls to a few of the longtime faithful members of their church as the family remained seated in the cool central air living room. Seeing how calm and collect his cousin Bishop Joe was handling the family's crisis Joshua knew that his pastor himself would need a little cheering up. Debbie was an active member of their church. Always smiling as she happily ushered and hosted being a greeter as one of the founding members of the church posted at the entrance door at times. She supported her cousin from day one when he opened the doors of his church in Mobile, Alabama and she would even bring Cousin Derrick to the church once a month. Knowing how her absence from the church membership would be emotionally felt, a little spiritual intervention from the church family today wouldn't hurt anyone. It's their livelihood. It's their job. It's Bishop Joe and Joshua's daily responsibility not only to the church members to the community as well. The great blessing is that in their eyes spiritual intervention works. That was the main reason Joshua stayed twenty-four seven by his first cousin's side. Not only does the pastor need assistance from time to time but Bishop Joe's job is extremely beneficial in crisis management. Bishop Joe was very excited about the new project that he is working on at his church which is the band he has hired to play during their Sunday morning worship service. It had brought back some of the members who may have stopped coming to the church for their own individual reasons. Though every Sunday the church always has a significant number of attendees because of Bishop Joe's charismatic style of preaching on what he believes, the band was bringing in a good crowd of folks to his church. It was a plan well executed. Especially for Cousin Jill. The band sound was balancing out her vocal ability even the more. Their Uncle Bucky's recording band was always over booked or not available to play for Bishop Joe's Sunday morning worship. Few years ago, Jill auditioned for her uncle's band The Bucky Blues Band however they chose another female singer to perform with them. Uncle Bucky's recording band has recorded two well selling albums in the past two years. The Greenlit Lounge is where the band plays faithfully in Mobile, Alabama. The Bucky Blues Band brings a lot of revenue to the Greenlit Lounge on Friday and Saturday nights.

Jill was faithfully committed on Sundays singing for the church. Tiny and Jemena together felt it was their Cousin Joe's clever way of promoting Jill's professional singing career with the sound of his new band. Joshua knew it was his Pastor's great marriage intervention tactics to repair the past wrong. As Joshua continued texting the members of their church steadily seeing that his family was emotionally exhausted, and Tye's mother was seriously grieving Joshua asked some of the church woman to bring their delicious, cooked meals to his uncle's house. Knowing that would upset Aunt Rebecca because that had always been her role in the family loving to work the kitchen Joshua contacted a few of his close clergy female friends who also had a gift to gab to come over to the house to talk. Joshua felt even, his aunt needed a break.

Rebecca's restaurant is well known and always has been well liked since they were kids. The mere fact that not only is she still managing a restaurant but that she is still hands on in the kitchen cooking and baking sweet potato pies is a great blessing to the family. However, Joshua observed that his aunt had been in Tye's mom's kitchen cooking and baking ever since she arrived at the house so it may be time for a little church family intervention. Joshua Listening to the advice of what his Uncle Willie James had suggested to Bishop earlier about not focusing on the question of what's the parcel delivery drivers hidden motives may be with the family. Joshua informed his Bishop on the plans of his church members coming by the house to visit and serve the family.

Bishop Joe knew the breaking news in Tye's parents' house of Georgia Mae's young family member being gunned down and murdered in a store on today was bothering his cousin Joshua. *"Great Josh, let the new church band come set up and play in the backyard"* Bishop Joe loudly suggested including his latest project into Joshua's plans. *"Family we've invited few of our church members along with the band to the house so we can have a prayer vigil for Cousin Debbie as she rests in peace"* Bishop Joe announced in the living room of Tye's parents' house.

CHAPTER 25

CONFESSION OF A
LOYAL FRIEND

Three of Tye's mothers' closest friends stopped by the house to visit her because her neighbor next-door who is also a close longtime friend had called them earlier in the morning after the Chief along with his deputies left the house, informing Tye's parents of the sad news about Debbie's tragic death on the highway. As Tye's mothers' friends consoled her a detective of the Mobile, Alabama police department came to the house knocking on the door. As the detective announced who he was and his reasons for coming to Tye's parents' house Jill's husband met the detective at the front door.

The Chief of police, Chief Reginald had turned up surveillance around Mobile, Alabama once he was notified about the murders of Argentina and Georgia

Mae's young nephew inside the small grocery store. The Mobile, Alabama police department was now more concerned for the safety of the Vendridge, family because the suspect of the double execution style murders that took place inside the local grocery store is still at large. Where or who could be the next target at this moment is Chief Reginald's biggest concern. As the detective remained standing in the doorway, he explained to Jill husband along with Tye's father who had joined them in conversation that the homicide unit witnessed his son Tye a little while ago at the crime scene. The detective continued to share Tanya's outburst of anger over one of the dead victims. The detective's specific reason for coming to the house was because the police department of Mobile, Alabama is trying to get some answers as to why or what is the connection with the murdered victims and the family members.

As Tye's father explained to the detective about the loss of his daughter due to the unfortunate accident on the highway caused by the deadly tornado and how he sent his son along with Tye's first cousins for moral support downtown to the police station to meet with Sheriff Wesley, the detective observed the family members sitting in the living room. Due to the nature of the crime in the local grocery store that afternoon the detective was impressed that Tye's parents were not alone.

Tye's father expressed to the detective of the family's suspicion about Georgia Mae's shaky background in Mobile, Alabama and her shady history dealing with his family. His biggest worry is Georgia Mae's undiscipline behavior endangers his now grieving son Tye who is very upset because of the tragic loss of his only sister Debbie. Tye's father continued to share with the detective how he's aware of Tye's travels throughout Mobile, how they had talked with Tye and are in communication with his cousins because their parents are also seated in the living room of his house as the family gathers in bereavement. But the family still fears for the youngster's safety as they travel around Mobile, Alabama handling the final arrangements for Debbie and the family business.

The detective continued to be impressed by Tye's fathers' knowledge of the tragic events that have occurred on this day involving or even now may have involved his family. As the detective left the premises of Tye's parents, he assured the family that the Mobile, Alabama police department would be working around the clock to find the gunman and anyone else who may be involved in the grocery store murders. The detective alerted Tye's father about the police patrol that will be circling around his house and Tye's house for the next few days until the homicide unit gives any further instructions on the investigation.

After the detective had left the house Libbie finally contacted Assemblyman Rogers on her cell phone explaining to him everything, she had observed riding in the back seat of Georgia Mae's vehicle since she had left her father's parents' house earlier that morning. Libbie also told Assemblyman Rogers about the female undercover officer who purposely blocked Georgia

Mae's Chevrolet Silverado with her car in the hospital parking lot and how vocally nasty she responded to the undercover officer. While Libbie continued talking to Assemblyman Rogers on the cell phone her best friend Robin came clean by confessing to Bucky in conversation who had taken a seat next to her when he came back to the house from talking on Brenda's cell phone with Assemblyman Rogers. Bucky figured that all the continual police presence all day surrounding Libbie was now making Robin nervous, which was her reason for sharing her personal business with him in light conversation. For Joshua it was all the negative energy taking place in his uncle's house that pressed him to make the plans for Bishop Joe's church to come to the house providing spirituality. As Bishop Joe listened to Robin's conversation with his Uncle Bucky as she insisted on curing his own curiosity so did Assemblyman Rogers, listen over the cell phone while he and Libbie was having their phone conversation. Overhearing Robin talking about her acquaintance with the parcel delivery driver whose truck is parked across the street. Assemblyman Rogers listened through the phone intensively. Robin shared about her boyfriend of two years whose loving, cool personality started switching up on her when his neighbor's family brought in a migrant through their church's adoption program, and her boyfriend had befriended him. Robin shared how her boyfriend introduced him to his own friends around the neighborhood, but the migrant started to hang around a different crowd. She perceived the reason was because the Haitian migrant was much older than her boyfriend. Robin continued to explain how sexually promiscuous the migrant neighbor had been with a lot of the girls around town and how she had her own suspicions about her boyfriend now cheating on her. That was probably the reason they bonded so well. She shared that her boyfriend's older brother is a parcel delivery driver with a lot of girlfriends who brags about even sleeping with the women that he delivers to on his daily route. What stood out to Assemblyman Rogers was when Robin mentioned to Uncle Bucky that her boyfriend's older brother is a race car driver. As Robin continued talking with Bucky Libbie disconnected with Assemblyman Rogers because she wanted to check in with her grandparents to see if they've spoken to her dad. Bucky was puzzled of why Robin would share personal information of her boyfriend's adulterous behavior to him when she's supposed to be consoling her best friend who just lost her mother. What really had Bucky baffled was Robin's intel of the migrant. And what did any of that have to do with her being startled by the appearance of a parked parcel delivery truck. Already beginning to feel the pressure of the events occurring in his brother's house as well as the murders involving his niece, Robin's babbling wasn't helping Bucky at all. Jill, who was also listening to the conversation automatically picked up that Robin's secret affair with the migrant and probably Robin's secret affair with her boyfriend's brother in an act of revenge was her connection with the parcel delivery truck. Jill knew that her pastor's religious presence in the room provoked Robin's adulterous confession. Bishop Joe had taken his cell phone back from Joshua to text his cousin Tiny regarding the information that Robin had shared. Bishop Joe perceived that the parcel delivery driver is working for Larry and that was the leak about the auto parts not being delivered to Tye's house but to his parents' house that Larry needed. Knowing his cousin Tye's love for cars and flashy automobiles Bishop Joe felt that whatever value the parts are worth is probably his cousin's reason for changing the shipment address. Bishop Joe shared with Tiny in the text on the cell phone that what his cousin Tye fails to realize is that Larry seemed to have all hands-on deck for Tye's treasures. Bishop Joe feels that is why the detectives are now posted at the door and the reason for the Chief of police coming to the house along with the sheriff earlier that morning. Tiny replied to Bishop Joe's text feeling that was the connection with Cousin Tanya and Larry's personal visit on yesterday to her workplace. Tanya is Tye's mechanic, and everything concerning Tye's vehicles takes place at her shop located downtown in Mobile, Alabama. Bishop Joe replied in a text to his cousin Tiny that Larry being a convicted criminal whose recently been released from prison is going to send out his soldiers to do any of his dirty work, so he won't lose his freedom. *"Now her girlfriend has been murdered"* Bishop Joe shouted out as he lifted his head from reading the display screen on his cell phone as everyone in the room turned and looked at the pastor.

CHAPTER 26

THE FINANCIAL DEPOSIT

As the clock continued to countdown the hours of the day and the humidity continued to control the climate in Mobile, Alabama steaming up its residents in the sweltering evening heat Georgia Mae finally got a hold of her older brother. As angry as Georgia Mae was with him for not informing her of his other son Georgia Mae was now more concerned with all the undercover agents that had been surrounding her throughout the day. The mere fact the detectives were making themselves visibly known to her was alarming. Taking into consideration what Officer Juanita said to her at the hospital in front of her nephews isolated room, Georgia Mae felt slight nervous concluding that the police were most likely building a case against her family that involves her current business transactions. Now with the murder that has happened inside the small local grocery store that involves not only her other nephew but Tye's Cousin Tanya. Georgia Mae knew the homicide detectives were canvasing around Mobile, in search of possible suspects, leads and motives to the deadly shootings. The Chief of police standing in Tye's kitchen is a notable sign he has now probably activated his units in search of persons of interest. Georgia Mae didn't share with her older brother any of the conversation that she had with Tye and his cousins as they rode around Mobile, Alabama in Quincy's BMW. Diamond being an eyewitness to the double homicide, Georgia Mae didn't want to raise any red flags of Diamond's whereabouts especially if she is riding in the car with Tye and his cousins. What raised Georgia Mae's evenly shaved eyebrow was that Eric had not called her at all throughout the day. Even when Georgia Mae contacted Shane knowing that he would relay the message to his secret lover Eric that she was looking for him. He still has not reached out to her. Georgia Mae also knowing the code of ethics in the streets that when incidents of this magnitude occur there is talk. If the streets were talking, then she knew the players had already received the word that her family had been hit.

Listening to the angry tone of her elder brother Georgia Mae knew that something else was happening that she has no knowledge of. Considering what had happened to one of his sons, she knew whatever her older brother was secretly conspiring, he was not going to share it with his baby sister. Georgia Mae also knows his protection of the family empire. An execution warrants a host of goons to strategically hit the streets reinforcing the perimeter that has already been set around the queen. But the sound of his tone unfortunately says to Georgia Mae that he wants bloodshed. As she disconnected the phone call with her older brother Georgia Mae quickly called Tye's cell phone. Questioning his current location Tye honestly shared with her that they were in slow moving traffic on the highway now headed toward the restaurant where he works as the head chef. Knowing that a gunman is still out in these Mobile, Alabama streets not apprehended Georgia Mae was concerned for the safety of everyone who was riding inside Quincy's BMW. Tye turned their conversation into a three-way call making it now a family conference call with Assemblyman Rogers, Georgia Mae on the phone and his cousins who was seated in the car listening on speaker phone. Assemblyman Rogers who was still at his natural mother's house along with his older sister Sally which no one had any knowledge of was glad Tye reached back out to him by phone.

"Assemblyman Rogers, I have my girl on the phone, and you are on speaker phone with the family in Quincy's car" Tye sternly spoke.

Georgia Me pulled her vehicle into the bank parking lot as she kept her eye out for undercover agents who might be tailing her white truck with their unmarked cars. Checking all her mirrors and looking out all of the truck's windows Georgia Mae parked her car in an available parking space in the banks parking lot as she listened to the conference call with Tye on her cell phone.

"Tye, I know that was heavy news that I shared with you earlier but there's a lot going on in these streets of Mobile, that I was even unaware of. The one person who I'm really convinced has a broader sense of what is taking place is Uncle Bucky" Assemblyman Rogers clearly spoke.

"Why do you feel that my father has any knowledge of any criminal behavior that has taken place on today man?" Blaire loudly asked overhearing the conference call on his Cousin Tye's cell phone that had been placed on speaker while seated directly next to him inside Quincy's BMW.

"Hey, Blaire I'm glad you're on the phone too it's really good to talk with you" Assemblyman Rogers replied.

"You have my condolences man" Blaire loudly replied. *"I'm terribly sorry about the loss of your wife Debbie, Assemblyman. I know today isn't a good day for you. Seems not to be a good day for any of us. We met with the funeral director today to make the arrangements for Debbie, and I really wish you were there. Seeing Cousin Debbie's lifeless body like that is a hurtful feeling. Your daughter Libbie is devastated! Her precious tender heart has been severely broken on today, Assemblyman Rogers. I had to assist Georgia Mae in almost carrying her out of the morgue. I don't know if Tye mentioned it to you but we have the information and office phone numbers for you so you can go over to the funeral chapel to see your wife, Debbie. They will go over to the morgue today to transfer and collect her body. You're a part of our family and you're included with any of the planning regarding the final*

arrangements. But I need you to explain why my father's name is coming out of your grieving mouth negatively" Blaire loudly spoke.

"Blaire, I don't mean any harm to you, Brenda or your mom Aunt Rebecca but your father has a serious gambling habit. I'm sure Tye is aware of it if I know about it. Not only does the word travel fast in the streets but even the upper social class like to spread the latest gossip. Now Chief Reginald and I are friends socially and we attend quite a few of the same benefit functions and banquets but so does your cousin Derek. Derek is well respected as a fashion designer and a fashion consultant nationally. And all of you'll know the close relationship Derek and my wife Debbie had. Now Derek lives with Chief Reginald, that's why Derek called me and informed me you were at the crime scene a little while ago. Because the detectives are and have been watching all of us for quite some time. I was unaware of that until this morning when Chief Reginald detained me in his office" Assemblyman Rogers clearly responded.

"So, Cousin Derek is sleeping with the Chief of Police?" Tiny shouted out to ask as he slightly turned his head towards the back seat of the BMW.

"No, Tiny he's not" Georgia Mae softly replied over her cell phone joining in on the conference type call. "Your cousin Derek and the Chief of police godson DJ Gan have been in a relationship for a few years now. Gan is a greyhound bus driver and from what I heard he's a local popular Jamaican DJ" Georgia Mae lifted her voice and responded.

"I didn't know they were living with him. I knew that was

the Chief's Jamaican godson, but I was unaware of their living situation" Tanya lifted her voice and spoke.

"That's the Jamaican DJ at Candice's party Cousin Jemena was talking about earlier in Cousin Tye's kitchen. Man, it's a small world isn't it" Tiny loudly responded.

"I really can careless who is sleeping with who. Murders are being committed now with no one in custody. Your safety in that car is more important at this exact moment than anybody's bedroom business. We don't need the gunman to hurt anyone else until he or they are picked up. Tye now you have a better understanding of why the Chief of police himself came to your house this morning to deliver the news to your family personally about your sister Debbie" Georgia Mae loudly said.

"Yes, I appreciate him for taking the time out of his busy schedule to meet with us as a family concerning Debbie's death because of that tornado on yesterday. I'm sure the Mobile, Alabama police department has activated every one of their crime units to work on the homicide case inside that grocery store" Tye raised his voice and replied. "It's just a matter of hours when the detectives will be contacting Diamond to go into the police station for interviewing and more questioning since she is an eyewitness of those deadly shootings. I'm sure the surveillance cameras inside the grocery store not only caught the murders but captured the suspects' faces and will give the investigators a photo lead on apprehending the gunman. The homicide detectives are probably working on the photos as we speak trying to download the data and pictures they have retrieved from the grocery store cameras to their own computers. There was a lot of police officers and agents on that block and *in front of the grocery store at that crime scene today"* Tye clearly spoke.

"Very true you'll" Assemblyman Rogers said. *"But the detectives have been looking at our families' daily routines for some time. Like I said to you earlier Tye, that was the reason my friend Chief Reginald detained me in his office as you went over to the morgue to see my wife's dead body. Now why did he only talk to me about something as serious as this, what we're now visibly starting to see, I'm not sure brother. Only reason I came up with is the sudden news of the death of my wife Debbie is tragic enough and I'm assuming he didn't want to overload you with worse news about an investigation. Because we socialize together on a weekly basis it might have been easier for Chief Reginald to speak with me, especially when it comes to discussing details of a case that is currently under investigation. As me being a political figure in the Mobile, Alabama community our conversation publicly displayed the police departments aware of crime in the community and some of their tactics on how the Mobile, police department is handling the matter.*

Blaire I truly thank you man from the bottom of my heart for considering my feelings on today when it comes to my wife Debbie. I thank all of you for thinking of me and allowing me to be involved in the final arrangements of my wife Debbie. Though we weren't legally married I know all of you'll understand the seriousness of our committed relationship. I loved that woman! Blaire, I seriously wish I was there earlier at the hospital with Tye too. I wish to see and be next to my wife again. I'm missing her warm smile as we speak. Not hearing from Debbie twenty-four hours ago was very nerve racking. *When I received the call from Derek late last night it relieved me somewhat of the stress I was feeling. I was used to her and Derek hanging out some nights at one of his fashion events. But even after Derek told me the heartbreaking news of what happened to Debbie I still couldn't go into our bedroom. Her absence from inside my house is too overwhelming. That's why I'm here at the house with my family now. My heart is crushed! Your Cousin Derek is still constantly calling me. He is worried about Tye, and he is aware of the danger that seems to be preying on our family. You'll already know Derek is taking the news of Debbie being killed on yesterday hard. As close as they were Dereks reaction is probably extremely emotional like my daughter Libbie's display of behavior in the morgue. I just hung up the phone with Libbie and she told me everything that took place with her today. Blaire I also thank you for being there for my daughter Libbie earlier at the morgue. Today is so unreal everyone. To answer your question Blaire, after listening to the highlights of the verbal police report earlier this morning at the police station and watching the breaking news on television as the crime spree escalates involving members of this family, I am persuaded to believe that your father a great playing musician at the greenlit lounge is not only the popular band leader but a major player on the card table of Larry's bosses"* Assemblyman Rogers assertively explained.

"Bucky is a card shark Assemblyman Rogers I agree but what Eric is after is far more valuable to him than to whoever Larry is out here in these streets with his idiot goons breaking the law in search for" Georgia Mae loudly responded.

"How would you know this vital information Ms. Big hip Sexy" Tiny sarcastically responded.

"Because she is obviously out here in these hot Alabama streets herself conducting top secret business with her gangster brother! Isn't that right Ms. Georgia Mae" Quincy sarcastically asked as he continued slowly driving his vehicle on route to the restaurant. *Swerving his BMW around some of the huge chunks of debris that remained on the detour road off the highway from the large tornado yesterday.*

"One of my brothers took a major hit today! He has now tragically lost his son. I'm not even going into detail of the pain he's experiencing but his response is what your cousin Derek and I are afraid of. I can't even intervene in whatever his planned response is going to be" Georgia Mae quickly replied as she reached her hands and long fingernails inside of her stylish pocketbook.

"God sure Can!" Tiny shouted as he quickly threw up his hands over his head while seated in the front seat of Quincy's BMW.

"God already has. Isn't that right Ms. Georgia Mae? That was the topic in the conversation you were speaking to Cousin Joshua regarding while we were seated inside the lobby waiting area in the hospital this morning" Quincy loudly spoke.

"After being an eyewitness to some of this madness today I know God has placed my pastor Bishop right into his aunt's house for Cousin Tye" Tiny loudly shouted. *"I've witnessed more than enough news cameras, paramedics and too many detectives in one day"* Tiny said.

"My pop is over at Tye's parents' house as well" Blaire, joining in loudly spoke giving his response in the conference type conversation.

"Yeah, but Cousin Blaire, seems like from what I'm hearing is my uncle out here in these Alabama streets making bad moves that any of us was unaware of." Tiny shouted. "Bishop text me a little while ago saying he is convinced that Larry is out here in these Alabama streets making moves that Cousin Tye is unaware of" Tiny loudly shared.

"I really appreciate you calling me back Tye" Assemblyman Rogers joined in the conference type conversation and spoke. "Earlier my assistant Kyle called me with a message that he retrieved on my office voicemail from an individual named Keith whose message was that he's after the turbo parked next to your Bentley's inside your garage. Keith wants your niece Libbie to leave him with the keys" Assemblyman Rogers shared.

"What? Keith! Nah these guys out here wildin! They shot up and murdered my girlfriend in cold blood this afternoon like she was some kind of wild animal caught in a game of hunting. Left her bleeding lifeless body lying on the cold store floor for a host of strangers to photograph and observe. That's why I got so angry Cousin Tye. Soon as I saw all those suits flashing their equipment all around not saying anything to me, I just lost it man. Argentina was a beautiful soul with a bubbly personality. Now these guys want to drag my little cousin Libbie into the middle of their gunfight! Yo, they straight wildin on us Cousin Tye!" Tanya shouted.

"What I'm thinking is they don't know exactly what happened to Cousin Debbie" Quincy lifted his voice and spoke while driving his vehicle along the detoured road.

"That was my impression as well Quincy. The Chief and

Sheriff patrol cars around our vehicles this morning got them idiots on edge" Georgia Mae loudly replied.

"No, they know about Debbie because Jamie showed up at Tye's parents' house today. Which set Cousin William off in a rage earlier in front of my family as well. They also are aware of Chief Reginald and Dereks' family relation I'm sure of that" Blaire, quickly responded. *"What is unclear to someone is what exactly happened in our family that would bring the police department including Chief Reginald to Tye's family houses. Which means that they're probably more watch parties involved than Larry's two thugs"* Blaire explained.

"So, Larry knows about what happened to my sister Debbie, but this Keith surveillance squad doesn't know all the details of what happened to my sister yesterday" Tye loudly replied.

"Is this the card table squad you were referring to that may involve my pop or is there another gambling watch party posted outside our homes" Blaire asked.

Diamond lifting her head slowly glanced over at Blaire who was seated next to her in the back seat of Quincy's BMW. *"I wonder who the man with that deep voice is, that was trying to get my attention before I walked into that grocery store just around the corner of my apartment complex"* Diamond spoke joining in on the conversation.

"Diamond, I must admit when you mentioned that episode in front of the store to me earlier over the phone, I knew Larry was going to pull something on you. For me that was an indication he, they whoever was about to attempt to run up on you. Which was the reason for us coming to get you"

Tanya loudly spoke as she sat next to Diamond in the back seat of Quincy's BMW.

"Blaire, the reason I'm sure your dad has more insight on the criminal aspect of what is transpiring here in our neighborhoods is because of the different card players he's been interacting with lately. Even if there is a new breed of hustlers or shysters out here in Mobile, Alabama I'm pretty sure Bucky has come across them in a game or two. I'm sure playing his saxophone at different venues with two well liked albums Bucky has come upon a host of hustlers. The Greenlit lounge is a hot bed for that type of lifestyle. I know the manager of that club personally and for the past three years they have been trying to present a better image. I must applaud their efforts with the reconstruction of the place and the new line-up of talent from the latest recording artist down to the hottest up and coming local talents. But with rivalry gangs seated in the crowd, hidden motives walking around in the lounge and dirty gamblers looking for potential pockets to rip off in a crowded establishment, that lounge is still a hotbed for mischief. Bucky being the leader of his popular band might have been preyed on from the beginning. That I don't know Blaire. However, he loves to play cards, and the stakes have been extremely high. Now that unfortunate news Debbie and I knew. And his hand has not been as lucky as Tye's consistent wins" Assemblyman Rogers clearly spoke.

"That's the disturbing news Derek knew. So, while idiots may have been casing the joint for customers, you'll Cousin Derek kept his clientele eyes on his uncle for bad company" Georgia Mae said.

Tiny slightly turned around in the passenger seat

of the BMW as his cousin Quincy slowly pulled up in front of the restaurant for his cousin Tye. *"Once again Big hip sexy, I must ask you how is that you know all of this vital information"* Tiny loudly asked.

Diamond slightly leaned forward in the back seat of the BMW towards Tiny's left ear *"she knows because of my neighbor Shane who happens to be Bucky's male lead singer and is my very good friend"* Diamond replied.

As Tiny slowly turned back around in the front seat, he turned his head and looked at his cousin Quincy.

"Thanks for driving me to my job Quincy" Tye said as he looked through the windows around the outside perimeter of the restaurant. *"I'm going to wait for my buddy Jason who I have asked to meet us over here. He should be arriving any minute"* Tye spoke looking down at the watch on his risk

"You think that maybe the safest place for you and Diamond to be at right now baby?" Georgia Mae softly asked over the cell phone as she slowly opened the white envelope that was now in her hands which she had pulled from out of her stylish pocketbook.

"Yeah Georgia, as bad as I want to see my parents, I'm thinking there is still some personal business we may need to handle before we go by the house. We may also need to switch cars, but I'll make that decision a little later while Jason is with us. That message from Keith gave me a good idea of what some of this other madness may be about" Tye replied.

"But that double homicide outside of Diamond's apartment complex is definitely your family stuff Georgia Mae!" Quincy

shouted as he pulled out his cell phone to call Jemena and give her an update of where they were now located.

"Well, I'm going to hang up the call and let you all finish conducting your family business. Once again thank you brother for reaching out to me and calling me back. For what it is worth talking to all of you on today has been somewhat soothing and comforting when my heart has just been badly broken. Just hearing from family has relieved a lot of my pain of abandonment. Blaire, your pops called me before I spoke to Tye earlier and from his detailed conversation as a man, I knew he was involved. My political guess is that your father is the target. Blaire, I never had the chance to say this unto you personally, but as a man and a respectable active political leader of the Mobile, Alabama community I'm very proud of your business decisions. What you have done for your own children, the opportunities that you have offered the children of many parents in Mobile, Alabama with your Karate school is phenomenal. As a man you have guided and supported your own household respectably. As a good son you have patterned yourself wisely after your father's business endeavors. As well as after your mother's excellent business skills. I know your cousin Debbie unfortunately is not alive now to commend you herself for your success but many nights you were the applaudable topic of our conversation in our home. Your family has businesses here in Mobile, Alabama, Blaire. And that is how I know Bucky is the primary target" Assemblyman Rogers clearly explained as he disconnected the three-way call leaving now only Georgia Mae and Tye on the phone line.

"Your cousin Derek has a good eye on your pops Blaire" Georgia Mae softly said as she slowly continued pulling

the money and receipts individually out of the envelope quietly adding the bills up in her head making sure the amounts were correct. *"He mingles with both sides and is well liked with the upper echelon business associates. In my opinion it's probably DJ Gan, his boyfriend that's assisting him with the lookout. Because not only does DJ Gan have to look out for his own welfare and business affairs at the lounge events but his boyfriends' surroundings as well. Like you and me Tye. Everyone knows I have your back baby"* Georgia Mae said.

"Yo, Cousin Tye, hang up with her" Blaire whispered to his cousin Tye.

"I understand, Georgia. Thanks so much for the intel baby you always come through for me. I love you even more for that. Today everything really seems to be messed up and I'm truly sorry about the murder of your nephew Ron and his friend who's now laying in the hospital wounded from gunshots" Tye responded to Georgia Mae.

"His brother Tye. My nephew Ron was shot and killed today as his brother Jermaine watched the gunman execute his only brother in one of the isles at the grocery store. My older brother now has one dead son headed to the morgue and Jermaine his other son laying on the hospital gurney suffering from severe shock whose mom is the friend and former coworker with the star eyewitness seated next you inside Quincy's BMW. And Blaire, I heard what you just said to Tye, but don't get mad at everyone else because your daddy doesn't know how to bet on his hands right" Georgia Mae loudly said as she quickly disconnected the cell phone call with

Tye continuing counting the money that was inside the envelope from her pocketbook.

As Tye continued to look out of his Cousin Quincy's car windows for the arrival of one of his good friends Jason, Diamond's cell phone began to loudly ring. detecting by the sound of the ring tone that the call was coming from an unidentified number Diamond refused to answer her cell phone. Tanya recognizing the signs of anger and frustration Diamond was now probably internally feeling, Tanya kindly reminded Diamond that the homicide detectives would be contacting her to investigate the murder of her girlfriend Argentina. When the phone rang again Diamond quickly answered the phone call that was from the homicide investigation unit asking her to come downtown to the office to answer a few questions about what took place at the grocery store earlier that afternoon while she was shopping for the tornado relief items. Diamond agreed to the interview and told the detective that she would come downtown to the police headquarters within the next three hours.

Tiny slightly turned around again in the front seat towards Tye and Blaire. *"You know Cousin Blaire before you say whatever it is your feeling that needs to be discussed with us. I must say that I have more respect for Assemblyman Rogers on today probably than I did in the past. The man just unexpectedly lost his wife due to high winds from a tornado funnel cloud that touched down in our city. And in less than twenty-four hours from being notified of the horrific news, he's also told by the Mobile, Alabama police department that there may be a potential hit on the lives of his family. So, what does the Assemblyman do? The man calls us Blaire. Now thanks to your brother-in-law Tye, we have been thoroughly informed about our family's possible safety being threatened. Now I understand Cousin Blaire you may have a few things you might want to get off your chest, but in my opinion that what Assemblyman Rogers just displayed is heroic"* Tiny said.

"I have to agree with Cousin Tiny because what he shared shed a lot of light on things that we probably all been witnessing in our own individual day to day lives" Quincy spoke.

"Listen guys, I salute him today. I can identify with him on the pain he feels right now of losing his wife. When I pulled that white sheet from off Argentina in the store and saw her face covered in blood the rage and sadness at the same time just engulfed me. I mean they didn't have to do big booty Argentina like that. She was a sweetheart. My heart is heavy man. I can literally feel his pain. I salute Assemblyman Rogers for even wanting to talk to us in his state of grief. That shows you how strong he really is. Cousin Debbie made a good choice about who she wanted to spend her life with. Now I wonder how Libbie's father is going to handle all this rivalry. That dude is licensed and trained to handle military firearms" Tanya responded.

"Yeah, Blaire I know that's your pops and that kind of personal information Assemblyman Rogers shared with us is something you might not have wanted to hear. Our parents are our heroes and that's the image, we expect everybody to acknowledge. Our grandfather was strong and as a family we all take pride in publicly upholding that image. But my girl Georgia and my brother Assemblyman Rogers at the end of

245

the day are just looking out for the welfare of our family" Tye spoke.

"All you punks seated in this car need to be quiet and let me say what it is that I wanted to say" Blaire shouted.

"The last several weeks my pops started acting different towards the family. Brenda and I noticed it. With Delores included one night we took our mom out for a little family style dinner and a little family meeting. But you'll know how Aunt Rebecca is, she loves to talk so she spent half the night telling us all about everybody else's business. Now mom did share that pop's schedule keeps mysteriously switching up on her and it was really beginning to aggravate her. After all these years with them being married, running a successful business mom told us that suddenly, Bucky either disappears without letting her know of his whereabouts or he doesn't come home at the time he used to without any explanation. Now I know Pop handles the financial banking of mom's bakery as well as most of the financial inquiries of his own bands business. A couple days ago, Delores and I were discussing that fact because she even noticed this guy is always standing around outside of my school. We both kept on receiving calls from some guy calling from different phone numbers asking us both the same nonsense questions about our insurance policies. We were both wondering if it was that same guy stalking my school and family. Now you'll do know that Mobile, Alabama has some characters wandering around here too. However, I was unaware of all the fiasco until Tanya notified me yesterday about Larry's unplanned visit to her job" Blaire loudly explained.

As Tye looked at his cell phone contemplating whether to call his parents or not a silver Hyundai with Kentucky license plates pulled up in front of Quincy's parked car. A tall muscular man exited out of the driver's side of the car. Tye quickly hoped out of the backseat of Quincy's parked BMW walking over to the silver vehicle to engage in conversation with his friend Jason. As the two of them slowly walked back towards Quincy's BMW, Diamond asked Tanya to open her side of the backseat door and let Diamond out so that she could also speak with Jason. That was the actual reason Tye asked Jason to meet up with him so that Tye could get a better understanding of what his cousin William may have encountered while working at the docks with them. While the three of them were standing outside of Quincy's vehicle talking, two black BMW'S came screeching from around one of the corners tailing each other driving at high speeds. Thankfully, the vehicles didn't stop, passing the restaurant as they continued high speeding down the street onto the next block. As a measure of precaution Tye made Quincy move his car into the small restaurant parking lot while they all went inside of the restaurant together. A SUV quickly pulled up and three muscle fit men quickly jumped out of the Black Range Rover. It was the Olympian takeover squad. Tye's long time gym buddies. Jason had shot them a text to come stop by the restaurant after Tye shared with him earlier concerning the sad news about his sister Debbie. Leaving their Range Rover SUV parked in front of the restaurant, the Olympian takeover squad joined the fellas, Tanya and diamond inside the restaurant. Since Diamond was going to need a ride over to the police department headquarters to meet with the homicide unit Tye asked his friend Jason if he wouldn't mind taking her downtown to the Mobile, precinct. Of course, Jason agreed because of their descent work history together and past cool friendship. Tye called Brenda asking her to persuade her father Bucky to drive William over to the restaurant to briefly meet with them. Brenda informed Tye that some of the church members had arrived at his parents' house and that cousin Joe was planning on conducting a memorial for Debbie with the church band in the backyard of the house.

CHAPTER 27

LONG TIME FRIEND

Tye's friend Jason along with Williams' close friend Diamond sat at one of the tables together inside the restaurant with Tye's cousins Blaire and Tiny who seemed to be more interested in the two's work history at the docks. As Tye was standing next to his cousins Tanya and Quincy by the restrooms briefing his gym buddies of all the events that occurred his father called him. Worried and now concerned about Tye's whereabouts after the detective showed up at the door, his father called Tye's cell phone in the hope that they were headed to the house. Tye handed his cell phone to his cousin Quincy who spoke briefly to his uncle updating him on the reason for their current location at the restaurant. Bucky observing his nephew's behavior towards his pops perceiving the state of anger that Tye was now in after all these senseless deaths that's now surrounding him in these few hours, Bucky took his brother Willie James and his nephew William by car over to the restaurant to check on Tye.

Tye expressed to his cousin Quincy and the fellas why he didn't speak to his pops that he knows his cousin Joe well and he understands his cousins' spiritual intensions, but Tye was not in the mood to pray. Tye felt that was his cousins' thing so let them be a blessing to his parents and do their prayer thing while he does his street thing. Tye also expressed for him to hear that his brother Assemblyman Rogers being involved in some street mess was fueling his anger the more. He loved his sister Debbie and Tye felt that he owes it to her to handle the heat that was now coming from the underground bosses concerning some of his investments.

Tye quickly called Assemblyman Rogers and asked him if he could meet them at the restaurant and he agreed to come. Then Tye quickly called Georgia Mae back to ask her if she could also come to the restaurant in hope that it would somehow bring Tye face to face with Larry knowing that in any event, he would be tailing her. However, the calls kept on going to her voicemail.

CHAPTER 28

THE MEMORIAL SERVICE

After Bucky, his brother and nephew left Tye's parents' house on their way to the restaurant for a surprise checkup visit, the new church's band members arrived. As Rebecca and three of the senior women from Bishop Joe's church hosted the people in the backyard along with Tye's mom five of the woman who were also from the church worked diligent in the kitchen preparing dinner for everyone. Joshua along with a few of the younger fellas and his cousin Brenda were setting up the chairs around the yard that Jills husband obtained from the garage. Bishop Joe, Jill, two of the ordained leaders and Tye's father met upstairs in one of the bedrooms about the order of service. Even though Joshua's original plans were for a small intimate spiritual gathering to help comfort his uncle and aunt from the pain of the loss of their daughter, word had quickly spread among the congregation. The keyboardist invited the main choir, and his choir members brought their family members with them to the house so the number of people in the backyard began to increase. Tye's moms' friends each made phone calls around the neighborhood to some of their own closest friends who brought more food over to the house. As the crowd continued to gather in the backyard of Tye's parents' house Cousins Bobby, Bam and Tommy arrived at the house along with their friends. Earlier while everyone was still seated in the living room Delores had called two of her husband's staff workers from Blaire's karate school to bring some folding chairs over to the house.

As the evening humidity sat still in the hot Mobile, Alabama air, Cousin Jaquie walked in with her husband who was a famous renowned pianist and the two of them, after showing love to Tye's mom walked directly over to the church's new band members as they were still in the process of setting up the equipment. Cousin Jaquie began singing her favorite gospel hymn acapella soon followed by her husband accompanying her playing the keyboard that had finally been setup. Jill who didn't want to be out staged by her cousin Jaquie quickly left the meeting with her pastor upstairs as she could hear her cousin hitting every note and hurried down to the backyard to sing along with her cousin Jaquie.

Quincy had called his wife Jemena while he was at the restaurant and advised her not to come out of the house with their children because of all the criminal activity that was taking place around the family. After observing and witnessing the aftermath of the double homicides at the grocery store, Quincy didn't want to endanger his own family. Quincy had suggested to his wife Jemena that she probably needs to miss out on the memorial for Cousin Debbie tonight specifically because of the active shooters and screeching BMWs scurrying around corners in the streets of Mobile.

As Cousins Jaquie and Jill continued to duet together singing another gospel song on the backyard patio in front of the small crowd seated in Tye's parents' backyard, the choir joined in with them slightly lifting the tempo while the new church band accompanied them. Tye's Father eventually made his way back downstairs to join his wife and the family as they sat close together near the backyard patio where the performances were taking place. Libbie and Robin sat together as Robin held Libbie close comforting her best friend tightly in her arms as they both cried sadly missing Debbie's presence. Seated next to Robin was Jill's husband who was sipping on a cold glass of freshly squeezed lemonade trying to cool down from the humid temperatures outside and unwind, being exhausted from assisting everyone as well as assembling the chairs from out of the houses garage. Debbie's Cousin Joshua couldn't contain himself because of the overwhelming joy he was feeling that his planned event had turned out successfully. Joshua kept on smiling even though hearts were heavy around him because of the sad occasion. Bishop Joe and the leaders from his church that was with him finally assembled themselves back downstairs sitting with the family in the backyard of the house. Bishop Joe kept his eyes on Libbie's best friend Robin feeling a little uneasy knowing that Robin was very upset and emotionally vulnerable seated directly next to Jills husband. Joshua observed his pastor, but remained excited for what he had envisioned earlier about the changing of the family's atmosphere for it to become spiritual was now taking place as some of the gifted family members led the memorial tribute for their beloved Debbie.

Two more families from the church arrived at the house bringing more food and their own chairs as they were ushered in by a few of the active young men also from Bishop Joe's church. Chaplain Davis along with another detective of the Mobile, Alabama police department showed up to the house unannounced. As they were escorted to the backyard of the house, Delores seeing chaplain Davis recognizing him from earlier at her Cousin Tye's house immediately text her husband Blaire letting him know the police officers were there. While Chaplain Davis was standing in the yard Tye's mom fastened her eyes on him as the other Mobile, detective standing next to Chaplain Davis stared directly at Robin. Tye's father noticed his wife's constant stare at chaplain Davis, so he arose from out of the chair and quickly walked over to both officers while Jill's husband followed him

Joshua quickly ran up onto the backyard patio to join in singing with his cousins Jaquie and Jill as they sang one of Debbie's favorite church songs. Bishop Joe stood up and Joshua handed him a microphone as Joe sang the next two lead verses of that song by himself. Everyone in the backyard stood up on their feet responding to the bishops' sharp vocals with the clapping of their hands as the church's new band played their instruments in the background keeping the beats. The choir started harmonizing their voices making the background sound symphonic. As Joshua, Jill and Jaquie joined Bishop on the lead Tye's father walked towards the garage area with the two police officers.

"I failed to mention this a few hours ago while the detective was here at my front door asking questions concerning my son. A young man named Jamie came here to my house earlier this morning attempting to offer his condolences to the family. My biggest problem was that we didn't know him and had never seen him before today. I seriously doubt Debbie knew him like he stood on my backyard porch with his lying lips claiming she did. This Jamie guy really upset my brother and my nephew. He upset me so bad I ended up sicking my dog on the skinny guy. My nephew William attacked him, and I threw Jamie out of my house. All this fighting on the worse day ever. It led to a family meeting because he wasn't the only visitor we had that was suspected today. Very upsetting to my family that some thugs would be bothering my son on this particularly. He really doesn't need aggravation. He's still young and today emotionally my son Tye might not be as strong as everyone is used to seeing him" Tye's father loudly explained.

"Listen detectives, none of us are perfect and we all have our flaws. As humans we make mistakes. Now as believers of God we learn from our mistakes apologize for them and with our faith move on hopefully doing it differently. I say this

because I love my cousin Tye and I've watched his relationship with his girlfriend Georgia Mae over the years develop. Her reputation here in Mobile might not be squeaky clean but when they are together the two of them become role model citizens in this community. Her business sense and Cousin Tye's expert culinary skills serve this community well. Just like my Uncle Bucky and Aunt Rebecca" Jills husband clearly spoke.

"I appreciate everything that you have shared with us about Tye, and I will definitely relay this information to the investigation team" The detective loudly replied. *"However, gentleman we received another anonymous tip from a reliable source that there's a possible suspect seated here in your yard which is what brings us out here this evening. Once again, we truly do apologize for having to come to your house with this type of news during this occasion. Knowing that dealing with the challenges of grief can be cumbersome. We do applaud your efforts as a family to have come together and throw this type of event lifting each of your spirits as you collectively morn the tragic passing of your loved one. But as a possible lead in the double homicide investigation that took place this afternoon in a grocery store, now bring the investigation out at this location to one of your guests. So as detectives we must do our job to help this case"* the detective loudly explained.

"If you don't mind me asking how Tye is" Chaplain Davis politely asked.

"The fellas are with my brother Bucky; officers and I do believe he has taken them out to get something to eat" Tye's father replied.

"How is your niece Tanya feeling? It's my understanding that she was extremely close to one of the victims that was

murdered this afternoon inside the store. The homicide unit witnessed her emotional breakdown at the crime scene as well as your son Tye comforting her" Chaplain Davis asked.

"She is also with my brother Bucky. Ever since they were young Tye and Tanya have been side by side. As they console each other, my family is embracing the two of them" Tye's father replied as he slowly walked back to his seat.

"Detectives may I ask you who the suspect guest is since everyone here is practically family in one way or another" Jill's husband loudly asked.

"From a reliable source that we do now have in custody, we believe the young lady Robin who is here seated with your cousin Libbie has some valuable information that is needed for our homicide case" the detective replied.

"Let me ask you is Georgia Mae with Tye right now" Chaplain Davis asked Jill's husband.

"I have no idea where she is! Georgia Mae dropped Libbie off here at the house earlier as Tye asked her to do! She apologized to us while we were standing in front of the house for not coming inside and Georgia Mae quickly drove away in her white truck" Jills husband loudly replied as he turned walking away from the detectives heading back to his seat next to Robin. The detectives slowly followed Jill's husband as everyone in the backyard was still standing, clapping their hands to the spiritual singing come from the four cousins on the backyard patio and the choir.

As the detectives escorted Robin outside of the house to their unmarked vehicle officer Juanita along with the tall grey haired female detective with the badge around her neck wearing blue jeans had also arrived at

Tye's parents' house to speak with Robin. Stepping out of the car, officer Juanita introduced herself to Robin as the lead detective in a burglary and robbery case. The other male detective that escorted robin out from the backyard to the end of the driveway in front of Tye's parents' house where their unmarked police vehicles were parked introduced himself as the lead homicide detective in the double murder case that took place inside the grocery store. The tall grey haired female detective with the badge around her neck wearing blue jeans slowly walked over to Robin with a file folder in her hand.

"*Good evening, Robin, do you remember me from earlier in the hospital parking lot*" *the female detective asked.* "*I'm a detective that works in the crime unit here in Mobile, Alabama and your father is a person of interest to that deadly shooting inside that grocery store. Now you're not under arrest or in any serious trouble we just have some questions to ask that will help our cases. We seem unable to locate any of your older brothers. Do you happen to know where your younger brother Ben is at this time*" *the female detective asked Robin.*

Robin's head dropped down towards her sneakers. She slowly lifted her head and looked over towards Chaplain Davis who was standing next to Officer Juanita. Robin then turned and looked out at the house across the street down where the parcel delivery van had been parked earlier.

"*The last time I may have seen him, he was robbing that house down the block along with my boyfriend*" Robin sorrowfully confessed.

"*Your boyfriend was arrested on a warrant three hours ago on another charge. He's in our custody now and must have seen you here because he's the one that tipped us as to where to find you. However, he has no idea of where we can locate his buddy, Ben. Your boyfriend said to the arresting detectives of the crime unit in the interview room that you can help us with that information*" the female detective clearly replied to Robin.

CHAPTER 29

THE SHOOT OUT

As the sun hid itself from hovering over the city of Mobile, Alabama given way to the moon that clearly began to glow brightly showing itself in the darken Alabama skies, the evening rush hour traffic that once cluttered the highway and streets of Mobile, dwindled drastically.

Georgia Mae sat inside of her air-conditioned white Chevrolet Silverado 1500 parked outside of the empty bank in the parking lot talking to Shane on the cell phone while escaping the hot humidity. A red pick-up truck quickly drove into the empty banks parking lot pulling up alongside Georgia Mae's parked white truck. As the short beautiful blonde haired young woman eased herself out of the driver's seat of the red pick-up truck, Georgia Mae unlocked her trucks door so the blonde-haired young woman could get into the passenger side of her vehicle.

"My boyfriend Tye is going to be upset with me because I'm not answering any of his phone calls" Georgia Mae spoke while the beautiful blonde-haired young woman made herself comfortable in the passenger's seat of Georgia Mae's white Chevrolet Silverado 1500.

"That's why I don't have a steady boyfriend because I don't have time for the check-in" the young blonde-haired woman replied as she pulled down the passenger side sun visor looking into its mirror to check the curls in her long blonde hair.

"I've had some manly looking female detectives trying to check in on me at certain locations around town throughout the day" Georgia Mae loudly said as she put her cell phone away inside her stylish pocketbook.

"I hope you giving them the same attitude that you've clearly been giving that boyfriend of yours Tye" the young blonde-haired woman replied as she comfortably leaned her petite body back into the butter soft leather passenger side seat.

"I have never in my life given the police much of my attention" Georgia Mae quickly responded.

"As hot as it has been today, I'm not sure why someone would want to give any kind of attention to anybody. Despite a message that I received of one my runners getting picked up by the police today, everyone else is in place Georgia Mae, the shipment has come in aboard the huge vessel and I verified it with my own eyes" the young blonde-haired woman spoke.

As Georgia Mae slowly handed over to the young blonde-haired woman the white envelope full of cash and receipts inside of her white Chevrolet Silverado 1500, two black BMW'S quickly pulled up screeching its tires into the empty banks parking lot stopping directly behind Georgia Mae's parked vehicle. As the young blonde-haired woman immediately reached inside her purse attempting to pull out a gun she owned that was tucked way down inside, four young men dressed in all black wearing sweatshirt hoodies immediately stepped out of the cars and began shooting their automatic weapons directly at Georgia Mae's vehicle. One of the gentlemen shooters quickly ran to the front of the white Chevrolet Silverado on the passenger side and fired four shots from his gun through the tinted window striking the young blonde-haired woman directly in the chest. As the shooter made his way back to the rear of Georgia Mae's vehicle, three more BMW'S quickly pulled inside the empty banks parking lot also screeching their tires simultaneously one behind the other, several individuals also wearing black hoodies jumped out of the cars and started shooting directly at the four young men who were standing behind Georgia Mae's parked truck. Two of the young men got hit from the exchange gunfire and fell to the ground. Another young man jumped out from one of the black BMW's parked behind Georgia Mae's truck and started shooting in the direction of the three BMW's. As the crossfire continued Georgia Mae who had not been hit by any bullets, quickly put her trucks transmission into reverse as she pressed her driver's foot down hard onto the gas pedal backing up the white Chevrolet Silverado hitting one of the men and pinning them between her truck and one of the black BMWs as Georgia Mae's white truck slammed into the black BMW. A large black van also pulled into the empty banks parking lot driving past the three BMW's speeding head on and crashed into the other black BMW that was stationed by Georgia Mae's white truck. Georgia Mae's uncle stepped out of the large black van with his shotgun blasting the windows out of the BMW with his gunfire, shooting and killing the driver seated in the front seat of the other BMW. Georgia Mae put her trucks transmission into park, turning off the engine as she quickly snatched the white envelope off the lap of the now deceased blond-haired young woman whose body was seated next to her inside of the Chevrolet Silverado 1500. Georgia Mae quickly put the envelope inside of her stylish pocketbook knowing that whatever just took place was not about the business transaction that was taking place between the two women inside of her vehicle. Specifically, if her uncle is now visible on the scene. Jumping out of her white truck and leaving her shoes inside of the truck Georgia Mae quickly ran towards one of the three BMWs stationed close to the entrance of the parking lot. Soon as she sat down in the back seat of the first car, the BMW sped off maneuvering around to the other side of the parking lot exiting out onto Mobile, Alabama street. The heavy exchange of gunfire must have alarmed citizens of Mobile who were either driving by or in one of the surrounding stores by the bank location, because police patrol vehicles with their sirens blaring immediately came racing up to the empty banks parking lot as the black van and the two remaining BMWs started pulling away from the scene.

Georgia Mae quickly reached inside her stylish pocketbook, pulling out her compact size cell phone to call her youngest brother as the young male driver of the black BMW turned the speeding vehicle onto the entrance of the highway.

"Thank you, Ben baby, you're a life saver. You'll really came through for the queen on tonight" Georgia Mae yelled out from the back seat to the young male driver of the BMW as he sped down the highway switching lanes.

"Your brother sent us to you Georgia Mae because he knew what Larry was planning to do after a few of my team was picked up by the police earlier today. Your uncle surprised me just now I didn't know their van had been tailing us until he pulled up in that banks parking lot blasting everyone" Ben replied as he swerved in and out of lanes on the highway speeding in the black BMW.

"Your team" Georgia Mae shouted in response!

"My team, that's how I knew who you were with and where you were actually located" Ben loudly replied.

Georgia Mae ended the attempt phone call to her younger brother and slowly put her cell phone down onto her lap. Staring at Ben through his rear-view mirror of the BMW, Georgia Mae took two deep breaths before she picked up her compact cell phone again this time calling her eldest brother. Her sister-in-law Orange answered the phone call.

"*Hi, Orange where's my brother I need to speak to him right now!*" Georgia Mae demanded!

"*He's not here. He left a while ago on his way over to the restaurant where Tye works to look for you*" Orange softly responded.

Georgia Mae quickly ended the phone call.

"*Ben, take me to my boyfriend's restaurant near downtown Mobile, now*" Georgia Mae demanded as she started texting Tye a message on her compact cell phone.

"*Assemblyman Rogers was absolutely correct*" Georgia Mae softly whispered as Ben immediately swerved the black BMW to exit off the highway onto the detoured local road.

CHAPTER 30

THE CONVOY

As Bucky pulled his car up to the restaurant with his brother Willie James and his nephew William seated in the car, Tye's buddy Jason walked out of the restaurant. Soon as William spotted Jason walking in front of the restaurant from out of the backseat of his Uncle Bucky's car window, he jumped out of his uncle's car acknowledging his former Mobile, Ports dock worker. When Diamond saw her best friend William standing in front of the restaurant speaking with Tye's buddy Jason, she quickly dashed outside of the restaurant right into William's thick stocky arms. Screaming into his ear, while continually crying because of the sudden agonizing fear the gunman executed when he called out Diamond's name as he murdered her friend Argentina directly in front of her earlier inside of the grocery store.

"Oh, man little brother she's here too. This is why we needed to be here with our nephew Tye" Bucky loudly said to his brother Willie James as he turned off the ignition to his car.

"My son William and his Diamond girl. Hopefully she'll lift his spirit somewhat" Willie James said to his brother Bucky as he opened the car door and eased his large body out of the car.

Stepping out of the parked car into the hot humid Mobile, night air Bucky and Willie James slowly walked over to Diamond as she sobbed sorrowfully in Williams arms. Jason turned himself towards the two older gentlemen as he begins explaining the situation of the homicide detectives request to speak with Diamond as an eyewitness to the crime scene earlier inside the grocery store and William immediately decided to go over to the police headquarters along with his best friend Diamond. As Willie James and his son William assisted Jason in getting Diamond into the silver Hyundai, Bucky noticed the Kentucky license plates on Jason's car. As the Kentucky license plate silver Hyundai finally pulled off from in front of the restaurant down the Mobile, Alabama street Willie James noticed a Dodge Charger that was parked little ways up on the opposite side of the street as he stood in front of the restaurant.

The two older brothers proceeded to enter inside of the restaurant where their nephew Tye worked as the main chef. Willie James stopped in the restaurants doorway swiftly turning around to observe the Dodge Charger again that was parked up the street, checking

267

to see if there was any body movement through the dark tinted windows as the streetlamps glared on top of the car. As Willie James instantaneously observed the parked Dodge Charger the car's trunk popped open. Willie James slowly turned back around and entered the restaurant. Joining their family and Tye's gym buddies who were seated at a table inside towards the front of the restaurant, Bucky embraced his nephew Tye in a tight bear hug.

"Pop, what brought you guys down here to Cousin Tye's job" Blaire asked his father Bucky.

"Your father and I are very concerned for everyone's safety tonight after hearing from the detectives of the double homicide inside that grocery store this afternoon" Willie James replied to his nephew Blaire.

"I'm sorry to have heard about the loss of your lady friend, Tanya" Uncle Bucky said as he slowly embraced his niece Tanya also in a tight bear hug.

"That was so unfair to Big Booty Argentina! Them losers didn't have to kill her Uncle Bucky" Tanya somberly spoke.

"Lately there seems to be a lot of retaliation happening around Mobile" Willie James loudly spoke.

"Yes, it's a serious mess even today Uncle Willie" Quincy loudly replied.

"No what is a mess is that friend of little Libbie. That was the main reason I rushed us over here to see you all. That bag of lies she was trying to sell to me as if I was born yesterday. Robin is not even half my age, and I could smell the crap coming out of her young teenage mouth. I could tell from everyone in the room who witnessed her reaction to the delivery

mans parked van up the block from my brother's house, there was a serious concern" Bucky loudly explained.

"Pop, Delores text me that the detectives are over at Tye's parent's house now. She also text messaged me not too long ago that Chaplain Davis escorted Cousin Libbie's friend Robin out of the memorial service to the front of the house" Blaire loudly shared.

"That might of all happened way after we had left the house. However, what you just shared nephew, doesn't surprise me because the detectives were at my brother's house door earlier asking him questions. There is some serious trouble surrounding itself around our family today" Willie James spoke as he took a seat next to his nephew Tiny.

"Georgia Mae texted a message that her truck was sprayed by heavy gunfire tonight. Her friend was shot and killed seated right next to her. Georgia feels that my brother Assemblyman Rogers was correct in his perception of all the criminal activity which is taking place that involves our family on today" Tye loudly shared.

"Now that bit of alarming news doesn't surprise me at all either. Her brother's recent activity at the Greenlit lounge when I've been performing is nothing but trouble" Bucky loudly replied as he and Tye finally sat down in chairs next to each other.

"Pop, Assemblyman Rogers expressed to us earlier that you may have bid on hands that you couldn't win in more than one card game" Blaire spoke.

"He expressed his concern onto us that someone is trying to collect their earnings that you may have placed on the betting table Uncle Bucky" Quincy spoke.

"*Is that the main reason you drove down here to Tye's workplace Uncle Bucky? Perhaps there is some important information that you want to share to your loving family privately*" Tiny loudly spoke as he put his hand on his Uncle Willies leg.

"*Wait a minute cousin, don't team up against Uncle Bucky. If Tanya's girlfriends' job was sprayed with bullets and Diamond miraculously survived on today. If my girlfriends' vehicle was sprayed with bullets and Georgia just miraculously survived on today. Then that threatening message to my brother from his assistant today about my own vehicles that are parked inside of my house garage may be even more relevant than solely Uncle Bucky's off bet at the card table*" Tye spoke.

"*Exactly Tye, like the bag of garbage that little girl Robin was sharing in my brother and sister-in-law's living room earlier. I walked down to that house and checked as I was on your sister Brendas', cell phone Blaire, while talking to Assemblyman Rogers. As I spoke with him, I heard where his head was at. But, in my opinion that house was either being robbed, or burglarized and Libbie's school friend was an accessory to the crime somehow this afternoon. I've had houses and businesses since all of you were running around in dirty diapers. I know what signs to look out for. My wife Rebecca is an active member on our neighborhood watch committee so there are things together we have been professionally trained to watch out for. Why that family's house was targeted is none of my concern. That's what those detectives knocking on my brother's house front door are paid very well for and that is their job to investigate. That is for the crime unit to solve not me*" Uncle Bucky loudly explained.

"I called Assemblyman Rogers and asked if he could meet us here at the restaurant and he agreed. I'm going to need Keith's personal information along with the instructions he left for me. That is so I can contact him to straighten out this automobile parts business he's inquiring about" Tye loudly spoke.

"What's going on with the automobile camped out across the street from this restaurant? That Dodge Charger parked and sitting outside of the restaurant has a potential drive by coming from out of its trunk" Uncle Willie James loudly said.

"Dodge Charger? Really uncle! That's probably the same car that Diamond was shaking up over, as she walked to the grocery store before the murders occurred as she claimed" Tanya shouted, jumping up out the chair as she quickly hurried over to the restaurant's front door to observe the vehicle herself. Tye's gym buddies quickly arose from the table and followed behind her also to check out the car.

"Yes, the driver side window is down, and I see a cloud of smoke coming out it" One of Tye's gym buddies loudly shared to the family inside of the restaurant.

Blaire jumped up from the table and hurried towards the restaurant's kitchen to collect some large knives. Quincy immediately text messaged his wife Jemena telling her to call the police and send them to Tye's restaurant asap. Tiny, Willie James and Uncle Bucky quickly rose up off the chairs headed towards the restaurant door to also see the car. Tye called

Assemblyman Rogers to see if he was within the vicinity of the restaurant's location.

"Hey, Tye I'm almost there you should see me in a black pickup truck" Assemblyman Rogers shouted out to Tye as he answered the phone and then quickly disconnected the phone call.

Tye, putting his cell phone into his shorts pocket, ran after his cousin Blaire towards the restaurant kitchen to see what he was up to. Before he could get to the restaurant's kitchens door, his cousin Blaire came rushing out of the kitchen with two giant knives in his hands. They both ran to the front of the restaurant to join the others outside.

A large white SUV came screeching down the street as the passenger door of the Dodge Charger and the trunk opened. As the white SUV sped past the Dodge Charger veering left headed directly towards the restaurant Uncle Bucky quickly stepped up to the curb between his car and the gym fellas Range Rover. The white SUV partially pulled up to the restaurants driveway before coming to a screeching complete stop as a fat man wearing jeans and a shirt hoped out of the passenger side with a shot gun in his hand. The driver side of the white SUV swung open as well as a woman wearing a long black shirt, and jogging pants hoped out with a gun in her hand.

All of a sudden in the other direction two black Chevrolet Silverado 1500 pickup trucks came speeding down the mobile street one behind the other as the passenger window and the backseat windows were down on the first black pickup truck heavy gunfire rang out directly towards the white SUV, everyone that was standing in front of the restaurant immediately hit the ground to cover themselves from the hail of bullets that was now loudly ringing in front of the restaurant. A skinny white man with no shirt on standing in the back of the first black Chevrolet Silverado 1500 pickup truck started firing his shotgun directly towards the Dodge Charger parked across the street striking the tall skinny guy that was standing outside of the car on the passenger side. As the two black trucks slowed down in front of the restaurant parking lot directly shooting at the white SUV that was stationed halfway in the parking lot, the white guys that occupied both vehicles started yelling as they opened fired on the Dodge Charger and the white SUV killing the woman wearing the long black shirt. The first black Chevrolet Silverado 1500 quickly sped off down the mobile, Alabama street as the tall skinny white guy standing up in the back of the pickup, continually opened fire on the blue Dodge Charger. The second black Chevrolet Silverado then slowly moved up towards the now bullet marked and shot up white SUV as the fat man was now lying on the ground by the passenger side door of the white SUV covered in blood gasping for air. Standing up in the back of that Black Chevrolet Silverado 1500 pickup truck there was Gus, the very large white bearded man also wearing no shirt with an automatic assault Rifle in his hand. As he aimed for the head of the fat man lying on the ground, he turned his head to the right looking towards Bucky who was on the ground between the front of his car and the rear of the parked Range Rover.

"When are you niggers going to learn to keep your dirty hands off the white man's Diamond" Gus, the very large white bearded man wearing no shirt yelled out as he fired his gun directly at his head, shooting and killing the fat man as he laid on the ground covered in blood by the passenger side door of the white SUV.

The black Chevrolet Silverado 1500 then quickly sped off down the Mobile, Alabama street as the white men inside the second black pickup truck yelled, screamed and continued shooting at the parked blue Dodge Charger across the street from the restaurant.

As everyone slowly got up from off the ground in front of the restaurant, where they all had dropped down low trying to shield themselves from the hail of gunfire coming from out of both pickup trucks, the police quickly pulled up. Uncle Bucky kept his eyes on the blue Dodge Charger across the street as police vehicles arrived on the scene from both directions. While the once empty Mobile, street now began to fill up with law enforcement vehicles blaring their loud sirens and flashing their bright lights into the dark Mobile, night Tye's coworkers came outside of the restaurant to investigate the now crime scene.

As police officers started asking everyone that was standing in front of the restaurant questions as eyewitnesses trying to collect enough information on what had taken place, the black BMW that was driving Georgia Mae slowly pulled up two blocks away. Seeing all the flashing bright lights, Georgia Mae immediately called Tye as the young driver Ben parked the car cutting off the lights so their BMW wouldn't catch the attention of the local authorities that were now filling up the Mobile, street surrounding the Restaurant. Tye answered her call confirming that he had not been injured and explained to Georgia Mae that there were two vehicles that had been struck with bullets killing all the occupants inside both vehicles in front of the restaurant where his family was probably their original target before being intercepted by another team. Tye had suggested for Georgia Mae to leave the area and to go to his house to meet up with him later tonight. As Georgia Mae kept her eyes on Ben through the rear-view mirror inside the car, Georgia Mae told Ben to pull off and quickly leave the area.

As detectives arrived at the restaurant Tanya, Willie James and Bucky kept their eyes on the blue Dodge Charger that was now surrounded in yellow tape by the police officers who were all in the street. Tiny turned to Blaire when the tall grey-haired detective with the badge hanging from his neck wearing blue jeans and short-sleeved shirt got out of his unmarked vehicle walking towards the white SUV stationed in the entrance of the restaurants parking lot. As the police Sergeant who was wearing his police vest walked over to Tye and his gym buddies along with another detective that had arrived in front of the restaurant the coroners' vans slowly pulled up along with the news media vans.

Uncle Bucky walked over to Tye and his gym buddies to hear what the police Sergeant had to say to them as Quincy slowly followed.

"You have five dead bodies out here in front of your job chef in two different vehicles. The White vehicle here in your parking lot is the vehicle of interest of the double homicide that had taken place earlier at the grocery store. One of the dead bodies is the murder suspect of that double homicide taken place earlier inside of the grocery store. Across the street is one female deceased in the back seat of the blue Dodge Charger, one male deceased in the driver's seat who we have identified as Larry and the other male deceased on the ground with a gun lying next to the car is identified as Jamie. Do you personally know any of these individuals Tye" the Sergeant loudly asked as he looked at Tye directly into his eyes.

"No sir, I'm just the head chef here at this restaurant" Tye loudly responded as Uncle Bucky put his hands on his nephew's shoulder.

As the two Mobile, Alabama police officers turned and slowly walked away towards the other detectives, Quincy's cell phone started to ring so he went inside of the restaurant to answer the phone call from his wife Jemena.

"Nephew, I love you man and I'm very proud of your culinary success." Uncle Bucky turned towards Tye and spoke. *"I hid the jewelry inside a small black case which is now located inside of your new car's trunk last week when you picked me up from the barber shop. After my band's rehearsal that afternoon, I had my lead singer Shane give me a ride to the bank in his Posche, where I withdrew the jewelry and some other personal*

items from my safety deposit box. I first placed all the valuable items inside my Saxophone case so if I was being tailed then whoever would have suspected what I may have done with the diamonds would have led them to the visible Saxophone case. I then made the quick switch after Shane had dropped me off at the Barbershop to get my hair cut and you then picked me up in your new car that you've been working so hard on upgrading it to a race car. I placed the small black type of case behind the bundle of rags inside the race car's trunk as you drove me to your aunt Rebecca's restaurant that afternoon. I used Shane as my driver because I knew Eric had all eyes on his secret lover Shane. Shane and your girlfriend Georgia Mae are good friends however, her family is notorious. Georgia Mae's brother had his eyes on your Bentley and your cousin Derek has his eyes on her brother because of his undercover relationship with his best friend Shane. When Georgia Mae's brother began frequenting the lounge I kindly asked your sister Debbie to start occasionally visit the lounge to keep an eye on her favorite Cousin Derek and his lover DJ Gwan. I had a feeling Georgia Mae's brother might try to hurt Derek so he could then secretly lay with DJ Gwan as he and Eric rivalry battle continues. Both are creeps. But at the end of the day whether I play my Saxophone live before the crowd or secretly play cards in one of the back rooms with hoodlums it's still my family in the building who I keep both my senior eyes on. Tye, you thought it may have been your hand that you played which upset your opponents. No nephew, I'm the card shark in this family and everyone in town is aware of that" Uncle Buckly said to his nephew Tye as they stood in front of the restaurant.

"Yes, Uncle Bucky that's good to hear. However, I'm the baller in Mobile, Alabama and my hand always wins" Tye responded as he walked away from his Uncle Bucky towards the Restaurant front door.

Tiny and Tanya, seeing the expression on their cousin's face quickly followed their cousin Tye back inside the restaurant as Tye's gym buddies came inside behind them. As they all sat back down at the table the tall grey-haired detective with the badge around his neck wearing blue jeans and a short-sleeved shirt also came inside the restaurant, walking over to the table where they all were sitting including Quincy.

"Good evening, family and friends. Family I see we meet again today under unpleasant circumstances. From all the dead bodies surrounding you guys on today I do need to say that you all may need to thank your cousin Bishop Joe for his continuous prayers over the family. Tye from what I see here tonight at your workplace, you need to go over to your parents' house and embrace them in a loving hug. You will all benefit from that. In all my years as a professional police officer seeing not only the dead bodies outside of this restaurant but the weapons also lying next to their bodies. Tye, you are one lucky brother" the tall grey-haired detective spoke.

THE END
Written by; Peaches Dudley

Printed in the United States
by Baker & Taylor Publisher Services